# AHAB
### AND
# JEZEBEL

# AHAB
## AND
# JEZEBEL

A MATCH MADE IN HELL

JOSEPH BRINGMAN

BRINGMAN PUBLISHING

**Ahab and Jezebel: A Match Made in Hell**

Scripture quotations are from the *King James Version*.

Quotation of Leo Tolstoy's *Anna Karenina* is from Constance Garnett's translation.

Cover designed by Miblart

Map created with Bible Mapper (biblemapper.com)

This book is a work of fiction. Any references to historical events, real persons, or real places are used fictitiously. Other names, characters, places, and events are products of the author's imagination, and any resemblance to actual events or places or persons, living or dead, is entirely coïncidental.

Publisher's Cataloging-in-Publication data

Names: Bringman, Joseph, author.
Title: Ahab and Jezebel : a match made in Hell / Joseph Bringman.
Description: Seattle, WA: Bringman Publishing, 2024.
Identifiers: LCCN: 2024902841 | ISBN: 978-1-963006-01-8 (hardcover) | 978-1-963006-00-1 (paperback) | 978-1-963006-02-5 (ebook)
Subjects: LCSH Ahab, King of Israel--Fiction. | Jezebel, Queen, consort of Ahab, King of Israel--Fiction. | Queens--Israel--Fiction. | Israel--Kings and rulers--Fiction. | Historical fiction. | Christian fiction. | BISAC FICTION / Historical / Ancient | FICTION / Christian / Biblical | FICTION / Christian / Historical
Classification: LCC PS3602 .R56 A43 2024 | DDC 813.6--dc23

*Maximo feli et optimo amico Rhubarb,*

*qui mihi peramanter assidebat dum scribebam.*

*Tui semper meminero.*

*"Happy families are all alike; every unhappy family is unhappy in its own way."*

Leo Tolstoy, "Anna Karenina"

*"And if it seem evil unto you to serve the LORD, choose you this day whom ye will serve; whether the gods which your fathers served that were on the other side of the flood, or the gods of the Amorites, in whose land ye dwell: but as for me and my house, we will serve the LORD."*

Joshua 24:15

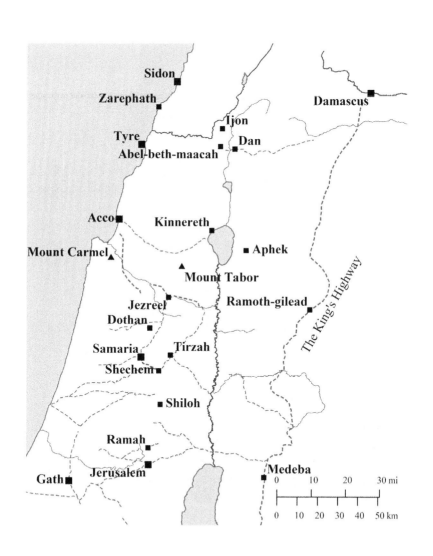

Sidon

Zarephath

Damascus

Ijon

Tyre
Abel-beth-maacah
Dan

Acco
Kinnereth
Aphek

Mount Carmel
Mount Tabor

Ramoth-gilead

Jezreel
Dothan

The King's Highway

Samaria
Tirzah
Shechem

Shiloh

Ramah

Gath
Jerusalem
Medeba

| 0 | 10 | 20 | 30 mi |

| 0 | 10 | 20 | 30 | 40 | 50 km |

# CHAPTER ONE

J EZEBEL MADE HER ENTRANCE just as the first rays of the sun peeped through the palace windows, making the corridor's ivory pillars sparkle amid the shadows like fireflies in a moonless sky. Striding briskly down the corridor, each muscle exuding firmness with every step she took, Jezebel stared straight ahead like a lion surveying his domain. She kept her pointed chin elevated; strands of her long, silky black hair flowed freely behind her slender neck.

She reached the end of this corridor and was about to make the habitual leftwards turn towards the palace sanctuary when a shrill voice cried out:

"Wait, my queen! Wait for me!"

Jezebel halted mid-step. With her whole body stiffening, her clenching chest shot forth a spurt of stomach acid; but, swallowing the sour fluid, she craned her head around and trained her slowly-narrowing eyes, bulbous and green, onto the man with the shrill voice. "A-hab," she said, enunciating each syllable with an individualized scowl.

Her husband, panting, scurried down the corridor. He wore soft, sumptuous, billowing robes whose Phoenician-made cloth shone with the rich purplish-red hue secreted from Tyrian snails;

1

golden tassels, their metal mined in Ophir, fringed his bell sleeves as well as the hemline that dangled above his bejeweled sandals. A thin diadem of gold inlaid with three sapphires, which had graced Omri's noble brow at the conquest of Medeba, hung a tad lower on the left side than the right of the narrower, wrinkly forehead of Omri's son. When he caught up with her, Ahab immediately bent over, clasping his knees while his rotund stomach sagged. "Jezebel, darling," he wheezed while straightening up, "I wanted to talk with you."

"Make it quick; I'm about to worship Baal," said Jezebel, resuming her stride at a slower pace so that Ahab could keep up with her. "Which reminds me"—she locked her unblinking eyes onto his—"has the king performed his morning prayers today?"

"Oh, yes, of course," answered Ahab, eagerly nodding his head. Smiling, he added, "My day always starts at Baal's altar. I honor the god before doing anything else."

Without bothering to look back at him, Jezebel reached backwards and ran her long fingers across his stubbly face. "Before you shave, at any rate."

Ahab, his fat lips fleeing from one another and high cheekbones reddening, quickly felt the brown fuzz on his chin. "I didn't realize..." His gaze fell to the tiled floor. "No!" he exclaimed, slapping his upper left arm as he was accustomed to do whenever he thought of something clever (or, as the more cynical would say, whenever *he thought* that he had thought of something clever). "This is actually good: it illustrates the point I wanted to make."

*Oh, just what I needed,* thought Jezebel, her lean aquiline nose crinkling. *Another of his* illustrious *illustrations!* She stopped and turned to face him. *Let's hear what this one is...*

"O my dearest and entirely beloved wife, dedicated mother of two fine sons, daughter in whom her father's eyes delighted, exemplar of queenly propriety—do you not see that even the hairs on my chin cannot properly be taken care of, cannot look their best, cannot thrive... without that tender love and care which only you can provide?"

Jezebel, moving it swiftly but adroitly underneath her dress so as not to betray any motion, slammed one foot upon the other's toes. Frowning from the pain running up her tibia, she managed to stifle the laugh that was about to escape from her swelling lungs.

"Jezebel, when I wake up in the morning and do not see your beautiful face, smell your lovely scent, feel your warm body pressing up against my own... I'm just not able to function as well, to think as straight." He raised his hand. "I *need* you..."

She stared blankly at the hand stretching out towards her. It was a big hand. The clean skin, immaculate and never-calloused, testified that this was indeed the hand of a hereditary monarch. As it inched towards its queen, passing through the air like a slow-moving moth, it rained several droplets from its moist underside. The index finger almost made contact with Jezebel's waist.

She swatted it away.

"I am sure any one of your concubines could do an adequate job at reminding you to shave," huffed Jezebel, her eyes becoming slits. "If the king's bedchamber is too frigid in the morning, perhaps he should play King Daniel and fetch a Shunammite virgin."

"I think you meant King David."

"Whatever!" *As though I care at all about old decrepit Hebrew kings...*

3

Ahab shook his head. "My dearest, you know I would never bring another woman into our special room, profane the sacred temple of our love, desecrate the site where our sons originated..."

*Baal, either strike him dumb or me deaf!*

"Besides," he added as he leaned his head forwards, his almond eyes twinkling and fat lips quivering, "no Shunammite could ever equal your beauty."

Jezebel felt his hot breath on her face. As the corners of her lips curled downwards, she groused, "This beauty will wither if deprived of water. Unless you wish to see that, what are you doing about the drought?"

"Well, we've still got enough water for human consumption—"

"And what about the animals? Shall my prized stallions starve from lack of fodder, or the speckled bulls my mother bred?"

"Of course not! I'll send Obadiah out at once to search for grass."

"If the king can procure this treasure," said Jezebel softly, leaning in and planting a single kiss on his cheek, "he'll discover how grateful his queen can be."

His pupils dilated. Licking his lips, he murmured, "Oh, he'll get it..."

Jezebel watched her husband scamper back down the corridor. *Finally*, she thought, letting out a sigh as soon as he was out of sight. *I never thought he'd leave...*

Resuming her gait, she soon reached her destination: the palace sanctuary. It was a large room filled by several rows of pillars. Four giant oil lamps, one burning in each corner, illuminated the room; the altar's incense perfumed the air. The walls were decked with tapestries depicting various episodes from the life of Baal:

wrestling a seven-headed serpent, creating tidal waves to obliterate a fleet of ships, marrying his sister Anat, building a heavenly palace, and fighting Mot the god of death. In the center of the room, seated upon a gilded throne, towered the seven-foot image of Baal himself. He had a thick beard and braided hair falling over his back and right shoulder from under a helmet that was decorated with the horns of bulls. The sole garment he was depicted wearing consisted of a striped kilt fastened by a finely carved belt, from whose end a curved dagger protruded up onto his chiseled abdomen. He held a mace in his raised right hand and in his left hand, which he held stretched out to his worshippers, was a thunderbolt in the shape of a spearhead extending towards the ground.

Jezebel approached the image. Kneeling before her god, she stretched her arms up to him and clasped his cold, muscular bronze legs. "God of Gods, Lord of Tyre, grant victory to your servant Jezebel over those vexatious dissenters. I have filled the land with your altars, rites, priests. But pockets of infidels persist in our backwaters, stubbornly clinging to their Hebrew superstitions, led by... *that man*. How he blasphemes your holy name and the name of your faithful servant, too! Deliver him to me, O Baal, and may the last embers of resistance die with him."

Thus she prayed her daily prayer, requesting the same request. She remained there for several minutes in this posture, silently meditating; her eyes, though closed to this world, gazed blindly up to the god. Then a bass voice, booming and articulated with a tone of aplomb that has resounded through the mind's ear of many a mortal, pierced the quiet:

"Hi, queenie."

Jezebel snapped her eyes open. She unbent her knees. With her trembling hands still pressed against the god, she eased herself up from the floor. Her heart beating faster, the blood rushing into her cheeks, and silken tresses jostling beside the temples of her head, she turned away from Baal's image and said:

"Hello, Pygmalion."

Wearing white priestly robes that hung loosely around his sides, not belted as they were meant to be, Pygmalion leaned against a pillar about twenty paces behind her. His hand was casually working a toothpick; his sleeve fell down to his elbow, revealing not monstrously huge biceps. When her eyes met his, he cast his toothpick upon the floor and swaggered over to her like a tomcat down his alley.

Jezebel stretched out the top of her hand towards him. But when he took hold of it, far from kissing it as any other priest would, he instead yanked her against his body, wrapped his arm around her waist, tightly clasped her right buttock, and with his free hand corrected the angle of her head so that he might plant a mighty kiss onto her squirming lips.

Her nostrils flaring from the struggle, Jezebel gasped, "Stop, Pygmalion, stop!" She managed to free herself from his clutch. Glancing around the room, her eyes completely dilated, she exclaimed, "If my husband had seen this, he'd kill you on the spot!"

"Ahab kill me? Hah!" He slapped her lower back. "Maybe if he sat on me he could."

Although the corner of her lip began to form a spontaneous smirk at the image forming in her mind, she consciously forced a frown and moved several steps away. "Be that as it may, he has his servants and lackeys: like all men, they'll obey the one who feeds them." Whipping her head around, her eyebrows scrunched, she added, in an icy tone, "Besides, I'd have thought that of all men you, a priest, would have acted more properly in Baal's holy sanctuary—to know decorum, unlike those vain fellows who shamelessly uncover themselves around the handmaids."

Without blinking, Pygmalion met her eyes. "I'm Astartë's priest, not Baal's. If Baal's got any objections"—he cupped his hand around his ear and, standing tiptoe, pressed it close to the statue's mouth—"he'll have to speak up for himself." When no objection was forthcoming, he said, "I guess the god approves."

"You think you know just what to say in any situation. You think you're so clever, don't you?"

"Obviously. Of all men, we priests know how to act as though we were all-knowing."

*What a rascal you are!* Jezebel crossed her legs and flipped her hand through her hair while finalizing the counter retort she was about to make; but before she could, footsteps resounded outside the door. *Oh, great... I hope it's not him again...*

An older woman in her fifties, dressed in black garments and sporting a black veil atop her grizzled hair, ambled into the room. Observing Pygmalion before settling her beady eyes on Jezebel, she bowed and said, "Good mistress, your presence is needed in the Reception Hall. There is no one to receive the petitioners."

"What do you mean, Elishat? This time of week, the king ought to be there receiving the peasants' petitions."

"I am sorry, Mistress." Elishat shook her head. "The king quitted the palace five minutes ago with a troop of men."

"HE DID WHAT?!" exclaimed Jezebel, the spittle flying from her mouth. *He told me he was going to send Obadiah... He never said he was going himself—just get up and go, leave his wife without a word...*

"The peasants are getting restless."

*Damn the peasants!* "Fine, fine, I'll go." She flicked her hand towards the entrance. *I have to do everything else for him... I might as well placate his subjects for him, too...*

Elishat bowed her head and withdrew to just outside the entry-way.

Jezebel turned to Pygmalion. "I'm leaving now..."

"That's okay. It's probably for the best. There's a sacrifice I was supposed to be at ten minutes ago and they can't begin until I arrive." Closing the distance between them, he put his arms akimbo—his thumbs facing outwards and thudding up and down on his abdomen—and bent down his head until he was at eyelevel with her. "But when will I see you next?"

Throwing her arm behind his neck, Jezebel thrust her ruby lips against his. She worked her lip muscles hard, like a crazed horseman beating his steed. Pygmalion's lips were chapped, but the saliva welling up in her mouth had soon moistened them. The taste of bacon, cooked before sunrise in the palace's kitchen, still lingered upon them and a hefty scent of myrrh filled her flaring nostrils.

Five seconds passed, then ten, fifteen, twenty, twenty-five, and finally a total of thirty seconds had elapsed.

Unpuckering her lips, Jezebel began a leisurely withdrawal. With his hazel whiskers still tickling her chin, she whispered, "Come at the usual time."

Leaving him where he was, she sauntered gracefully over to the entryway.

Elishat was waiting for her there. "And is my regal mistress happy this morning?"

"Yes," said Jezebel with a smile, "she's a very happy mistress indeed."

# CHAPTER TWO

A HAB STOOPED OVER AND scooped up a handful of pale dirt. It was completely stripped of moisture. Some brittle remnants of yellow grass were intermixed with it. As he manipulated the desiccated soil between his fingers, it evaporated into a fine dust that the gentle breeze soon bore away. Nodding to his servant, he received a canteen of water which he used to wash his hands.

"Are you sure none of our men found any?"

"No, my lord," answered the servant. "Not so much as a creek remains in these parts."

Wiping away the sweat on his forehead and shielding his almond eyes, Ahab stared up at the cloudless sky. *How long can this go on?* He turned his gaze to the endless expanse of wasteland that had bloomed with olive bushes and amber wheat a mere three years ago. Now, languishing from drought, the landscape was dotted with the carcasses of wild animals. *Were it not for the Tyrians, the people would starve too... Yet, even with the costly grain imports, the lack of grass is devastating the livestock. We may lose all the horses and mules in the kingdom if we can't find grass soon. I hope Obadiah and his scouts are faring better.*

At the same moment that Ahab's thoughts had turned to the steward of his palace, the selfsame man appeared on the horizon. Whipping his horse hard, Obadiah dashed across the desert. He dismounted and promptly bent his knee and bowed his turbaned head before the king.

Keeping his wrinkly brow aloof, Ahab glanced down at his steward. "Obadiah, why do you return alone? Have your men found water or grass?" He waved for him to stand.

"No, my lord," answered Obadiah, standing. Though the rest of his body was shrouded by heavy white robes, his tanned face was visibly nervous. As his yellow teeth chewed his lower lip, he said, "Instead of finding them, I found Elijah."

*Elijah!*

Ahab shielded his uncovered mouth with his hand. Goosebumps ran up his limbs despite the heat. "You've captured that outlaw?" *Ooh, Jezebel will be so-oooo thrilled...*

"No. He came upon me while I was apart from my men. I was in no position to capture him. But he charged me to deliver this message to you: he wishes for you to come this evening to the place where I saw him in order that he may speak with you in person."

Stomping his jewel-encrusted sandal on the ground, Ahab screeched with his shrill voice, "It's been three years now, *three years*, since that so-called prophet predicted this accursed drought! He's turned one single prediction, which blind luck made accurate, into a cudgel to agitate the peasantry, to blaspheme Baal and all the gods, to attempt to turn my subjects' hearts against me and my queen... And after all that, that man has the gall to demand that *I*, his king and sovereign lord, should go to him? No!"

Obadiah bowed his head. "My lord the king burns with an anger hotter than the desert sun and he has every justification for it. But I know, when he reconsiders, that he will realize the advantages of such a meeting."

"What advantages?" said Ahab, cocking his thick neck.

"For three years the king has scoured the countryside for Elijah, even exacting oaths from our neighboring kingdoms not to grant him refuge. He did not find him. But now Elijah has revealed himself. We know where he will be tonight."

"You may be right..." Ahab rested his hand on his chin. "Where would this meeting happen?"

"About a mile northeast of Dothan."

\*\*\*

A HAB NIBBLED ON HIS fat lips.

The sun had nearly set on the horizon. Long streaks of crimson light, radiating from the star as blood gushing from a slaughtered pig, filled the cloudless sky. To the northeast of Dothan lay a hill, grassless and about thirty feet high, where Elijah had instructed the king of Israel to wait. So Ahab waited at the base of the hill along with Obadiah and the men, twiddling his thumbs, alternating his weight on each foot, and increasingly crinkling his nose as the minutes passed.

Finally a figure, having ascended from the other side, appeared on the hill's summit. The setting sun behind him cast a glorious aura around him like an angel's halo; but because he was standing directly in front of the light, the features of his face were unperceivable to Ahab and his men.

*Is this what Moses looked like when he spoke with God on Sinai?* wondered Ahab, gazing upwards. *No, no, no. Baal is our lord and god. The Other One does not exist. Or... if He does exist, then He's just one god among the rest. There's nothing special about Him.*

"That's Elijah," whispered Obadiah, pointing upwards.

Ahab, gulping, called out with his shrill voice, "Are you the one who has been troubling Israel all this time?"

The cloaked figure gazed down at them. His long, unkempt hair billowing in the gentle breeze, he thundered with a mighty voice: "My name is Elijah! Yahweh is my God and I am His prophet. What I have done I have done as the Spirit of God led me. If you question whether I am 'the one who has been troubling Israel,' then you are mistaken and utterly ignorant of things divine. For I have not troubled Israel"—he snapped his arm out and pointed at Ahab—"it is *you* who troubles Israel! You and your father's House! Both of you have forsaken the commandments of Yahweh! And you yourself serve Baal—or should I say the Baals? (For you not only worship one false god like your father but you feel compelled to worship your idol under multiple aspects as well: Baal-Zebub, Baal-Peör, and Baal-Perith are but three of the countless names you ascribe to him.) Therefore the wrath of God is kindled against Israel on account of the sins of their kings."

Ahab had taken a step backwards as soon as the booming baritone soared down the hillside towards him; when Elijah pointed to him, his legs had begun to wobble. But, stretching out his sweaty palms and grasping Obadiah's shoulder to steady himself, Ahab inched forwards.

"You say that the sins of me and my father are to blame. If so, why does the whole kingdom suffer? Whatever trouble you allege we caused pales in comparison to the miseries this drought has inflicted on the people. Why, then, has your God seen fit to punish the king's subjects rather than the king himself?"

"Because the people have followed their king in his transgressions," answered Elijah, raising both his hands heavenwards. "Abandoning the God of their fathers, they worship the idols brought into the land by that wicked woman Jezebel. They bow down before false gods made of wood and iron, offer up cakes to the 'queen of heaven,' and commit the most unspeakable abominations the heart of man has ever devised. Israel partakes of her king's sins and therefore justly suffers God's holy judgment."

"Don't blame my wife!" Ahab formed a fist, the veins bulging on his hand, and shook it in the empty air. "Jezebel is the greatest woman in the world! She wants the best for this kingdom and knows that this means we must pay our respects to all the gods of heaven. You deny there are more gods than one? Fine. I cannot change an obstinate man's opinion. But do not single out my Jezebel for your condemnation. She didn't even introduce these gods to us! You forget that Israel's got a long history of worshipping many gods: even in Moses' day, our ancestors are said to have worshipped a golden calf. If that solitary God of yours can't inspire loyalty in His own chosen people, don't try and shift responsibility onto Jezebel. Have you ever wondered if, maybe, His style of leadership might be to blame for His unpopularity? Sending droughts upon the land and threatening to kill everyone with famine strikes me as a bit off-putting, to say the least."

Elijah simply snorted. "Yahweh is the Creator of Heaven and Earth: He can uncreate whatsoever portion of it He so wishes. Unlike Baal and the other dead statues before which you and your wife grovel—so-called gods who rust and need men's hands to wipe the dust off them—He is a living God! And He has the power to accomplish what He wills!"

"Baal is a living god, too. He also has great power."

"If he's so powerful, then why hasn't he ended this drought for you?" asked Elijah, raising a single eyebrow.

"Umm..." Ahab's pupils wandered to the corner of his eyes.

"Jezebel beseeches him every day to demonstrate his 'power.' Does she not?"

"Yes, but..."

"But dead metal can do nothing! Only the God of Israel can make the gentle rain drop from the heavens upon the ground beneath."

"Well, supposing that your God did have this power... what would I, uh, have to do for Him to send some rain my way? Is there any kind of sacrifice or offering He especially likes?"

Elijah started moving down the hill. Looking neither at the ground before him nor the members of the royal retinue, he kept his unblinking eyes locked strait on Ahab's. He stopped about ten feet away from him.

Ahab glared at the prophet's scraggily beard, his disheveled head, the dirtied mantle hanging about his body, his thin arms gyrating from side to side, and his frenzied bug-eyes transfixed on him. "I repeat: What do you propose I do?"

"Renounce the Sidonians and their false gods! Return to the religion of your forefathers! If you repent, then salvation is yours; persist in idolatry, and perdition lies at the door."

"How can I renounce the Sidonians? They feed the people!"

"They feed you lies!" bellowed Elijah. "Your stomachs are full of pabulum, your hearts yet fuller of wickedness. But if you return to Yahweh and beg His forgiveness, He will not only heal your land and cause your fields to flourish: he will confer on you the Bread of Life that will stop you from ever hungering again."

"This drought—which you claim is the result of your God's judgment—is what made us dependent on Sidon in the first place! All because... because we couldn't grow our own food. If you want to convince me your God has the power—to convince me that Baal's false, then why don't you call the drought off? Just call it off right now and let us have rain! Prove that you can really communicate with this 'almighty' God and speak on His behalf!"

Elijah chuckled. "If the king desires proof from the God of Israel, then send and gather to me all Israel unto Mount Carmel one week hence, and bring with you the prophets of Baal and the prophets of the groves who eat at Jezebel's table. Then all shall see whose God is true!"

"Fine! I will!" shouted Ahab, his face flushed red with anger. *I'll expose you for what you are... everyone will see you're just a fraud, a charlatan, an imposter...*

Without turning his back on Ahab, his unblinking eyes still glaring at him, Elijah retraced his steps backwards and slowly disappeared from view over the hilltop.

"Obadiah, make the arrangements."

"Yes, my lord."

As Ahab walked back to his chariot and prepared to return to his palace at Jezreël, he contemplated the gravity of accepting the prophet's challenge. One thought kept recurring in his mind. It was not the sturdiness of his own religious convictions; nor what sort of alleged proof Elijah might present to try to win over the people; nor even the logistics of convening within a week, from every quarter of the kingdom, all the priests of Baal and Astarté (who numbered almost a thousand men), but rather this question:

*What will Jezebel think about this?*

# CHAPTER THREE

"OH, YES, MORE," PANTED Jezebel, her whole body flushed with heat. She wiped the sweat off her forehead; the blood was surging through her arteries.

"It's getting late," said Pygmalion, sitting up in her bed which gave off the strong aroma of myrrh, aloes, and cinnamon. "I'll need some sleep if I'm to make that journey tomorrow."

"Oh, that stupid journey."

Pushing aside the gold-fringed coverlets, Jezebel slipped into her translucent red tunic and dashed across the room. On the silver-legged table set against the wall opposite her bed was a rich array of foods left there by the maidservants: olives, pomegranates, red grapes, cheeses, honeyed biscuits, cakes, ham sausages, smoked eagle legs, roasted stork breast, and several bottles of spiced wines. She shoved a few biscuits into her mouth, carelessly letting crumbs rain here and there upon the white marble floor. After folding the front of her garment up to make an impromptu basket, she piled an assortment of the foods in it. Grabbing a bottle of wine, she returned to the bed.

Jezebel tossed her pickings onto the sheets before crawling back under them.

"You're quite ravenous tonight," remarked Pygmalion as he plucked a couple grapes off their vine.

"You wouldn't believe it," said Jezebel in between greedy glugs of wine. "Ahab was a total pig at supper. He just went on and on whining about his gout, about how much 'pain' he's in. And whatever his physicians are giving him made him fart non-stop; the whole dining room—you know how large it is, right?—it all stank worse than the runny dung in the stables. He completely murdered my appetite." Her teeth tore some flesh off an eagle leg.

"Then I'm glad I'll be in the open air if I have to be by him."

"I don't understand why you even have to go." She leaned over and bit off the cucumber tip that was sticking out of Pygmalion's mouth, simultaneously chewing the vegetable while she massaged his lips. "He was so foolish to agree to that arch-rebel's demands."

Stroking her soft cheek, he chuckled, "I have no doubt you told him that to his face."

Jezebel allowed a giant smile to stretch from ear to ear. "Of course," she whispered as she began stroking burly portions of his body. "I told him exactly what I thought: he should have captured that man when he had the chance instead of agreeing to put on some theatrical 'battle-of-the-gods.'"

"Do you doubt Baal will triumph over the Hebrews' God?"

"Baal is so much greater..." She rolled over and climbed atop him, ignoring the food her movement was causing to roll off the bed. "He slew the mighty god Yam. He even defeated the god of death himself. It's insulting even to ask him to compete against that heathen deity, like suggesting a strongman wrestle a mewling child."

"I'll tell you what Elijah looks like when he loses."

"I'll look at him myself," said Jezebel in between kisses.

Pygmalion cocked his head. "You're coming?"

"Of course not." She crinkled her aquiline nose. "But I've given Ahab instructions for how he can arrest Elijah. I'm sure that man will have some fellow rebels with him. While you and the priests are defending Baal's honor, our troops who'll escort you shall position themselves well. Then, as soon as the sacrifices conclude, Ahab gives the word and our troops shall isolate that man from his followers and bring him to me. What do you think?"

"So you're basically turning the whole event into a trap," said Pygmalion, narrowing his eyes.

"Exactly! I'll finally have that man where I want him." *At least so long as Ahab manages not to screw things up...*

"Will Elijah's capture really be that important? He's just one man."

*Just one man?! How can he say that?* Jezebel, her nostrils flaring, whipped her body into an upright position. "He's the face and embodiment of the native opposition! All of the Hebrews who hate me, who refuse to bow before Baal, who utter hateful words against Tyrians and all foreigners (while being too ignorant even to know the difference between Tyre and Sidon!)—they all look to Elijah for leadership! If we take him out, we'll be on the verge of extinguishing the last embers of resistance."

"But the opposition is a small, powerless minority; I reckon there can't be more than a few thousand dissenters left in the whole kingdom. If all they do is worship a different god than me, and murmur their discontent in the privacy of their own homes, why should I care? Flames, clubs, arrows all hurt my body; a Hebrew whispering his God's name does not."

"Kingship is legitimized by Heaven! Resistance to Baal is treason to the king!"

Resting his hand on her shuddering shoulder, he gently guided her back beneath the covers. He put his arm around her waist and whispered in her ear, "Don't look now but, unless I forget, it's also treason for the queen to sleep with other men."

"I meant the monarchy in general!" protested Jezebel, picking her finger. *Our government rules because Baal sanctions our rule; anyone who denies him implicitly questions our right to rule. Any priest ought to know that...*

"Yes, yes, I know. Nobody in his right mind should oppose you." Pygmalion yawned and leaned back on his side of the bed. "At least it'll be over tomorrow. Then Baal will reign supreme, the king will still have his throne, and Jezebel will be able to sleep in peace."

"And will you be okay with that?"

"Why wouldn't I?"

Jezebel articulated her words curtly. "A moment ago you almost sounded like a Hebrew-sympathizer."

"Woman, I have such great sympathy for the Hebrews that I'm gonna circumcise myself in the morning." Closing his eyes and laying his head on the pillow, he added, "You can watch, if you want."

Jezebel silently shook her head. She patted down her hair that had become messy when she had bolted upright. After sucking on a couple olives and spitting their pits onto the floor, she nuzzled up against Pygmalion.

"You know," she ventured a moment later, running her long fingers through his coarse chest hair, "it's not only treason for the queen: the adulterer who seduced her is equally guilty."

"But you seduced me."

"That changes nothing."

"Yeah, there's no justice in the world. A man runs a great risk when he penetrates a king's harem."

"You must really love me to have risked everything."

"Nah. I was already guilty of that treason several times over. I figured I couldn't be executed a second time if I slept with the queen, too."

"What do you mean?" said Jezebel curiously. "You don't mean you've been at it with Ahab's concubines?" *Not that those whores could equal me...*

With his long bangs flopping into his eyes, Pygmalion blew upwards to move the hair before responding. "Why is your first thought about his concubines?" He gently elbowed her side and smiled wryly. "You forget that his mother lives in the harem, too."

"His mother!" She snickered at the thought of him and the queen mother. *Oh, Pygmalion, you're such a cad...*

She slept wrapped in his warm embrace, her body pressed up against his like corn in its cob. It was a peaceful sleep, free from all night tremors, nightmares, and night sweats.

While it was still dark outside, the larks uttering their familiar and intense chant to resurrect the sun, the warmth of Pygmalion's body began to pull away from Jezebel. She awoke with a shiver.

"Pygmalion..." She stretched out her arm to him as he slipped out of the covers. "Don't go."

"Can't you hear the larks?" he replied, having already slipped on his sandals.

"They're nightingales. Come back under the covers."

"No, they're larks." He bent over and kissed her forehead. "The sun's almost up. I've gotta set out for Carmel."

Jezebel's naked feet hit the cool marble floor. "Forget about Carmel." She slithered up behind him and interlocked her arms around his waist. "Stay," she whispered as she nibbled his ear.

He gently stroked her arm with his thick, muscular hand. "Trekking across the hot desert in a priestly caravan ain't my idea of a fun outing. But I'm under orders of the king."

"Screw the king!"

"Frankly, I'd prefer not to." A wily look flashed in his eyes and his facial muscles formed a smirk. "He's just not my type."

Jezebel giggled. Unlocking her fingers for barely a moment, she moved her arms and slid her body around so that she could face him before entrapping him again. "The king will have hundreds of priests with him. He'll never know if one's missing."

"But I'll know." Pygmalion put his hands under her armpits and easily lifted her up. "How can I shirk this task when all my priestly brothers will be out there? As much as I'd like to lounge around with you, I can't turn my back on them. I've got to go."

He kissed her, nearly sucking the air out of her lungs when he pulled his lips away from hers. Setting her down on the floor, he crossed the room and was about to step out onto the balcony.

"But you can't go..."

Jezebel's low, plaintive voice stopped him midstep. Turning only his neck around, he raised one eyebrow and casually asked, "Why not?"

As she sashayed across the marble floor, her translucent tunic shimmered in the first rays of the rising sun. "Because," said Jezebel, placing two fingers on his right temple and playfully walking them down his cheek, "I say so."

"And I say I'm going. So what can you do to stop me?" scoffed Pygmalion, pushing her hand away in an equally playful manner.

"All I have to do is scream and a dozen armed guards will instantly burst through the door and surround you. And lest you forget, any man found in the queen's bedchamber—it's a capital offense."

Pygmalion did not respond to her threat. Instead he rested his hands on the balcony's railing and leaned over the side. "Just look at that sun," he mused, gazing at the horizon. "The rich red and orange rays, the fluffy pink clouds... gradually giving way to a cerulean blue playpen in which the doves dance with their mates. Can you feel the breeze?" He held his head up and shook his curly hair, which the zephyrs struggled to elevate to the heavens. "It's so peaceful, so beautiful..."

Before Jezebel could reäct, Pygmalion threw his legs up and leapt over the railing. "All men must die, my sweet," he said nonchalantly while nimbly wrapping his legs around the supporting column. "And if I have to die, then I want to die on a day like today!"

"Pygmalion!" She threw out her hand to grasp him but he had already begun his slide down the column.

"I'll be seeing you!" he called out as he reached the ground.

She gazed down from the balcony and watched him dash across the vast courtyard which was still empty at this time of day. When he disappeared behind the wing housing the palace's kitchen, Jezebel let out a gentle laugh.

*Oh, Pygmalion, what would I do without you?*

# CHAPTER FOUR

S ILENCE REIGNED IN THE palace parlor apart from the shuffling of clay tablets. Jezebel sat at her ornately-carved cedar table, grimacing while she made her way through a stack of foreign correspondence. Streaking across the polished tabletop and pawing at her wrists were long shadows cast by the candles on either side of her, whose gooey wax oozed a pungent scent that choked the air.

"What kind of candles are these?" said Jezebel irritably. She crinkled her nose. "They stink like shit."

Behind her silver chair stood Elishat. "I apologize, Madam. The cargo ship from Tyre sank, so we had to purchase from the local artisans."

*These Hebrews can't even make candles right.* Jezebel sneezed and sprayed the table. "Then open a window," she snapped.

Elishat scurried over to the doorway that lead outside to a patio. Pushing the double doors open, she gasped. "It's raining, Madam!"

*Raining!*

Jezebel went over to the threshold. She stretched her hand outside and felt the steady flow of rain falling from the dark gray, cloud-filled sky. "So the drought is finally broken," she mused, licking her lips with delight. Listening to the water humming as it impacted the patio's pavement, she thought, *And at the most opportune time! That man Elijah will be proved to be a fraud and the murmuring of the dissidents will be countered...*

She returned to her desk, a great smirk on her face that quickly turned into a frown. "Damn it!" she muttered, having reached the next tablet.

"What's wrong?" said Elishat. She trained her beady eyes on the cuneiform inscribed in the tablet that was shaking in Jezebel's hands.

"Baal-Eser and Ummashtart are coming. They write that they'll arrive next—"

*CRASH!*

Jezebel whipped her neck around while Elishat shrieked. The blue glass vase, which had been perching atop the cabinet beside the hallway door, was now reduced to shards upon the floor, intermixed with broken stems and saffron crocus heads decapitated by the broken glass. In place of where the vase had stood was the big hand that had displaced it. Panting heavily, stinking gobs of sweat trickling down his sickly pale face, Ahab leaned against the cabinet.

"Ahab, what's the matter?"

"Oh, Jezebel, it's terrible, terrible..." moaned Ahab, staggering over to her.

"Did you capture Elijah?"

"Ohhhhhh..."

Clapping her hands, Jezebel said, "Elishat, leave us."

With a bow, Elishat closed the hallway door as she left the room.

Jezebel grabbed her flask and thrust a cup of wine into his hands. "Take this." *And stop balling like a child...*

He greedily slurped the wine, draining the cup in a mere three seconds. While reaching for the still half-full flask, Jezebel slapped his trembling hand.

"Not until you tell me what happened."

Inhaling deeply, Ahab's distraught eyes stared into his empty glass. "Mount Carmel... what happened... it was the most frightening thing in my life. When we arrived this morning, Elijah and several hundred of his followers were already encamped upon the mountain. Probably three thousand men, women, and children from the surrounding towns and countryside assembled around the same time as we did; they thronged all sides of Carmel, cutting us off and preventing us from stationing our guards in the places your plan called for."

"So you failed to arrest him." Jezebel's left forefinger labored at picking her thumb's skin. "Is that all?" *Did the sight of your own subjects instill such servile fear in you?*

"No! Then the prophet came down and started addressing the people, saying, 'How long will you waver between two sides? If Yahweh is God, follow Him; but if Baal, then follow him.' The people greeted his challenge with silence. Then Elijah solicited two bullocks from the people, proposing that your priests choose one of them while he chose the other, and that each side cut it in pieces, and lay it on wood without any fire underneath it, and call upon the name of their respective gods. He said, 'whichever god answers by fire, He is God.' The people voiced their approval.

"Baal's priests went first. They selected a bullock, prepared it without fire, and began calling upon Baal. The priests stretched their necks up to the sky, straining their vocal cords by bellowing to Baal, and dancing around the altar so much that their vestments were on the verge of falling down. They kept this up for several hours. But Baal never answered. Then Elijah started mocking them, speaking horrible blasphemies against Baal."

"What did he say?" demanded Jezebel, clenching her fists. *As though I can't imagine…*

"He stood before the people and, laughing haughtily as though it were the greatest joke in the world, said to the priests, 'Keep on calling him, boys, for Baal absolutely is a god! Perhaps he is hard of hearing, or is away on a journey, or is busy using the latrine! Or maybe he's just asleep and needs you to awaken him! So keep on a-hollering and don't let up!' Elijah's ridicule angered the priests, and amused the people to no end, which incensed the priests even more. In response, they disrobed and whipped out their knives and lancets. It was a gruesome sight, watching their naked bodies—hundreds of them!—drip with blood as they repeatedly cut themselves in the name of Baal. But despite their self-laceration, which continued until the evening, Baal did not answer them, nor did he send fire, nor would he."

Jezebel gnashed her teeth. *Pygmalion, your piety will not be in vain! Though Baal ignored you, I will shower you with more honors than god ever gave mortal!* "Well, Elijah may have just set up a little contest—with no possibility of either side claiming outright victory—so he could have an opportunity to mock Baal and agitate the peasants against him." She petted Ahab's still-trembling hand. "But we'll capture him eventually, and then he'll learn that—"

"NOOOO!" screeched Ahab, jumping up so fast that his stool tipped over behind him. His whole body heaving, his breathing resumed its fast pace. As Jezebel stared in astonishment at him, he said shrilly, "It wasn't a draw! Elijah's God won!"

"What do you mean? How can you say that?"

"After the priests gave up, Elijah went up Mount Carmel. He took a dozen stones and formed an altar; then he dug a trench around the altar. He put the cut-up bullock on the altar and ordered the people to fill the trench and douse the sacrifice with water. Twelve large barrels full of water! Elijah then lifted his hands to the sky and declared, 'Yahweh, You are God in Israel and I am Your servant. All that I have done was done at Your command. Hear me, and let the people know that You are the true God and that they are to worship You alone!' And then..." His mouth remained open, and his tongue and fat lips moved, but not a sound came out.

*And then what?* She stared at him without blinking as the seconds passed.

Suddenly Ahab lurched over and grabbed the wine flask. Tipping his head back, he glugged half the contents while the other half rolled down his still-sweaty neck and wetted his purple robes. "Oh, Jezebel," he murmured, slightly slurring his words. He leaned over her, pressing his twitching face against hers. His hot, moist breath exhaled the scent of alcohol all over her. With his pupils dominating his fearful eyes, he whispered, "There was fire-rain!"

A flash of lightning lit up the room, followed by its boom.

"There was what?"

"Fire! Flames! Hot stuff!" Ahab dug his nails through his robes, making a huge tear across his front and revealing his sweaty chest. "Fire rained down from the cloudless sky! From the *sky*! It consumed the sacrifice. It consumed the wood... the stones... the dust... It even consumed all the water in the trench!" He fell on his knees. "O Jezebel, Yahweh is real! My forefathers were right after all! He *is* God! We must propitiate Him before He destroys us all!"

*No!* Putting her hands on his shoulders, Jezebel rose from her chair. "Get up!"

When he managed, by holding on to her for support, to rise to his feet, Ahab was hyperventilating; his face twitched violently.

Jezebel slapped his left cheek hard. "You can't honestly believe that!"

"But it was a true miracle! I saw it with my own eyes!"

"A *miracle*? *Miracle*?! You want to see a '*miracle*?!'"

Brushing past him, she stormed out of the room. Her heart was beating loudly in her ears and her palms grew moist as she trudged purposefully down the corridor. From further within the palace rang the sounds of mourning and women crying; but Jezebel ignored the noise, too busy concentrating on what she was about to do.

She arrived at a storeroom. Inside there were shelves filled with jars of all shapes, sizes, and colors. She seized an empty glass pot and set it on the dusty floor. Without needing to pause to examine each of the hundreds of jars, Jezebel quickly selected what she wanted. From this jar she dumped a handful of yellow powder into the pot; from that one she took a pinch of mulched roots. After assembling the dry ingredients, she then took a pink tube from a top shelf and poured out a black, viscous glop. A rancid smell, reeking like rotten fish boiled in cat urine, arose as soon as the glop hit the other ingredients. Jezebel picked up the pot and stirred the mixture with a spoon, making it bubble and fizzle with a crackling sound.

*If that man thinks he can use some cheap tricks on my husband,* she thought as she exited the storeroom, biting her lips, *to make him defect from Baal and restore the Hebrew heresy... He will realize how badly he underestimates Jezebel, daughter of Ithobaal!*

"Ahab!" she yelled while reëntering the parlor. "Get over here!"

"What?" Ahab stumbled over to the patio doorway where Jezebel was standing.

She pointed to an empty plant container about fifteen feet away, which the downfall by now had filled halfway with water. "Do you see that flowerpot?"

"The big round one? Yes."

"What's in it?"

Peering out, the rain hitting his head, he replied bemusedly, "Water."

"Yes, water." She walked over and dumped her pot's contents into it. A hissing sound erupted when the mixture entered the water but quickly quieted down as it dissolved. "Hand me a candle."

Ahab, holding his large hand over the flame to shield it from the rain, trudged over through the downpour. He passed the candle to her.

*You want to see some 'hot stuff?' Then prepare to be burned!*

Jezebel turned the blazing candle upside down in her hand and dropped it into the now-blackish water. Immediately the surface of the fluid exploded into flames. They shot five feet upwards as a solid mesa of fire. Despite the steady downpour of rain, these flames would not die. For a moment they even glowed white before quickly subsiding into a foot-high, albeit slow-burning, red blaze. The heat of it washed over Jezebel's face, tickling her cheeks.

While her body remained taut and unruffled by the conflagration, Ahab's legs pulled him several steps back inside. His widening eyes stared unblinkingly and his yellowish teeth, poking out of his gaping mouth, glistened from the light. "I can't... believe what I'm seeing!"

"And yet you believed it whcn Elijah ignited water," said Jezebel, approaching his side.

"H-how...?"

She touched his face and gently turned it towards her. "As you can see, he's not the only one who can perform that trick. I too know a thing or two."

"I didn't realize it was possible to ignite water..."

"All it takes is the right ingredients and a little expertise."

Ahab glanced again at the inferno. "But, but... when Elijah did it, I didn't see him throw any ingredients into the water." His wrinkly forehead rose. "In fact, he didn't even put the water in the barrel! He had the common people fill the barrels from the Kishon River, in the sight of all. He never even got near them."

"Did the people supply the barrels, or did he?"

"Uh... he did, I guess. But what does that have to—"

"Well, there you go," sneered Jezebel, patting him on his back. "It matters not one whit whether you add the ingredients to the water or the water to the ingredients! Obviously, he put them at the bottom of the barrels ahead of time, before he even offered them to the people. When they filled them with water, and the water made contact with the concoction lying at the barrels' bottoms, the water dissolved it and became combustible—all without anyone seeing what he had done. I'll commend Elijah for his legerdemain. That was a subtle thing he did, very masterfully. It's like when you poison someone's drink, not by waiting until the drink is already poured and then trying to add a poison without alerting the victim, but rather by first lacing the empty cup with a clear powdery toxin and then allowing the victim himself to pour his drink of death. No man suspects poison in his wine when it is he himself that pours. But answer me this: how many suspect the cup into which they pour?"

Gulping, Ahab placed his hand over his mouth. "I never thought about it like that... The possibilities you raised—they're terrifying in their simplicity. But..." He glanced at the crackling fire again. "Even if he did what you say, the fire—the fire came down from the sky! Yours shot upwards from the ingredients; his came down from the empty sky... How could he possibly fake that?"

She narrowed her eyes and, without any further motion of her body, nonchalantly asked, "Who says it came down from the sky?"

"I saw it! With my own eyes!"

"You *thought* you saw it." She shook her left index finger while resting her right hand on her hip. "Did you not say that he performed his rite atop Mount Carmel while you and the crowd remained at the bottom of the hill?"

After he nodded affirmatively, she exclaimed, "Of course he did! From the audience's viewpoint, one couldn't see him take out a flint and strike one of those rocks he'd set up. You yourself just saw how fast this plant container caught fire and how high the flames rose. With twelve full barrels of water, teeming with who knows how much—I can only imagine how high his flames leapt! And in the split second it took for the fire to rise and then subside—the whole thing transpiring in an instant—it would truly look, from your vantage point, as though the fire came down from heaven instead of the simple truth: that it went up from the earth."

"By Baal!" exclaimed Ahab, clasping his cheeks. "You're right! That makes complete sense. Oh, I can't believe I almost fell for that false prophet's trickery." He hugged her from her side and gently rested his cheek on hers. "Thank you, my dear. I know no one can deceive you."

Jezebel gave him a quick peck on his chapped lips. "That's right, husband." She linked her arm with his and began leading him across the room towards the hallway door. "Although the deceiver may have escaped our clutches today, he shall not prevail tomorrow. His deceptions stand exposed, his false prophecy exploded, and when our priests explain all this to the people they'll—"

When he was about two feet away from the door, his wife already reaching out to open it, Ahab suddenly stopped as though an invisible wall had run into him. His sudden halt jerked Jezebel, causing her arm to fall out of his and causing her to fall against the real wall.

*You stupid fool!* "What's the matter now?"

"Your words just reminded me," answered Ahab as he bit his fat lips and twiddled his thumbs, "that I'd forget to mention… about what happened to our priests."

She cocked her neck and blinked. "What happened?"

"Well, the people, not being as perceptive as us, were completely taken in by Elijah's deception. The putative miracle really shocked them. When it occurred, they fell to the ground in acknowledgement of Elijah's God. Then, having thus reduced them to putty in his hands, he told them..." He stared at the floor with closed eyes. "He told them to kill all the priests."

A fierce pang seized Jezebel's chest and her widening eyes consumed her face as the adrenaline hit her bloodstream. Clasping her stomach, she bent over, sputtering, "What?!"

"At Elijah's command, the mob seized our priests and led all of them down to the Kishon. There Elijah and his associates beheaded them with swords, slaughtering them one-by-one in the name of their God until the brook was dyed red and clogged with hundreds of heads." During the course of his speech, Ahab kept stretching out his shaky hand to his bent-over wife, repeatedly withdrawing it without making contact before reaching out again. In the end he refrained from ever touching her.

"Surely they couldn't have killed *all* of them?" A cold sweat dripped down her forehead as she straightened up. *Oh, Pygmalion, my Pygmalion! He can't be dead! He just can't be!* "There must've been some survivors..."

Ahab shook his head. "I'm sorry, darling. They're all gone."

Jezebel stared blankly at the wall. "Our kingdom's without priests..."

"Remember, you recruited all the original priests, my dear," said Ahab soothingly while inching rearwards out the hallway door. "I have complete confidence you'll be able to recruit their successors, too. Perhaps you could ask your brother to send us some of his?"

He left.

Jezebel, however, stayed where she was, her body swaying back and forth and her head pounding from an abrupt migraine. After several moments in this condition, she stumbled over to the patio door. With the gloomy rain continuing its depressing downpour, causing her black mascara to run down her dour cheeks and pool beneath her bleak mouth, she stopped in front of the plant container. The once raging fire had just about died down; only a few crackling embers remained.

Falling on her knees, she stretched her neck heavenwards and yelled:

"NOOOOOOOO!"

Her hands formed fists. Her teeth grated against one another to steady her mouth. Shaking her silky black hair out of her reddened eyes, which glared like those of a hate-filled crow eyeing the murderer of its fledglings, Jezebel pounded the ground so hard that her skin bled and shot red droplets several feet away.

"You may have slain my priests, Elijah," she hissed, rising to her feet, "but you will *NEVER* oust me or my gods! This land is ours now!" She placed her clenched fist over her heart, its bloody droplets staining her dress. "I swear by Baal and all the other gods that I will butcher you with the very sword you used to steal Pygmalion from me! Tremble, Elijah... tremble like all your coreligionists shall tremble tomorrow! By the time I'm through with this land, there will not remain one soul who remembers the name of your God!"

# CHAPTER FIVE

"**Y**ESTERDAY WAS THE WORST calamity," murmured Ahab, shaking his head whose brow wrinkled with especial anguish. "The absolute worst..."

"Yes, my king," answered Obadiah as he led the way down the gloomy corridor.

*It's made Jezebel so upset. She has lost her appetite for all but vengeance. My innards twist with pain whenever I see her like this...*

Obadiah stopped at the intended room. Turning the door handle, he glanced over his shoulder. "To distract from yesterday's travesty, you will find my latest acquisition inside. I hope this gift will please the king and make him forget his worries." He opened the door and a brilliant light from glowing lamps streamed into the hallway.

"Oh, my..." All the anxieties plaguing his mind evaporated. Ahab's heart intensified its pace. His mouth went dry at the same time as his already moist palms openly flooded onto the floor. Goosebumps dotted his heated skin; every part of him was moved by the sight.

There were two gilded chairs, a cedar nightstand topped with wine bottles, and a large bed inside the perfume-scented room. Lying upon the bed's golden sheets was a gorgeous woman. She wore a translucent white dress that draped seductively over her long, lithe legs splayed across the bedspread. Strands of smooth sandy hair spread out beneath her head as an octopus' tentacles. A pearl necklace encircled her slim neck and a silver belt girded her supple waist.

Licking his fat lips, Ahab asked, "Who is she?"

"Her name's Nava," replied Obadiah. He strutted over beside the bed and took her roughly by the hand. "Rise for your king, girl!"

*Not so rough,* thought Ahab, grimacing as Nava was yanked to her feet. "Thank you, Obadiah. You may leave us now."

Bowing his head, Obadiah quitted the room.

Ahab, rubbing his large hands together, lingered where he was and marveled at the attractive figure before him. Her pretty eyes, modestly concealed by a forest of long lashes, were pointed towards the floor. Inhaling the fragrant scent of frankincense emanating from her, he crept towards her. She made no movement as he advanced. He stretched out his moist palms. She remained completely still like a doe ignorant of the approaching hunter. Encountering no resistance, Ahab gripped her firm, voluptuous breast. He placed his left hand underneath her chin and, lowering his head to her eyelevel, said:

"Has anyone ever told you, my sweet, how beautiful you are? As a king, I've had my share of beautiful women; but you surpass them all like a lily sticking out among a patch of thorns."

Nava merely sighed and shut her eyes.

"You look ravishing in your dress."

"These clothes and accessories were selected for me."

He put his arm around her lower back but felt her body go limp in his embrace. "What's wrong, my little pomegranate? Most concubines cannot contain their delight at being chosen for the king." *I didn't say something I shouldn't have, did I?*

"If my lord the king," said Nava, forming a triangle with her arms while leaning her exposed neck backwards, "wishes to take his bondwoman, then I will not refuse his advances. I understand my lowly place in this cruel world; my destiny has been adequately explained to me."

"No, no, don't say it like that." Ahab spoke soothingly while gingerly lowering her arms. "You make it sound so sordid and vicious."

"But is it not? Isn't that how these trysts go? My days are not mine but subject to your whims. Your servants drag me into the bedroom whenever the mood strikes you. So long as you find me pleasing, I subsist in this state; but then, once you grow bored with me, I am banished to a house of confinement where I must live as though a widow until the day of my death. For once a king has had his way with a woman, no other man may have her."

Clasping her rosy cheek and wiping a lone tear away, he said, "I don't know what tales you've heard, nor do I deny that many kings fall short in manners. But I am a gentle king. My women know how gently I treat them, and kindly too."

"Then I must confess my ignorance," whimpered Nava. "For my experience in these matters is limited to what I've heard from other slave-women. Their stories are many, their characters diverse; yet all follow the same recurrent plotline of masters who force themselves upon unwilling slave-girls and then discard them when they are done."

"You don't have to worry about such barbaric treatment here, my little innocent." Ahab sat down at the foot of the bed and bade her sit beside him. "I positively loathe the louts who think and act as though physical strength gives them leave to snatch and take whatever they want, to overpower those weaker than they, to ill-treat the defenseless... If men like that were the only ones populating our world, what kind of life would there be worth living?"

Placing her hand atop his, Nava murmured, "So you will not force me to..."

"Of course not." Moving his other hand to stroke the top of hers, he sandwiched her warm little hand between his bulging veins. "I am not like those masters who behave more like beasts than men, and like beasts crave only satisfaction of their animal wants."

Ahab brushed her long locks aside and gazed into her bashfully-blinking eyes. "I am more than that. I yearn for something more substantial than mere flesh—something deeper, something touching upon the human heart that fills us with such great joys when it's appeased but... pangs us with mighty sorrows when starved of affection." He kissed her warm cheek. "It is love that I am searching for—love which I know must be freely given. For 'like the ravens which never repeat the line you wish unless they are tenderly taught, women cannot be forced into love but must be charmed.' My mother taught me that. It's a good maxim, one which life has convinced me to be true."

"Your mother sounds like a wise and noble woman."

Nava rested her head on his forehead. Flushing, Ahab meekly murmured, "She is."

"And you seem to me to be a very noble-hearted son worthy of such a woman, far nobler than the men I've had the misfortune to know since..." She broke off and turned her head away from him, her whole body shivering.

"What's wrong, my dear?" His eyes widening with concern, he jumped up and moved beside the bed so he could face her. "No man has ever laid his profane hands on you, has he?" *Obadiah always checks to make sure they're virgins, so her problems shouldn't be because of that...*

Shaking her head, her sandy hair moving about like streamers blowing in the breeze, Nava dabbed her eyes. "No, it's not because of that. It's just... I've dreaded this night for so long, the one they kept preparing me for. I've been dreading the thought of what would happen to me, both now and in the future... fearing what I would have to endure to please my wicked master. And then, when this day finally comes, and I actually meet you, hear your words so sweet and friendly, and I, I..."

"There, there," soothed Ahab. Kneeling down, he looked up into her reddened eyes and patted her hand. "Nothing's going to happen until you want it to."

"I thank the king so much." She kissed his wrinkly forehead. "He's treated his handmaid so much better than she could've dreamed."

Ahab climbed back onto the bed and put his arm snugly around her. "Well, you're so much more different than I was expecting. I've never met a slave-girl such as you."

"I am still learning to adapt to my new lot in life. I've only been enslaved for four months."

"What?" Some drool fell from Ahab's open mouth in shock. "You mean you were originally freeborn?" *That would explain why you talk and act so differently from those girls Obadiah usually brings me...*

"Yes, I was freeborn. Until four months ago, I was a freewoman. And I remained free from all hardship so long as I lived with my father and my three older brothers in Shechem."

"What happened?"

"Men came and killed them, sparing only me so that they could sell me into slavery."

"That's terrible!" Ahab formed a fist and shook it about the empty air. "Sweetheart, just tell me who they were—point them out to me—and I'll see to it that the criminals pay for what they've done."

"But they were your own men who did it."

"What?"

"They were royal soldiers simply following their orders."

Ahab cocked his head. "I don't understand. My men were under orders to kill them? Whatever did your father and brothers do to bring this down upon themselves? Were they outlaws?"

Glaring at the floor, Nava hunched her shoulders and glumly said, "The only crime they committed was to abstain from idols, preferring persecution in service of the true God to the corrupt pleasures offered by the false gods. You see, my father, Ichabod the son of Eli, was a Levite and a priest of the God of Israel: the kind of man your queen has declared unworthy of life."

*Her family was part of the old priesthood?* Ahab gnawed his lower lip and bounced his fingers against each other. "So... are you a worshipper of your father's God, too?"

Her brown eyes locking intensely onto his, Nava firmly declared, "Yes, I am."

Ahab's body became paralyzed by her declaration: not even his eyes blinked. *God in heaven! Obadiah has brought one of Elijah's coreligionists into the palace! If Jezebel should find out, especially after what happened at Carmel, she would be so—oh, god, I can't even bare to imagine it...* Cracking his lips ajar, he tried to articulate something but stopped when Nava placed her head against his chest.

"My dear king," she murmured, snaking both her arms around his right arm, "I pray this revelation does not alter your gallant intentions or harden your noble heart against your maidservant." Her heavy, tearing eyes looked up to him. "But if it does, and my faith offends you so, then I am prepared to rejoin my father and brothers in death."

"No, no, no; don't think such dreary thoughts. You'll always be safe with me," said Ahab instinctively, not pausing even to reflect on what it was that he was promising. *I doubt this young, beautiful maiden could be at all dangerous...* He brushed her rouged cheek that felt soft as cream. *She's more like a delicate little rose, which needs a gardener to keep it safe.* "Just don't go around talking about your beliefs, especially not around Jezebel. To be on the safe side." *No reason to provoke her unnecessarily...*

"Whatever my lord thinks is best." She yawned.

"Oh, my little dove is tired." He gingerly extricated his arms out of her grasp and rose from the bed. Looking at her, he had to blink rapidly to cover up a tear trying to escape his duct. "You've endured so much for one so young and gentle. Rest now, dear one. Your king will be here when you awake. May the—" He was about to say "gods" but quickly pivoted to the singular. "May God grant you peaceful sleep."

Nava removed her necklace and laid her head on the pillow. "Thank you, noble king."

Ahab stood there admiring her for a minute. Then he exited the room.

As he reëntered the hallway, noiselessly shutting the door behind him, Obadiah hailed him from further down the corridor.

"And how did the king enjoy his gift?" he asked, bowing his head as he approached Ahab. "Did she prove satisfactory?"

Acknowledging Obadiah with a nod, Ahab casually remarked, "I left her intact," as he began walking away from the concubine's room.

"What?" The steward's eyes went wide and he covered his gaping mouth with his gold-ringed hand. "My king, I am sorry. Was there some hidden defect in her that I failed to perceive? If so, I'll quickly find you another—"

"No, no, no; nothing of the sort."

"Then... what, if I may be so bold to ask?"

Ahab's fat lips unrolled into a brimming smile and his blubbery chin undulated with a chuckle. "Obadiah," he said, putting his arm around his steward's shoulder, "this girl isn't like all the other concubines you've bought me. There's something different about her... something esoteric in her bearing. She exceeds the mere confines of flesh and overflows with a rich ethereal quality, exhibiting a lively innocence which greatly entices me. I want her! She promises something more substantial than a single night's delight. I can envision enjoying her company for many a moon. But to maximize this burgeoning garden of delight, I will need to take my time and cultivate her like a rose..."

# CHAPTER SIX

ezebel slammed her fist down on the table. Her cup
tipped over from the shock, unleashing a sea of beer to cascade
onto the white marble floor. Panting, she yelled, "If he was spotted
in Judah, then why wasn't he captured?"

"I'm sorry, my queen," answered the captain, his gray eyebrows
and wrinkled face sagging. He bowed his head to the beer-soaked
floor. "Our contact in Judah reported seeing him pass through
Beersheba, but he did not remain there; it would seem Elijah is currently taking refuge somewhere in the Judean wilderness. We're
still searching for his precise whereabouts, but... it will require a
bit more time."

*I am surrounded by incompetents!* Jezebel, flexing her hand to
dismiss him, collapsed in exasperation onto the couch. With her
silky black hair flowing over the couch's back, she gazed up at the
silvery animals skillfully carved into the ceiling.

While the captain was exiting through the parlor entryway, Elishat passed him, her long black garments trailing her as she entered. She approached Jezebel and made a deep bow with her
grizzled head covered by a translucent veil.

"Our men still haven't captured him!"

"Well, what can you expect from men?" said Elishat coldly. Her beady eyes narrowed. "Men have been assisting that rebel for a long time."

"What do you mean?"

Elishat bent over the couch and whispered into Jezebel's ear. "Madam, it has just come to my knowledge, after interrogating all our soldiers who accompanied your husband to Mount Carmel—and who therefore witnessed Elijah surrounded by his entourage—that among those followers of the false prophet were at least three men, three Hebrew prophets to be precise, who were previously condemned by you to death."

Jezebel sprang upright. "WHAT?! Which men?"

Elishat pulled out of her sleeve a papyrus scroll and pointed at the names. "These three."

*These men are still alive!* Jezebel's skin burned with rage as her long fingers angrily unrolled the easily-ripped scroll. *Alon of Beit El tried to recruit Hebrew priests from Judah; Zebulun of Ramoth was caught proselytizing the Hebrew heresy; Uziel of Jerash sacrilegiously violated Baal's sanctuary in Dothan...* Scowling, she exclaimed, "Alon, Zebulun, and Uziel were some of the worst offenders among the infidels we've captured. I personally sentenced them to death only last month!"

"Which is why the royal guardsmen recognized them when they spotted them."

"How did this happen?!"

Elishat interlocked her fingers over her liver-spotted hands. "Obviously, they could not have escaped without someone noticing. The only conclusion is that someone in authority interposed to save them and make it look as though they were not."

"Yes," murmured Jezebel, rising from the couch. She proceeded to pace up and down the room. "All the Hebrew 'prophets' are closely guarded in the palace dungeon prior to their executions, so no one could break them out without the guards discovering the prisoners were missing. Someone—some traitor—must have interfered by taking them into his custody and letting them go. Not anyone could have done it; it would require a high-ranking official's authority... Who had oversight over these men?"

"If you recall, Madam, after passing judgment and descending from your tribunal, you asked the king to arrange the details of their executions."

*Oh, there was my mistake.* Jezebel snorted. *Ahab can't even kill men shackled in chains!* "So whom did he appoint to have them executed?"

Elishat shut her beady eyes and sighed. "The king apparently gave verbal orders alone, and I was unable to find out from the palace staff which official received the task."

"Why didn't you go ask the king?"

"I tried but his guards turned me away: he's given strict orders not to be disturbed."

"Then I'll go and ask him." She clenched her fist. *When I discover whom he appointed, I'll know the traitor...*

Following behind her mistress as she exited the parlor, Elishat said, "I must warn you, Madam, I believe the king is with his new concubine."

"Of course he is," muttered Jezebel, gnashing her teeth. *What is this—the eighth day since he bought his latest whore? I guess there's still about six days to go before he grows bored of her and moves on to the next one; they usually last only a fortnight apiece...* "Well, I'll simply have to interrupt them, then! There's no time for the king to be embracing women he's not married to when there's betrayal and infidelity lurking in our home."

As she was about to turn down the corridor leading to the harem, Elishat halted her with her arm. "Madam, the king's not in the concubine's apartment. She's with him in the library."

"With him in the library?" Jezebel's soft-angled eyebrows leapt in surprise. Whipping around and placing her arms akimbo, she said, "Whatever are they doing in there?"

"They're reading."

"Reading," echoed Jezebel, smacking her lips. *Is that now all he can manage to do with his concubines?*

"The rumor circulating in the harem," said Elishat as though reading her thoughts, "is that the king has yet to consummate his lust with her."

Jezebel, shaking her head, let out a hefty laugh. "Rumors are such liars! Saying Ahab abstained from a beautiful woman in her bedchamber is like saying wolves abstain from the ewes which stumble into their blood-stained paws!" Still chuckling, she dismissed Elishat and turned in the direction of the library.

Continuing on alone, Jezebel was about to turn at the hallway juncture that would take her to the library. But as she passed the corner, without the running feet having made any sound to alert her ahead of time, a small mass collided into her.

"Urrrrffff!" she gasped, the air being pushed out of her lungs as another body slammed headfirst into her chest. Falling backwards, she fell into a sitting position on the floor. Her arms had instinctively grasped hold of what had hit her. She dazedly shook her head before exclaiming, "Jehoram!"

"I'm sorry, Mother," cried her fourteen-year-old son shrilly. He had landed in her lap. Standing up too quickly and without sufficient care, he bumped into the table that was against the wall. A ceramic vase proceeded to roll off and shatter on the floor. "Oops." He thrust out his small, grubby hands to help her up.

Having arisen, Jezebel ran her hands through her disheveled black hair. "Jehoram, look what you did! How many times have I told you and your brother not to run indoors?" She spoke crossly and glared icily at him with bloodshot bulbous eyes.

"I know, I know..." He looked down, crossing his legs and rubbing one naked foot with the other. His white, knee-length tunic was covered here and there with gray splotches of dirt.

"You boys are always getting so dirty," grumbled Jezebel as she exasperatedly brushed some of the dust off his clothes. She worked from top to bottom. Thrashing the smooth fabric hard enough that a cloud of dust appeared, her rough hand soon elicited a yelp from him.

"Okay, okay, that's good!"

He struggled to escape her clutch. But holding him by his shoulders, she pressed her face against his and stared unblinkingly into his huge eyes.

"Listen to your mother next time." She released him and started rounding the corner. But as she did, a hand tugged at her from behind.

"Wait," begged Jehoram, pulling on her scarlet dress. "I want to tell you what Ahaziah did to me this morning."

Jezebel pushed his hand away. "Not now. I have something important to speak with your father about."

"Are you gonna yell at him too?"

*The cheeky brat.* "Would you rather I just yell at *you*?!"

Jehoram gulped and shook his wide-eyed face. "No, Mother."

"Then scat!" She gave him a swift swat on his rump to prompt his hasty departure. *Children...*

Finally able to proceed on her way, she reached the library without further delay. Two guards were stationed outside the double doors. Despite being under orders not to let anyone enter, they meekly stood aside when the queen clapped her hands and held open the doors for her.

The walls of the library were cluttered by ceiling-high bookshelves, crammed with scrolls ranging from the pristine papyrus inscribed in Ahab's reign to the brittle, moth-eaten documents that were older than the monarchy itself. A stale odor pervaded the whole room. Ahab and Nava were situated with their backs to Jezebel. Leaning over a large flat table at the end of the room, they were perusing several unrolled scrolls. Nava, pointing to one of the scrolls, was murmuring something excitedly to the king; he in turn, his arm around her shoulder, was busily massaging her.

Jezebel rolled her eyes. Stamping her foot loudly, she hollered her husband's name.

"Jezebel!" Ahab spun around, transferring his sweaty hand from his concubine to his heart. His eyes were wide and mouth agape. "I wasn't expecting—"

Glaring at him, she swaggered over to the table and elbowed her way between the two of them. She glanced at the scrolls on the table and sniffed. "What's this?"

"It's a chronicle of my forefathers detailing the genesis of the Israelites."

"And not just the Israelites," said Nava, sidestepping Jezebel so that she could stand next to Ahab. "Moses recorded the origin of the world and all mankind."

"Well, sorry for interrupting your historical studies," said Jezebel sarcastically, flicking her hair, "but I've urgent matters to discuss with you." She pointedly stared at Ahab when she articulated the word "you."

"What are they?"

"They're for the king's ears alone."

Ahab's almond eyes toggled back and forth between his wife and his concubine. "I don't think there'd be any harm if Nava stayed: I trust her."

*What?!* Jezebel's nostrils flared. *He's unwilling to be alone with his wife unless he has his whore to hold his hand?* Gritting her teeth, she asked irritably, "Is it the vapors from these musty papyrus scrolls that's making you act like Abraham?"

"What?" Ahab confusedly glanced at Nava who shrugged her shoulders in response, causing her long sandy hair to sway.

"Surprised, are you? Did you think I was utterly ignorant of Hebrew lore?"

"Frankly, yes. You've never expressed any interest in my people's past."

"This has nothing whatever to do with interest. But it does befit a queen to know the rudiments of her people's past. I know in particular the history of certain ancient Hebrews... and their women too. Like Sarah. Oh, look!" She placed a finger on the scroll. "Here's that legendary line of hers." Squinting at the Hebrew letters, she read:

"'Cast out this bondwoman and her son: for the son of this bondwoman shall not share in an inheritance with my son!' What a wonderful declaration, so passionate, so forceful, so cutting... That woman certainly knew what she wanted and what she wanted was the best; even the Hebrew God Himself sided with her against her husband!"

Patting the other woman's hand, Ahab said, "Perhaps you could wait outside, sweetie."

"Yes, my lord."

As Nava headed towards the doorway, Jezebel fixed her hateful green eyes on her while flexing her fingers. *That's right, 'sweetie.' Wait outside like an obedient little doggie.*

"So, darling," began Ahab hesitatingly, scratching his big nose, "what is it you wanted to—"

"You never visit the library! Why all of sudden do I find you reading these old, heathen writings?"

"It's for the same reason you said. There's nothing wrong in studying the history of one's nation."

*Ooh, you're suddenly a scholar now, are you?* "That strumpet isn't luring you to the heathen scriptures to try to persuade you they're true, is she?"

"Why would she do that?"

"She is a Hebrew after all, right?"

Ahab gulped. "Yes, she is. What of it?"

"Elijah continues to stir unrest among our Hebrew subjects," said Jezebel, "agitate against our gods... I think it only safe for the time being to be weary of unknown Hebrews. You never know which of them will incline their ears to the dissidents."

"Nava is a wonderful girl. It makes no difference to me what her nationality is."

"If you don't care about nationalities, then why don't you get a Tyrian whore?"

"I already have one."

Ahab spoke coolly, his countenance calm as he gazed into her eyes. His wife, unmoved by his words, issued no retort. But suddenly, his serene expression contorting into a wide-eyed, jaw-dropped, gasping look of horror, he waved his moist hands while blurting out, "Arishat, I meant Arishat! She's from Tyre!"

*Arishat...? Why's he bringing up—oh.* She shook her forehead in her palm. "Listen, I didn't come here to talk about that Hebrew. I need you to tell me whom you placed in charge of overseeing the executions of the false prophets Alon, Zebulun, and Uziel."

"Umm... those were the ones tried last month. Yes, I remember, it was Obadiah. I specifically told Obadiah after the trial that he should see to their deaths; afterwards, he reported that the deed was done."

*Obadiah! I should have known it would be that man...*

Ahab cocked his head and scratched his blubbery neck. "Why do you want to know about dead prophets?"

"Because they're still alive," breathed Jezebel.

"What? How?"

She clasped both his chubby cheeks and held his gaze on hers. "Because whoever was supposed to oversee their deaths instead permitted them to escape with their lives. It also means he violated the Statute of Treasons that you yourself enacted three summers ago. That makes Obadiah a traitor to the crown!"

"I can't believe it," said Ahab, his voice muffled due to her hands scrunching his cheeks against his chapped lips. "Obadiah a traitor? Letting condemned prophets go? Why would he do such a thing?"

"Because he's a Hebrew."

"Jezebel, you can't assume that just because of his nationality. Remember, I too am a son of Abraham."

"You're a worshipper of Baal who happens to be Hebrew. But he's a Hebrew who wants Elijah to topple us from our earthly thrones and the gods from their heavenly thrones."

"Working with Elijah?" Ahab blinked. "How do you figure that?"

She let go of his face and crossed her arms. "Who supposedly 'discovered' Elijah after months of searching for him? Who relayed Elijah's request for you to meet him at Carmel? Who freed Elijah's fellow false prophets from their justly imposed sentences?"

With a sigh, Ahab hung his head and answered, "Obadiah."

"Yes," hissed Jezebel, the veins on her temples bulging, "Obadiah the traitor! He's been abusing his authority to free the Hebrew rebels we've captured—giving aid and comfort to our enemies—and he's been working in tandem with the rebel mastermind himself to kill all of our priests and debase us in the eyes of our subjects."

Ahab clasped his knees and shook his head. "He never struck me as anything but a loyal servant, eager to please; I really liked him."

"It was all an act on his part! He comported himself specifically to win your trust—the better to betray you." *He certainly knew with what baits he could stage-manage you!* "He wormed his way into our home—into the very heart of royal government—so he could carry out his treachery."

"What do you want me to do with him?"

She patted his sweaty cheek and whispered in his ear, "Not a thing. I'll take care of everything myself."

# CHAPTER SEVEN

THE OVERPOWERING STENCH OF several different bodily fluids staining the floor assaulted her aquiline nose before she was even through the doorway. Entering the bleak cell, which was lit only by a couple of oil-lamps, Jezebel looked around. The floor was littered with iron pokers, iron plates for roasting feet, iron combs for tearing flesh away, and other tools of the torturer's craft, including several racks and a couple ropes hanging down from pulleys affixed in the ceiling. Seven sets of iron manacles protruded from the cracked stone walls. Confined in the central one, wearing only a loincloth made from sackcloth and strips of crusty brown blood, Obadiah's disheveled head slumped low and he did not look up when she entered.

One of the two burly men on either side of the prisoner approached Jezebel. "My queen, we interrogated the traitor throughout the night. He's confessed to smuggling upwards of a hundred Hebrew prophets who were condemned or about to be arrested, as well as to nourishing them in a cave. (We've already dispatched guards to investigate the said cave, although he maintains that they are no longer there.) Among the prophets he released were the three that you told us were spotted with Elijah."

"Had he any collaborators?" asked Jezebel as she nonchalantly gazed at their handiwork.

"Per your instructions, we repeatedly"—he cracked his knuckles so loudly that a noise, like children's bones breaking beneath a rampaging horse's hoofs, resounded off the walls—"put that question to him. Regardless of whatever discomfort he experienced, or however many times he fell in and out of consciousness, his answer remained coherent and unaltered. He conceived the escapes himself and executed them through the abuse of his high office. Apart from several of the first smuggled prophets, he had no further assistance in rescuing the rest; he strongly maintains that he had no help from within the palace nor were any royal servants privy to his treasonous intentions."

"You are certain he's telling the truth?"

His scarred jaw forming a grin that revealed his crooked front teeth, the torturer said, "Confidence is high."

"Thank you, Hannibal," said Jezebel, stretching out her hand and deigning to let him kiss it. "You are one man whose expert hands I know I can trust." *And there are so few men who I can say that about!* She glared at the prisoner. "I wish to speak with the traitor alone. Leave us."

Hannibal and his colleague bowed their heads and exited the chamber of torture.

"Oh, Obadiah," she called slowly with a faux-sweet tone of voice as she sashayed over to him, "there's something I want to say to you."

He did not move his head, which was still flopping downwards. Several long streaks of dried blood were caked on his face; the skin where his beard had been was doubly red from the violent removal of the hairs and several spots where chunks of flesh had been combed away.

Jezebel grabbed the pail of water that lay beside several teeth on the floor and, cold droplets hitting her painted fingernails as she lifted it, hurled its contents onto him.

"Waaahhh urfff ugh!" exclaimed Obadiah. His whole body convulsed from the shock of the cold. Shaking his heavily bruised head which was also missing many large clumps of hair, he looked up and turned his swollen black eyes on her. "You!"

"Yes, me!" She pinched his mouth and started manipulating his charred lips. "The Sidonian whore, the witch of Phoenicia, the evilest of women, She-Who-Brings-Abominations—isn't that what you little Hebrews call me?"

Grimacing, Obadiah spat, "No matter how obscene your reputation is, it cannot equal the vileness of your soul, you bloody monster!"

"A bloody monster, am I?" She laughed. Then, narrowing her bulbous eyes into slits, she punched him in his groin. "You are the bloody monster, Obadiah! You and that accursed man Elijah! He massacred hundreds of my priests—the best of men!—and you helped him do it!"

"I never knew he was going to kill them," gasped Obadiah, panting heavily from the pain. His nostrils flaring and his fist-forming hands shaking their shackles, he exclaimed as saliva spurted out of his frowning mouth, "But I thank the great God of Israel that he did! Those heathen priests of yours were corrupting our land—just as you wanted them to, you pagan witch!" He spat on her. "My only regret is that I couldn't bring a sword against them myself."

Wiping the disgusting spit off her face, Jezebel thought, *This filthy beast needs some taming.* She turned her back on him and began scanning the instruments of torture strewn across the floor. "Emotions like love and hate gain in strength from our interactions with others. The foolish majority hates others only for the minor grievances of life: an unkind word spoken here, a pilfered purse there, a breach of etiquette upon another's spouse... Yet only a few can inspire the extreme revulsion I detect in you. You hate me with perfect hatred, don't you?"

"As every true son of Israel should!"

She picked up a scourge and ran her other hand through its many leather thongs. "That may be true. And I can abide most Hebrews' hate. But you're not any Hebrew," she said, dropping the scourge. "You were our steward, the highest ranking man in the palace besides the king himself, free to go and act in subversion of our government. I never liked you. My husband did (and we all know *why*). I'd have preferred a Tyrian nobleman to a Hebrew peasant. Yet up till now I had not suspected you of treason. What a fool I was! Your treachery was manifest for all to see: not the springing of convicted criminals, mind you, but the living, breathing means you employed to try to drive my husband away from me and Baal."

"I haven't the faintest idea what you're saying."

Jezebel picked up an iron poker and jabbed it into his ribcage between his ninth and tenth ribs. "Don't play dumb with me, you whore-pimp bastard! For far too long you've been satiating my husband's lust by procuring him youthful flesh of the female variety."

Coughing blood, Obadiah hoarsely said, "All I did was find concubines suitable for the king. It had nothing to do with politics or religion. After languishing with you, your husband needed an actual woman for a change."

"An indecent tongue in an indecent man!"

"There's nothing indecent about the services I provided the king. Under Moses' law, a man is permitted to take bondwomen to be his concubines, otherwise known as wives of the second class."

"Spare me Moses and his archaic rules!" growled Jezebel, striking him again. She bit her lip and growled, "I've heard enough about that damned rebel to last me forty years! Just tell me if that last whore you bought is one of you Hebrew heretics?"

Obadiah's eyes fluttered as he let out a gasp. His voice sank lower. "You suspect she's a believer?"

"Unlike the others you procured, who were content to perform their services in bed, she has taken it upon herself to lead him out of the bedchamber and into other matters. She seems, in fact, quite intent on filling the king's mind with ancient Hebrew tales." *And he's such a pig, he'd follow whatever sordid bait Beauty dangled in front of him...*

"She may or may not be a worshipper of my God. And I pray to God she isn't. For if I had known, I would never have brought her or any other worshipper of Yahweh into this demonic hellhole of yours!"

Suddenly he burst into laughter. His sides heaving in pain from the effort and his face groaning, he nevertheless managed to cackle heartily in between the bloody coughs.

"What are you laughing at?" She put one arm akimbo and rested the poker on her thigh. *Has he lost his mind?*

"I just realized something." He ceased laughing and stared past her. "I spent last night in agony, imagining that my coming death is owed entirely to devotion to my God. Yet after hearing you just now—you seem to hate me more for recruiting concubines than for saving the men of God!"

"Lies!" Jezebel thrust her arms out so fast the poker escaped her clutch and soared into the wall.

"Your reaction betrays your words." A huge smirk engulfed his partially toothless face. "Why do you hate the king for having a little harem? Are you *jealous*, Jezebel? Afraid he'll forget you? Your own father was legendary for his womanizing. I'd have thought you'd be accustomed to having other women around."

*My father never needed maggots to find his women for him!* Grinding her teeth, she grabbed his remaining clumps of hair and pulled his head back. She pressed herself so close to him that her whole face became covered by his foul breath. "You enjoy infuriating me? If you were other than a foolish man, you'd know not to irritate the one holding your life in her hands."

"Why? You'll kill me anyway."

"I assure you, a blow to the neck from a quick sword is far less unpleasant a death than others I can devise."

Obadiah snorted. "Then I guess I can't count on any possibility of mercy. You're always your nastiest around this time of the month."

Jezebel scratched his face from one cheek to the other, digging her long red nails into his flesh and ripping it open. Ignoring his howl of pain, she stormed to the door. "Hannibal!" she yelled, flicking the hue-matching blood off her painted fingers.

"At your command," answered Hannibal as the door opened.

"Unfasten the prisoner!" She turned around to shoot an icy glare at him. "We're going to take him to his execution."

Operating at a fast professional pace, Hannibal and his colleague removed the beaten man from his bonds and manhandled him out of the chamber. They followed behind Jezebel who—her mind overflowing with thoughts of the priests slain by the Hebrews, her heart racing with fear of what the rebels opposed to her might next do, and her palms sweating with a feverish hatred for Obadiah—held her head high and marched solemnly to the stables and outbuildings behind the palace.

Drawn by her grave countenance and the groans of the prisoner being dragged behind her, a crowd of maids, cooks, eunuchs, counselors, cupbearers, and others started trickling out of the palace. They gathered in a hush round the pigpen where Jezebel had halted. Stretching a hundred feet from the stable and about forty feet wide, this muddy and trash-filled breeding ground reeked with the stench of porcine dung.

The boars and sows were inside the stable, making their customary grunts. But at Jezebel's command, a couple of her Phoenician swineherds dashed into the outbuilding. Smirking while she waited for them to return, she watched as Obadiah was bound to a stake set up in the center of the sty.

"You may kill me today," he yelled, his voice almost drowned out by the murmuring of the growing crowd, "but God will remember His servant! My blood shall cry out to Heaven and Heaven's King shall avenge me upon you!"

Jezebel snickered, "Heaven's King *is* watching us but his name is Baal! In his name I do condemn you to death for treason."

Faint squeals erupted from the stable just as she finished speaking, a plaintive noise whose piercing screech shushed the crowd. Everyone turned their heads to watch the swineherds emerge from the building. With unsmiling faces and a strangled piglet in both their hands, they treaded over to Obadiah. The condemned man struggled violently despite his chains, shouting, "Unclean, unclean!" as the swineherds smeared his whole body with the piglets' blood. Having finished bloodying him, they left at his feet the piglets whose limbs and eyes scarcely remained clinging to their mangled corpses. As soon as the swineherds had jumped over the pen's fencing, Jezebel raised her hand and the stable door was opened.

A shrill, pained squeal roared from the stable at the moment that a large boar, completely midnight black apart from its sallow horns, dashed outside. Hot breath visibly shooting out of its snout, the craze-eyed beast jumped up onto its hind legs and thrust its tusks upwards as though intending to pulverize the sky. Falling back to earth, its thick hooves gouging the ground, the hateful boar galloped over to Obadiah and the bodies of its offspring.

Not blinking lest she miss a single glorious moment of it, Jezebel licked her lips whilst rubbing her hands. *Die, Hebrew scum, die! In the afterlife may Baal boil you in pig dung!*

"UUUGGHHHHHHHHHHHH!"

A scream and torrent of blood gushed from Obadiah's mouth as soon as the boar impaled him. Yet despite killing the presumed murderer of its offspring by the force of its first blow, the enraged beast did not stop. It kept up its furious onslaught. As the man's bowels came out along with the deadly tusks, tearing a giant gap in the abdominal flesh, the boar speared him again and again and again. By the time the boar eventually let up on its rampage, its black head had been turned completely red from the condemned man's blood and bits of intestines clung to its tusks.

The crowd had remained subdued throughout this unprecedented spectacle. For although Jezebel had previously slain many Hebrew men for prophesying in the name of their God or else for speaking out against her campaign of persecution, she had not concocted for them such a bizarre or ignominious method of death, calculated to violate native taboos, as she had done for Obadiah.

A wicked smirk engulfed her face. Raising her hand to signal the crowd, she declared, "So let this and more befall all who would betray the monarchy and Baal!"

Taking one last glance at the tattered remains of the condemned man, Jezebel snorted and turned to go. She made her way through the murmuring crowd, which quickly cleared the way for her, and headed for the palace. As she was about to enter, Elishat rushed out to greet her.

"Madam," she panted, bowing her head, "I've been looking for you."

"What is it?"

"Your brother and sister—"

"*Half*-sister!" Jezebel corrected her.

"They've expedited their journey: they're arriving tonight."

# CHAPTER EIGHT

"**T**HIS BREEZE FEELS SO cool," murmured Ahab, closing his almond eyes and lapping the late afternoon air with his tongue. "Astartë's priests say each breeze is a little goddess begotten by cloud-gathering Hadad." Gazing out the balcony doorway, he added with a chuckle, "But I heard Baal's prophets joke they're only Dagon's farts!"

His arms squeezed Nava's warm body tighter in embrace, attempting to solidify their lock on her. But she pulled away, squirming like an eel trapped within a fisherman's net, and retreated to the couch on the opposite side of the parlor. As she sat down, she released a feeble yet audible sigh.

"What's wrong, dear one?" said Ahab. His eyes grew wide and gazed past her long lashes in search of her round brown eyes as he sat down beside her. "Was it something I said?"

"Yes, my lord, it was." Nava laid her small hand on his. "You referenced the foreign gods again; and although I do not think you meant to, your words have upset me."

He grimaced. *O Ahab, you fool! You know she doesn't like to hear that.* "I apologize for forgetting, my beloved," he said, gently stroking her soft hand. "The gods stole my wits from me." *Damn it! I did it again!*

Nava brushed his hand aside and wandered over to the large table made of Lebanon cedar. Her long thin fingers ran over the intricate carvings of the elephant tusk set atop the table, which depicted several swans in flight. "I know you must think me a foolish girl for being so sensitive to mere words..." Ignoring his protestations to the contrary, she continued:

"Yet I cannot help how I feel. I am a worshipper of the God of Israel... one of the few left. Like my father before me, and my brothers too—all of whom paid the ultimate penalty for daring to keep the faith amid persecution—my heart is pained whenever I hear vain idols treated as though they were living gods, not the wood and stone that they are. And I am doubly sensitive today after the... atrocious indignities the queen inflicted upon your steward."

"That bothered you?" Ahab cocked his head. "I didn't realize Obadiah's death meant so much to you. I was under the impression you had a distinct dislike for him."

Her body swaying as she shifted her weight from one foot to the other, Nava fingered her sandy hair. "You speak truly, my lord. From a wholly personal angle, I considered Obadiah a most loathsome character. I can't know what you saw in him that led you to confide your affairs in him; all I know is my experience with him. Delighting in his dingy dealings, he only saw me as a means of gratifying his king. From the moment he bought me he treated me no differently than a farmer treats his flea-bitten, yellow-toothed jackass."

*The villain! Had I only known with what cruelty he could mistreat angels...*

"Yet, despite my own feelings for him," she continued, her voice crackling and a lone tear escaping from her right eye, "I remember that he was a fellow Israelite and, what's more, a coreligionist, one of the last. For him to be martyred for our God... and killed in a manner calculated to offend the precepts of Moses' law—I am moved with great compassion for him." Hanging her head down, she added, "I also can't help but fear that one day a similar fate will befall me. For if the king's own steward can meet such an ignominious end, what chance have I, a mere slave, a living corpse, to escape such a death?"

Ahab rushed to her side and clasped her hands. "No, no, banish such fears from your mind!" His heart beat faster and his face flushed when she laid her head on his shoulder. "I promise you, I will never do anything to you."

Her watery eyes blinked their long lashes and her large pupils bore into his. "I trust you, O kindest lord. But what of your wife? If she were to discover my faith, and seek my death..."

"Don't fear her, my love. Not even if she curses me with all three thousand curses that her father, a priest of Astartë, handed down to her will I let her damage one hair of your sweet head."

"You won't betray me?"

"Never!"

"You have gladdened your handmaid's heart beyond anything she could have hoped for!" exclaimed Nava. She hugged the blushing king. Skipping to the center of the room, she knelt down in a southerly direction so that her body faced Jerusalem's far-off temple. "I must thank the God of Israel for the king of Israel's mercy!"

When she closed her eyes, Ahab sighed. "Shall I leave you then?"

"Instead of leaving," answered Nava opening one brown eye, "why not pray with me?"

"With you?" He cocked his head. *Even though we worship different gods?*

"Yes! Let us unite in praise of the God Whom our forefathers worshipped."

Ahab did not immediately respond. *Is this permissible?* he wondered, turning her request over in his mind. Ogling the beautiful concubine, Ahab licked his chapped lips and rubbed his moist palms together. *Well, Baal doesn't mind if I worship Astartë; El is not irked when I offer sacrifices to Anat. There's a whole pantheon of gods, varying in name from nation to nation, whom humans cultivate with various rites and ceremonies... What harm could it be to worship one more god?*

Without a word, he moved beside her and fell to his knees. His hands were just about to touch in prayer when, his eyes popping open, he suddenly thought:

*The gods may not care, but what about Jezebel? She is annoyed at me for simply reading the ancient chronicles and sacred writings of my forefathers. If she saw me praying to Him...*

"Don't worry," said Nava, smiling at him. Her long fingers touched his thick neck. "Everything will be all well."

The soft tap of Nava's hand having dispelled his rising angst, Ahab thunderously clapped his hands together and bowed his head. *O Yahweh, I don't know if You even exist or are merely a name as Jezebel's people say; but if You do exist, and You exercise power in this land, then I thank You for letting me have this gorgeous devotee of Yours. Whatever god can claim her as his handiwork is truly one to be worshipped.*

The minutes passed in silence. Ahab prayed as much as he could think. Even after he had exhausted the thoughts he could share with the invoked deity, Nava taught him words to say which her father had taught her and his father before him. After spending almost half an hour in fervent silence interspersed with vocalized hymns, Ahab opened his eyes at the sound of Nava rising to her feet.

"Thank you so much for granting my request, dear lord," she said. "I never dreamt that one day I would be praying to my God beside the king of Israel."

He stroked her cheek and gave her a kiss. "Prayer is nothing, my little pomegranate. It was a painless thing to grant. And I'll be happy to pray with you whenever you wish."

"Oh, thank you, my lord," she exclaimed, embracing his neck and kissing his stubbly face.

"No, I thank you." Smiling giddily, Ahab stroked her thigh and added, "You know, worshipping the way my forefathers did felt kind of good; the words fell off my tongue so naturally. Maybe I should take it to the next level: I can get a goat and offer it up as a sacrifice for Yahweh. How about that? I might not look like it, but I'm actually pretty good at slaughtering sacrificial victims."

With a gasp, her long eyelashes jumping upwards, Nava pulled back. Her face had blanched and her lips were quivering. "No, you can't sacrifice!"

"Why ever not?" spluttered Ahab, covering his heart which was now throbbing as a result of her unexpected reäction. *If prayers are good, aren't sacrifices better?*

"It is only lawful for priests to sacrifice in Jerusalem. Don't you remember what happened after Moses led Israel out of Egypt?

God designated his brother Aaron and his descendants—and them only—as His priests. You may be a king, but it was by sacrilegiously performing sacrifices himself that King Saul was stripped of his crown. For no sacrifice is acceptable to God unless it is conducted by a son of Aaron, such as my father was..."

"I'm sorry. I forgot how great a difference in cult there is between our native religion and the one we imported from the Sidonians."

"Do not apologize, dear king." She rested her head against his beating chest. "Your heart was in the right place when you made the offer, however unlawful it might be."

Ahab opened his dry mouth to offer one last apology; but before the first repentant sound could sally forth, he was interrupted by a guttural "humph" from the doorway. He whipped his head toward the doorway and startled even worse than he had a moment ago.

"Jezebel!"

Glaring at Ahab with bulbous eyes that were unmistakably livid, her nostrils flaring, she curtly hollered, "Come, we've got guests to greet!"

# CHAPTER NINE

---

O N THE WEST SIDE of the palace, the ten mammoth windows of the Reception Hall offered a perfect portal through which the reddish rays of the setting sun could penetrate the room. Opposite each window was a polished bronze shield larger than a man; these served not to defend lives in war but to reflect and magnify the sunlight. The white marble floor glowed ruddy apart from the black mosaic square in the center of the room. It was on this square that the king and queen awaited their guests.

"Remember," said Jezebel, the bridge on her aquiline nose soaring as her fierce green eyes met Ahab's, "my brother may cite the slaughter of our priests by the rebels in an attempt to question the effective authority and stability of our government. Nothing could be farther from the truth! The chief rebel is in exile and our officers are making progress in silencing dissent."

The wrinkles on her husband's forehead nodding approvingly, he said, "And the spy within the palace is no more."

"Yes, but don't bring that up," chided Jezebel as the veins on her neck briefly bulged. "He doesn't need to know our government's *sanctum sanctorum* was ever compromised."

"But I should mention the weather, right?"

"Of course! With the end of the drought, we will soon have agricultural self-sufficiency again. With us no longer needing to import food from Tyre, that's a lot of money my brother is about to lose. We can use that money as leverage in the negotiations." *One way or another, I'll get his assistance...*

"I hear footsteps."

Jezebel ran her hand through her silky black hair one last time. Then she clenched her teeth, pushed out her chin, and fixed her bulbous eyes on the doorway.

"Sister Jezebel!"

A tall man, sporting a ruby-encrusted gold crown and loose-hanging robes that quivered from every muscular movement he took, burst into the room. Letting out a hearty laugh from his wide chest, he crossed the floor in only a few giant strides and towered over Jezebel. Without giving her even the opportunity to protest by the suddenness of his action, he seized her by her waist, lifted her up off the floor, and spun her around three times before plopping her down.

"Baal-Eser!" exclaimed Jezebel dazedly as she hurtled through the air.

"Just like old times, right?" he exclaimed with a grin as he set her down again.

*Yes, however did I survive without my brother's rough embraces?* thought Jezebel, catching her breath. While smoothing her ruffled dress, she cast a penetrating glance over Baal-Eser and frowned. *He's certainly looking well despite the burdens of kingship...*

"It's been too long since our last family get-together."

"Those were my sentiments exactly when I received your letter."

Awkwardly sidling up between them, Ahab began to say, "Jezebel and I are both delighted that you and Lady—where is—?"

"This is a nice palace you've got, Ahab!" interrupted Baal-Eser, who slapped his back so hard that Ahab yelped and jumped a half-pace forwards. "I particularly like this room. The reflecting shields have an aura of divinity about them, like they belong in the sun god's palace. Did you design the room's layout specifically for them?"

"It is great, isn't it?" With bright and alert eyes, Ahab clapped and shook his hands together. "Jezebel thought up this gorgeous room. While it's a particular favorite of mine, the whole palace exemplifies the new cultural style for Israel that I've sought to—"

"Maybe I'll have my architects build me something similar; I think an eastern alignment with the rising sun would be far grander, along with maybe twenty windows. Sounds extravagant, I know, but I can afford it. My coffers are overflowing, and I confess I owe much of it to Israel's considerable purchases of—"

"Our coffers equally overflow and shall overflow even more as soon as our cropland recovers," interposed Jezebel, flicking her hand. Narrowing her eyes, she added, "If you marvel at the strength and prosperity of our kingdom now, then you can only imagine what greater things the future augurs."

"You're sure it augurs prosperity?" he asked, raising an eyebrow.

Smirking, she put her arm around his neck and whispered into his ear, "I oversaw the augury myself; the priest wouldn't dare perceive anything inauspicious in the entrails so long as I was present."

Baal-Eser slapped his thigh while guffawing. "That's the little sister I remember! Tyre has lacked your unique sense of cunning since Father gave you to Israel. It may have solidified his alliance, but I think he miscalculated: we'd have been better off with you at home."

Ahab frowned and his forehead wrinkled exceedingly as the seconds passed without Jezebel contradicting her brother's commentary. But she said nothing because thoughts of the true reason for her brother's visit kept revolving in her mind.

*Does he think he can win me over with such unmitigated flattery? He never complemented me before unless I had something he wanted. He wouldn't have invited himself here if he didn't need something... But what?*

Thereupon a woman entered the room. From beneath a translucent cerulean dress, her long legs glided effortlessly across the floor. She held a pearl-studded fan which she gently flourished in front of her rouged cheeks; her long eyelashes blinked as she trained her eyes on Jezebel who blankly stared back at her.

"Ah, here at last!" exclaimed Baal-Eser, throwing one arm up for emphasis. "I was wondering what was taking you so long."

As soon as she was within distance, Ahab hastened to plant a kiss on her delicate, flawless hand. "It's always a pleasure to get together with Jezebel's relations, especially one as fair as you, the dearest sister of my wife."

*Half-sister!* Jezebel forced back a spurt of stomach acid and, suppressing a scowl, secretly clenched a fist behind her back.

"Hello, elder sister," said Ummashtart with her sweet voice. Her lips formed a playful smile as Ahab released her hand. "I have no doubt that you must thank the gods daily to have so polite and kind a man as Ahab for a husband."

Jezebel flashed a glare at her blushing and obviously self-contented husband before answering, "Yes, dear little sister, my admirable Ahab is unlike all the other men I've known. Were it not for his particular traits that so distinguish him, neither Israel nor I would be in the enviable positions we are today." Trying not to smirk, she added, "And how is your warlike husband, Lord Hasdrubal, faring these days?"

"You'll have to ask the worms," snorted Baal-Eser. He spat upon the marble floor to Ahab's visible disgust. "That traitor plotted to stab me during the Festival of Melqart. So I crucified him."

"Simply terrible," murmured Jezebel nonchalantly. She turned to Ummashtart and shook her head. "Your husband connived so villainous a plot right under your nose? And against your own brother? And you never knew?"

"On the contrary," interjected Baal-Eser, coming between them, "it was Ummashtart who exposed his treason; I owe my life to her." He took her hands in his and began stroking them. "She's always been a darling, always looking out for my best interests. That's why, after the incident, I decided that I should make her my latest bride."

*What?!* Jezebel's jaw dropped but she quickly closed it with a snap.

Ummashtart smiled and affectionately pinched Baal-Eser's cheek. "Yes, Jezebel, our brother is an infinitely better husband than Hasdrubal could ever be."

Ahab jerked his hands up in front of his face and thereby shielded his gaping jaw with his sleeves. Peering out with his wide eyes and raised eyebrows, he said, "Oh, you... married your sister? I didn't know Tyrians did that..."

"Sure. Why not? We're only half-siblings; it's not like we shared a womb or anything."

"Well, I, uh, guess that's, uh, a fine match," spluttered Ahab, alternating his gaze between Baal-Eser and Ummashtart. "It just seems a little strange in these parts."

Jezebel leaned over and whispered in Ahab's ear, "What's so strange? Don't those old writings your whore's been reading you—don't they say that your forefather Abraham married his half-sister, too?"

"But that was when the world was young. It's no longer a common norm nowadays." Blushing, Ahab whispered in his shrill voice, "I mean, I also have a half-sister, and the mere thought of it... Yuck!"

*It's not the incest that disturbs me,* thought Jezebel as she eyed her siblings acting affectionately towards each other. *Even if they came from different tribes from opposite ends of the earth, separated by shark-infested seas, tiger-filled mountain ranges, and bone-dry deserts untouched by even a single drop of camel's urine, why would he choose to marry HER of all people?*

"Now that we've given you our family update," said Baal-Eser, clearing his throat, "and gotten the small talk out of the way, are you two going to keep telling us about Israel's promising agricultural gifts or are you finally going to show us some of that good Phoenician food we've sold you?" As if to underscore the pertinence of his question, his stomach unleashed a loud growl.

"I see your appetite is as insatiable as ever! Well, come on. The royal table and its bounties await us. You may thank the gods that our kitchen staff, upon hearing of your early arrival, could work so hastily. Otherwise, you'd have to—"

Jezebel was interrupted by a sudden sound emanating from the outdoors; it did not die down but sustained itself.

"What's that?" said Ahab, his mouth hanging open as he turned his head from side to side.

"I don't know," murmured Jezebel as she started heading for the balcony. *But it doesn't sound good...*

The unknown sound grew louder as she approached.

"It sounds like a herd of angry cattle," remarked Ummashtart.

*Yeah, right. As though you'd know what cattle sound like—actually, on second thought, you would know cowness very well.* Jezebel stepped out onto the balcony and craned her neck into the distance. The blood in the veins on her forehead was thumping loudly. The evening breeze tickled her frowning lips but could not make her smile. Instead, her frown turned into an outright teeth-bearing snarl.

In the distance, coming down the north road from the city and advancing at an irregular pace that varied from a sluggish amble to sudden bursts of speed, was a large mob. There had to be at least five hundred men. Though they were still too far away for their expressions to be visible, their heated shouts were an audible testament to their foul mood. Their spades and pitchforks not only clanged angrily but were flashing from the glint of their torches, whose flames illuminated the impressive size of the mob. Still about a mile from the palace, the mob continued steadily on its way.

Jezebel clenched her fists around the balcony railing and exhaled angrily.

Baal-Eser came up beside her and glanced at the approaching mob. Without any noticeable change of expression, he folded his arms and casually asked, "Do your subjects always greet your guests this way?"

"Not until you arrived," she replied, glaring at him. "Do you often provoke this kind of response in your travels?"

"Comebacks have never failed you, Sis."

"You'll have to dine without us," she said as she strode back inside.

"Need any help?"

Her lips curling as though she were tasting sour lemons, she tersely answered, "No."

"Well, Ummashtart and I will leave you to this then."

# Chapter Ten

A s soon as she had come in from the balcony, Jezebel left her siblings and wide-eyed husband in order to seek out Abibaal, her chief of security. She had no need of informing him of the approaching mob, since word had already spread throughout the palace. Squeals, gasps, panting, and frantic feet running down the halls resounded on all sides. Many servants, their sweaty hands clasping their heaving chests, rushed past Jezebel without the usual salutations and marks of their humble status.

"Where did this mob come from?" demanded Jezebel, trudging down the corridor while elbowing servants out of her way. *They can't all be from the city...*

"Men have been pouring into the city from the countryside since this morning," answered Abibaal, matching her pace.

She cocked her head and glared at him. "No one informed me of this."

"Our spies monitoring them didn't report anything dangerous," gulped Abibaal, his baritone voice temporarily rising in pitch before returning to normal. "The rustics initially dispersed among the city; it was only forty-five minutes ago that they congregated in the town square and thence began their march on the palace."

"Why are they coming? What set them off, and why now?"

"From what little info we've gleaned, the rioters are furious over the execution of Obadiah this morning: that's a thing they've been constantly mentioning. As to why they're marching on the palace—it's a safe assumption they're not delivering a petition."

"Are these Elijah's people? Has the blood of our priests whetted his appetite for royal blood, too?"

Abibaal shook his head. "There's no evidence for that. They may simply be common Hebrew subjects who, despite being generally indifferent to your religious policies, were nevertheless enraged by the way you killed Obadiah, which violated a host of Hebrew taboos."

*Aw, my precious Hebrew peasants are upset over how I treat them?* She bit her lip and tasted blood while she clenched her fists. *I'll show them what sort of treatment filthy beasts deserve...*

When they reached the courtyard on the north side of the palace, they exited the building and went out to inspect the defenses. Fifty cruel-looking men, wearing polished bronze armor that encased all but their snarling faces, and each menacing a large curved sword, were lined up in five rows. Jezebel looked them over and smiled.

A faint peep arose from behind her.

"Jezebel," wheezed Ahab, his heavy feet thudding over to her side, "I've assembled the palace guards like you asked."

"How good of you," she murmured. Motioning to the guards' commander, she asked, "Captain, are you ready to engage the rustics?"

The grizzled officer, his face marred by a long scar that ran from one cheek straight over his nose to the other, bowed his head. "The infantry awaits Your Majesty's command, but the cavalry is unavailable."

Her face flushed red. "What do you mean 'unavailable'? Where the hell are they?!"

"Pursuant to the king's command, this morning we dispatched the palace cavalry to Mount Tabor to greet the foreign dignitaries as they were passing through the countryside. The horsemen have yet to return, presumably needing to rest the horses after having to make the last-minute trip at the briskest pace."

"YOU!" Jezebel, the veins on her neck bulging, spun around and trained her bulbous eyes on Ahab. "You sent the cavalry out—the palace's chief defense!—just to greet my brother? Why would you do that?"

Wringing his hands, Ahab could not bear to meet her gaze but turned to face the ground. "I thought it would be great if your brother could see our cavalry's strength... see how strong our monarchy is..."

"That strength surely does us a lot of good when we need it but don't have it!"

"Well, I couldn't know this would happen!" mumbled Ahab. *IDIOT!*

Sighing, Jezebel crossed her arms and began pacing. "If we lack cavalry," she remarked aloud, not addressing Ahab, "we can't charge the mob and crush it. Given the size of it, our ground soldiers... Captain, have we any more soldiers?"

He shook his head.

"Abibaal," said Jezebel, snapping her fingers, "round up the servants and arm them with whatever's at hand. When the mob reaches the palace..." She broke off, her fingers rapidly tapping her thighs as her mind galloped roughshod towards a solution.

"Jezebel," murmured Ahab, placing a hand around her tense shoulder and gently leading her aside. "As much as I respect the guards' abilities, there are far too many rioters for them to hold off. Before they reach the palace, I think we should leave while we still can."

"WHAT?!" yelled Jezebel, slapping his arm off her. She glared fiercely at him like a lioness defending her mewling cubs from hunters who are stained with the blood of her mate. "Abandon our home to these marauders' torches? Give them the satisfaction of watching their betters flee in terror? Never!"

Ahab's eyes were wide and a long streak of sweat ran down his cheek. "But the danger! A palace can always be rebuilt. But what if they kill us?"

Holding the hem of her dress up, Jezebel declared, "Royal robes make great burial garments, crowns excellent funereal shrouds."

"Don't be so dramatic! You must look at our situation realistically."

"It is *you*, Ahab, who must be realistic! You must think of not just these rioters but how your actions will be viewed by the whole kingdom. A people is like a wild stallion that is still in the throes of being broken: ease up for an instant, just one idle moment that allows him to forget who is in charge of whom, and his dormant ferocity will return and he'll throw you off so hard that you'll break your neck on impact. If you show weakness by allowing a motley mob of stinking peasants to drive you from the heart of government, you'll fan this spark of rebellion into a general conflagration, and then you can expect to join a long line of kings deposed by their own subjects, and... that's it!"

"That's what?"

Ignoring him, Jezebel rushed over to the captain of the guard. "Captain, your men may be too outnumbered to drive the mob off, but they could still exert enough pressure to steer their motion and corral them in the northern courtyard, could they not?"

"Yes, I suppose so. But what will that accomplish?"

"You'll see..."

\*\*\*

STRAIGHTENING HER DRESS, JEZEBEL stepped out onto the balcony. The courtyard lay beneath her. By now the sun had set; the only light to illuminate her view was the glow given off by the rioters' menacing torches. The mass of rioters were approximately two hundred feet away from the palace, their progress slowed by the palace guards diligently trying to hold them at bay.

Jezebel gazed straight down and called to one of her guards. "Tell our recalcitrant subjects that we offer them one—*and only one*—offer of pardon if they will immediately disperse and swear never again to threaten the glory of our reign."

The unfortunate guardsman hastened across to the frontline of the rioters. From the ferocity of his gesticulations, he was clearly trying to assuage the crowd's anger with the offer of a royal pardon. But the hail of hoes, buckets, and other metal instruments that came raining down upon him unmistakably indicated the response of the crowd. As the guardsman struggled back onto his feet and fled, cries of, "Storm the palace! Kill the Sidonian vermin! Burn the bitch down!" roared from the enflamed crowd and resounded through the air.

A devilish grin upon her face, Jezebel laughed inwardly. *I was hoping they'd choose this course...*

She turned to glance inside the palace and with a nod beckoned an archer lurking in the wings to step forwards. He joined her on the balcony. With a calm stoic expression upon his face, he raised his bow and strung it with a flaming arrow. He aimed the weapon at the ground beside the first line of the crowd and fired.

A crackling sound, exploding exponentially louder, screeched through the sky as a wall of flames shot up from the targeted ground. The fire instantly engulfed the men standing nearest where the arrow landed—luckless fellows who, in the darkness, had been completely oblivious to the thick layer of oil drenching the courtyard's pavement beneath their feet. For unbeknownst to them, Jezebel had ordered all the palace's oil lamps, the kitchen's overflowing bins of grease, and every other combustible fluid to be emptied out upon the stone at a distance far enough away from the palace that it would not be jeopardized by the ensuing flames. This her servants had swiftly executed before the arrival of the crowd. Now her trap blazed in full force: the center of the vast courtyard burned with the bodies of howling men.

Jezebel leaned over the balcony and gawked in silence as the mob writhed in agony upon the ground. Those who were in the heart of the crowd burned alive without hope of escape. Some of the men on the crowd's outermost ring wildly tried to break away from the general inferno; but armed with long pikes, the guardsmen who were encircling the crowd mercilessly forced back the individual bolters and hurled them into the human bonfire.

Having glutted herself with the sight, Jezebel turned to go back into the palace. As cries of agony filled the air reeking with the stench of burning flesh, she murmured under her breath, "Molech, accept these sons of Israel as a sacrifice. Mot, I transfer to your kingdom a host of new subjects...."

# CHAPTER ELEVEN

"J UST A FEW MORE steps, sweetheart."

"What exactly are you planning?" said Nava with a curious smile, continuing to hold her hands over her eyes.

"You'll see," cooed Ahab, holding onto her elbow as he guided her steps down the corridor. When they reached the destination, he gently led her into the room, placed his fingers over hers, and said from behind her, "Alright, look!"

She opened her eyes.

"Oh, my! I can't believe it!"

Standing opposite them at the other end of the room, a musty scroll tucked beneath one bony arm while the other arm suspended a silvery censer that was emitting fragrant puffs of smoke into the air, was an elderly man. He was dressed in a pure linen tunic that stretched from his neck down to his feet, the sleeves reaching to his liver-spotted hands. Over this he wore a twined linen sash that encircled his skinny chest. Crowning his thinning gray hair was a turban made of fine linen in the shape of a cone. All his garments were plain white without embroidery or any other colors.

Nava rushed over to him and excitedly grabbed his long sleeves. "Are you really a priest of Yahweh?"

"Yes, O daughter of Jacob," answered the priest throatily. He coughed before continuing. "I have attended to our God since the day I attained that age ordained by Moses for the priesthood."

Turning around, a smiling Nava asked Ahab, "However did you get a Levitical priest here?"

"I'm the king!" chuckled Ahab as he approached them. He slapped his upper left arm. "All I had to do was command my servants to seek out a Hebrew priest. They did admittedly have some difficulty because they had to go outside our realm to find one, owing to my wife's... policy of removing them from our land. But they eventually found Nathan and persuaded him to come. After that, it was just a matter of getting him into the palace without drawing attention to his presence." Biting his fat lower lip, he thought, *We don't need to antagonize Jezebel unnecessarily...*

"Nathan, you can't believe how ecstatic I am to see you—it's been so long since I could converse with a priest of our people! I didn't think I would ever see another Levite in this land. Tell me, what led you to willingly come into this place which is so inhospitable to our holy priests?"

"The king of Israel's men freed five of our brethren, languishing in prison, in exchange for my presence. I am an old man who has lived more days than I have deserved. Even if their guarantee of safety should prove as false as their gods, I reckoned my decrepit old age an acceptable sacrifice for their freedom."

*He certainly displays that arrogant self-righteousness Jezebel is always going on about...* With a quick shake of his head, Ahab clapped his hands and announced, "Now, now, Nathan, all will be well. As agreed, you'll have full inviolability whilst you're a guest in my home. But come, I did not invite you here to chitchat about such matters but to minister to my beloved Nava."

Eyeing the king with an alert but unreadable eye, he said, "I remember." Without a further word, Nathan set about his business. He laid his censer on a table and beside it he measured out his scroll to the precise spot he wanted without so much as needing to glance at it—a testament to how often he had unrolled this scroll and memorized the locations of its contents.

Beckoning to Nava, Nathan gestured her to kneel down and he placed his hands on her shoulders. He started reciting prayers and hymns to the God of Israel. Nava joined him in praising their God; after several moments of watching them together, Ahab knelt down beside his beloved concubine and lent his voice also to the hymns.

When the long session of prayer had ended, Ahab turned to Nava whose bright round eyes had been fixed on the ritual. "Dear, did it please you to have one of your ancestral prayers performed?"

Nava turned her eyes to him. Whereas before they had shined with the happiness of a young dog chewing on its first bone, now they suddenly blackened like a spring storm and overflowed with tears.

Ahab planted his shaking hands onto her shoulders and cried, "Sweetheart, what's wrong?! I thought this would make you happy..." *Oh, the fickleness of women!*

"No, no, you misunderstand," said Nava, resting her head on Ahab's chest, just beneath his chin and chubby cheeks. "These are tears of joy! You have given me something no diamond could equal. Before now I knew you loved me, but I could not be sure if it was for me or just for my beauty. Yet now I know you truly love me for my soul. For how else could you defy the spirit of wicked persecution choking this land, and provide me with wholesome nourishment for my immortal soul, unless you understood me and willed only true goodness towards me? You are a generous king, Ahab, but even more importantly than that, you are a kind man."

Sniffing, Ahab quickly wiped a few budding tears out of his own almond eyes and hugged Nava even closer. "Darling, dear, sweetheart... I'm so happy you're happy! I knew you'd love it, I knew it! I would have—even if you'd wanted—I would've gotten you a—"

"What's going on in here?" A female voice suddenly interrupted the king's blubbering.

Ahab swung his head towards the doorway where a woman was standing. His eyes wide and his mouth agape, he gasped.

*NO! What's she doing here?!*

While frenetically disentangling himself from Nava, the woman in the doorway exclaimed:

"Ahab, what are you doing with her—and more importantly, with *him*?"

"Ummashtart!" exclaimed Ahab. Wildly waving his arms this way and that, he dashed over to her and hurriedly said, "It's not what you think! I can explain!"

Paying no heed to his flailing reäction, Ummashtart strolled past him and went to scrutinize the priest. With her hands cupped behind her back, she leaned in closely to the elderly man and, clearly out of visible curiosity rather than religious reverence, remarked, "By the look of your strange costume, I'll wager you're one of those Hebrew priests I've heard so much about."

"I am," grumbled Nathan, his cloudy eyes glaring at her with unmistakable contempt. "By the look of that abominable amulet hanging around your neck, I'll wager you're a worshipper of Baal."

Ignoring his remark and him as well, Ummashtart glanced at the Hebrew characters on the scroll, which was still unrolled on the table, before she turned her gaze back to Ahab. "Is this some sort of Hebrew ritual I've intruded on?" she asked, flicking her head to one side. There was a nascent smirk hanging around the corner of her reddened lip.

"Well, you see," said Ahab, wringing his hands, "Nava here is a worshipper of the Hebrew God, and I just thought that it would be nice to—"

"Oh, so this must be the little Hebrew girl whom I overheard my sister berating." Narrowing her mascaraed eyes, Ummashtart gazed intensely at Ahab as he squirmed. She murmured, "This is so confusing... Here I was, thinking that my sister hates the Hebrew God and wants to eradicate his worshippers. Yet what do I find? A Hebrew priest conducting his rituals in her own home! Jezebel must surely have changed a lot since I last saw her for her to tolerate such behavior. She is aware of this ritual, is she not?"

"Um, well, I, uh, I..."

"Oh, she doesn't, does she?" The smirk that had been building in her cheeks suddenly burst and enveloped her face. "How delicious!"

"Dear sister," gulped Ahab, bowing his head as he looked down at the floor, "I would appreciate it if you could keep this matter to yourself. There is really no reason to disturb Jezebel with any of this. She has enough to worry about without having to add to her worries—"

"That her husband has become a worshipper of the Hebrew God!"

"No, no, you misunderstand..." *God in heaven! What am I to do?*

"Then enlighten me."

Before Ahab could begin to sputter a reply, Nava gently placed her hand on his trembling chest. "No, my lord." She turned towards Ummashtart. "He owes you no explanation: he is the king of Israel. Neither you, your sister, nor anyone else on earth is entitled to pass judgment on his actions. The God of heaven alone will be his judge. If the king wishes to allow Hebrew rites in his palace, he requires no one's permission to make it so—much less that of a heathen."

Her speech prompted Ummashtart to raise a delicately groomed eyebrow. "Is this how slaves in Israel address the freeborn? In Tyre you would have earned a bloody back for taking that tone of voice with me."

"Please don't say such things," said Ahab, putting his arm protectively around Nava and holding her tight with his hand. "Her heart is in the right place."

"It's *your* heart I'm interested in... and I'm sure my sister will be as well."

As Ummashtart strolled jauntily out of the room, Ahab staggered over to the window. He nibbled alternatively between his lower and upper lips while staring blankly into the distance. *Oh, my... This is terrible. Jezebel is going to be so furious...*

He became mindful again of his present surroundings when Nava nuzzled her head against his thick neck.

"Don't fear the queen's wrath, my lord. There's nothing she may do to you."

"Nava, *I* should be the one comforting *you*! Jezebel really is going to raise her hackles when she hears of this. If you think she's been ill-tempered now—oh, just wait..."

"It does not matter, my lord." Her brown eyes were wide and sparkled as she gazed into his. "My people have long faced persecution in this world and we will continue to face it long after I am dead. The thought of all the evils Queen Jezebel could do to me has been a constant companion of mine for many years. If I should now be forced to lay my life down for the God of my forefathers—like my own blessed father and brothers did—I do so gladly, content with the knowledge that kind men like you will still be left upon this earth."

Embracing her tightly and swaying gently back and forth with her, Ahab murmured, "Sweetheart, I promise you, I won't let any harm come to you. You will be mine and I yours. Nothing will be able to come between us..."

# CHAPTER TWELVE

"**W**HY HAVE YOU ASKED me to come here?"

Jezebel moved her hand to shield her eyes as the noontime sun bore down on her. Out here on the plain, only a few miles northeast of Jezreël, there was not a tree or any other shade-giving object to be seen. Shoots of new grass extended in every direction like a green sea and covered a land that had so recently been barren. Her brother Baal-Eser was seven strides ahead of her, inspecting with his foot a rusty spade that some peasant or other had abandoned on the muddy, oxen-made path.

Looking back at her over his shoulder, he nonchalantly remarked, "Can't a brother spend some time alone with his sister whom he loves?"

"So long as it is only *fraternal* love."

"What a fierce imagination you have!" exclaimed Baal-Eser, thumping his hands on his lungs as they convulsed with a hearty, deafening laugh. "I have another sister for that sort of thing, so don't you worry about that." Suddenly he narrowed his eyes and formed his mouth into a mischievous grin. "Unless," he added, bouncing his eyebrows, "it is *jealousy* fueling your insinuation."

Jezebel crinkled her aquiline nose and glared at him. *You're such a pig.* "Seriously, why here?" she asked, changing the subject. "What's wrong with speaking at the palace?"

"I find palaces have too many ears; each wall conceals a traitor."

She glanced back at the dozen bodyguards who were keeping pace fifty feet behind them. *Yes, this is the perfect place to discuss secrets.* "How true, Brother. Especially when one must be on guard against one's own family."

"What do you mean by that?" asked Baal-Eser, halting.

"Am I mistaken, but were you not referring to our common sibling? Isn't Ummashtart the one you fear will betray you?"

"Why should I fear my wife?"

Jezebel narrowed her bulbous eyes and pursed her lips. The words dripping from her mouth like poison from a hemlock-laced chalice, she murmured, "Because your wife's a whore: every whore sells out her man eventually."

"Really?" yawned Baal-Eser, cocking his head and placing his arms akimbo. "And what makes you imagine she's a whore? Has Mother's crystal ball allowed you to monitor her comings and goings to and from my sacred bedchamber? Or have the gods granted you a ring of invisibility so that you might, without detection, inspect my bed's sanctity yourself?"

She brushed past him and did not deign to face him during her reply. "Don't be absurd, Baal-Eser. Neither divination nor preternatural abilities are needed to perceive her duplicity. Even in this godforsaken land, cut off from all the refinements of civilized life in Phoenicia, I have heard of the tales and gossip which circulate among the gentlewomen of Tyre—such stories they tell about our little sister!" *Not to mention that I have sisterly knowledge of her character...*

"So what? Silly women also say lunar eclipses occur so the moon can hide her celestial trysts. Such balderdash! If fools wish to speculate about another's conduct, it reveals more about their own fantasies than verifiable reality."

Gritting her teeth, Jezebel curled her lip and stared angrily into her brother's eyes. "If it were about a woman well-known for her chastity, I would concede your point regarding empty speculation. But we are speaking here of Ummashtart, a proven adulteress! You of all men should know her deeds: it was into *your* hands that she betrayed her husband and for *your* sake she offered up her body."

"Which is why I needn't worry." Baal-Eser slapped his thigh in tempo to the guffaws coming out of his throat. Looking at her scrunching up her face, he said, "O Jezebel, my dear Jezebel. You speak from your experience as Ahab's wife; and your life with that most excellent man shapes your view of marriage. You ought to be thankful that Father gave you to so worthy a man as Ahab."

*I thank the gods a thousand times every minute I'm awake and twice that when I sleep!*

"Yet our precious sister was not as lucky as you," said Baal-Eser, wiping a single tear of mirth from his eye after his attack of laughter had ceased. "Lamentably, Father unequally yoked her to a man far below her station, a man—if it isn't blasphemy to bestow that hallowed name on him—to whom even rats of the female persuasion would turn up their excrement-covered noses if invited into his bed. Hasdrubal was a fat slob, an ignorant braggart, an arrogant backstabber, an abject loser who both fell short in passing the harsh rigors of manhood and also lacked those soft qualities which are so becoming in women. It would therefore be inhuman not to excuse our sister for straying from Hasdrubal's feeble marriage-bed."

"Yet how can you be sure she's not now cuckolding *you*? She has already proven herself unfaithful to one husband: past behavior is the surest prediction for the future. For as certain of my Hebrew subjects are wont to say, 'the bitch returneth to her vomit.'"

"Now why would she do that?" Holding his arms outstretched so that she could see his whole bulk and jutting his muscular legs apart, he asked, "Who in his right mind would trade in a white stallion, spirited and in his prime, who outpaces all other horses in the field, is bred from noble sires and himself sires goodly offspring that is the envy of every mare... for a broken-down, cracked-tooth mule swarming with farting fleas?"

"Well, when you put it like that," said Jezebel dryly as she glared at him with a single raised-eyebrow, "I'm surprised you're not drowning right now in a sea of drooling women."

"Oh, I would be if I hadn't donned a special amulet that repels females. I don't particularly like wearing the thing myself—it's made out of bronzed hyena bones and they do chafe my skin just terribly—but it's either that or having to physically fight off every woman and girl within a twenty-mile radius."

*When you say stuff like that, I almost think Ummashtart deserves to have you for a husband...* Choosing to ignore his last remark, she instead said, "Aren't you jealous in the least?"

"Nah, what's the point?"

"You're a man. I've found it to be almost a law of nature that you men jealously guard us and reäct most violently should another man become too familiar with us."

"And that is why I stand above the herd of men! I never give myself ulcers worrying about my wives' chastity; life's too short to fret about that which we cannot control. If a woman wants to cheat on her man, she will and there's nothing he can do about it. Some fools try to defy this fact by locking their wives inside their harems and appointing eunuchs to watch them. But these geniuses forget to ask one pertinent question: who will watch the watchers? Yes, eunuchs may be dried-up trees, but the fruit of the womb is not the primary thing you women desire from us men. Ooh... it most certainly is not."

"I don't know which is greater: your faith in your wives or your blithe indifference. Either way, Brother, you are a most peculiar man."

Baal-Eser crossed his arms and narrowed his eyes broodingly. Locking his eyes onto hers, he said, "If you really must know, I doubt Ummashtart would ever stray from me. But, just between you and me, if she ever did, I'd just replace her with another wife younger and even prettier than she."

Jezebel snorted. "I see you are as congenial as ever."

"Well, I am my father's son."

*No one can dispute that...* "I'm pleased you are so congenial, so generous and openhanded. It should therefore be easy for you to grant me priests, enough to replenish my priesthood."

"I've been expecting this request," said Baal-Eser, smirking. "But you've already had your priesthood wiped out once by your heathen subjects. If I were to entrust my priests to you, how do I know your little heathens won't simply massacre them too?"

"Give me priests, and the heathens will be converted into loyal servants of Baal."

He shrugged his shoulders. "I supposed I could ordain new priests for you."

Vigorously shaking her head, Jezebel moved forwards and planted her feet in the soil in front of him. "If I wanted novices, I myself, wandering Samarian streets, could find plenty of muddy children wrestling in the gutters, shoving cockroaches up their nostrils, pilfering worthless trinkets from hucksters' carts, pissing high against alley walls—doing whatever little boys do—and make them priests." She grasped his face with her long-nailed hand, holding his head steady so that she could bore into his eyes. "What I need are *men*, men dignified in their bearing, skilled in priestcraft from long practice, who know the minutiae of all the rituals, knowledgeable in every aspect of religion, and who are bold in their love for Baal. Those are the priests you'll send to me."

"And exactly how many do you wish me to send? Ten, twenty, thirty?"

"No. Eight hundred."

"EIGHT HUNDRED?!" With his mouth gaping, Baal-Eser freed his jaw from her clutch and took a step back. "Eight hundred? Are you serious? *That's half my kingdom's priests*! Do you realize how disruptive it would be to suddenly lose half of them?"

She smirked. "Yes: half as disruptive as losing all of them."

Baal-Eser repeatedly bounded his fingers off his chest whilst directing his gaze to a patch of clouds on the horizon. "What you ask for is astounding. If another had made such an outlandish request, I would have deemed him mad." His face becoming as fixed as a stone statue's, he looked at her. "But I know you, Jezebel. You wouldn't ask for it unless you reckoned you could get it. So why am I about to give you half of Tyre's priests?"

"Because, my dear elder brother," replied Jezebel in a coquettish tone as she sashayed several steps away, "I'm not the only one in need of sibling aid."

"What does that even mean?" huffed Baal-Eser.

"It means a deal is in the air."

"Oh, is that what I smelled? I just thought it was you farting."

Her skin flushing red from the blood boiling in her veins, the muscles in her face forming a terrifying scowl, and her bulbous eyes flashing the same hatred that a rattlesnake flashes at whatever fool had the misfortune to step on it, Jezebel whipped around and pointed straight at him.

"I'm not naïve!" she shrieked. "Since you arrived, you've implied, hinted, intimated, in every conversation, about a great proposal you would make. So don't even think of leading me on like some urbane rogue with an inexperienced country girl. Speak plainly and tell me exactly what you want!"

"You're right, Jezebel. There is a great request I seek from you. (That is the reason why I brought you out here.)" He took a deep breath before bluntly declaring, "I want Israel as an ally for a war against the Arameans."

Remaining for several moments in silent contemplation, Jezebel finally murmured, "That is a big request." *I should have asked for more than eight hundred...*

"I know war with Aram is a serious matter. Under Ben-Hadad's leadership, Damascus has forged the disparate clans and tribal lands of the Arameans into a mighty kingdom whose strength now rivals that of the Egypt of old. Hell, if he's not stopped soon, in a few years Ben-Hadad may decide to add that troubled kingdom to his empire too."

She nodded. "Ben-Hadad has greatly increased Aramaic influence these past few years. I am familiar with his list of conquests." *It is about time someone cut that upstart down to size.*

"I cannot allow him," continued Baal-Eser, "to grow any more powerful. His empire nearly surrounds my whole kingdom, threatening to choke us into submission. He's a threat who must be neutralized before we end up taking our orders from him like so many other kings."

"I too have been troubled by his ascendancy," agreed Jezebel, rubbing her chin. "Yet a war against Aram will not be effortless. Is your army capable of defeating his?"

"Not by itself. I have been augmenting it with auxiliaries from all the other Phoenician cities but even that is not sufficient to defeat the union of Arameans. That's exactly why I'm going to let you share in the spoils of victory after our combined forces vanquish Ben-Hadad. If Israel and Tyre combine our forces and launch a two-pronged attack on his territory, then together we can crush the Aramaic menace and reconfigure the balance of power in the region."

"Intriguing... How would we commence this war and how would we prosecute it?"

"Do you remember my first wife, Talitha? She brought to the marriage Arpad and its hinterland as a dowry. But ever since Hamath and Kinalua fell to Ben-Hadad, Arpad has been severed from my other territories: my shadow no longer covers it. Much turmoil has engulfed the city in the meantime as the Arameans have allowed it to succumb to brigandage and lawlessness. I've had desperate messengers come to my court, begging me to intervene. Using their plight as a pretext, I'll initiate hostilities by sending my armies into the northern part of his realm. When he leads his army against mine, I won't be able to defeat it alone. So that's precisely when Israel will reveal our secret alliance. You'll invade the southern half of his realm, making straight for his capital Damascus with little resistance. At that point, Ben-Hadad will have no choice but to divide his forces between the two invasion points: each of us will then simultaneously face and crush the divided, weaker armies."

Jezebel wordlessly paced around the plain. Kneeling down, she scooped up a handful of dirt. Allowing the dusty particles of soil to trickle through her fingers, she said:

"This strategy of yours sounds very promising. I like it. When do you want to launch your invasion?"

"After the Festival of Dagon."

"And once we defeat Ben-Hadad, what are your war aims? Do you seek his overthrow, or would you let him remain in a weakened position as a vassal? Are you content with annexing peripheral lands around Arpad, perhaps making it contiguous with Phoenicia, or do you covet his whole kingdom?"

"Well, I want his military might destroyed. Hamath, Qarqar, and all the lands surrounding Arpad must be mine as well. Depending on the gods' favor, I would not rule out taking more of his kingdom, even all of it."

"All that isn't awarded to Israel," reminded Jezebel, fixing her unblinking eyes on him.

Grimacing, Baal-Eser replied, "Yes, Israel will have its fair share of the conquest."

"And you'll send me all my priests before the war?"

He nodded affirmatively, whereupon Jezebel wiped her hands on her scarlet dress and said, "Then it is agreed. May Baal and all the gods look favorably upon our grand alliance!"

"Excellent! I knew you'd want in on this!" Rubbing his hands greedily, his eyes flashing from side to side like a lion before it pounces, he suddenly stopped. "I almost forgot about Ahab."

"What about him?"

"Shouldn't we consult him before we pronounce the pact complete?"

She snorted. "There's no need. When the time for war arrives, he'll hearken to my counsels as he always does." *With his loose lips, he's liable to divulge our secret plans... Best to keep him in the dark till the time for action comes.*

"You speak boldly of your influence. I have no doubt that you wield your influence effectively. Yet, formally at least, you are merely Ahab's queen: he is Israel's king, whose word is law, and who reclines in majesty upon its throne. If I am to conclude a pact with Israel, don't I need the support of its king?"

Her eyelids collapsing into a haughty stare while her right cheek rose, Jezebel cocked her head sideways and brusquely remarked, "If you believed that, you would have invited him here."

Baal-Eser chortled and slapped his thigh. Then, his whole body quivering as though he were struggling to contain his enthusiasm lunged forwards and hugged his sister with a rough embrace. Planting a wet kiss on her cheek, his teeth grazing her skin, he exclaimed, "If only Father could see us now! His children about to dominate the world!"

Having concluded their business, they began retracing their steps. When they were halfway back to the palace, Baal-Eser told her, "Now that I have your support, I'll be returning home. I have another engagement awaiting me there."

"Postpone your engagement till the morning. Tonight we'll enjoy a celebratory banquet to consummate the agreement."

# CHAPTER THIRTEEN

A FROWNING EUNUCH FINISHED the silky coiffure as a
maidservant applied the last coating of rouge onto her mistress's cheeks, her hands nervously following the brisk face as it shifted back and forth over a duplicated letter. Crumpling the papyrus, Jezebel handed it to Elishat, who had been silently waiting at the queen's right hand.

"This was an amusing find. 'Thy navel is like a round goblet, which wanteth not liquor. Thy belly is like a heap of wheat set about with lilies. Thy two breasts are like two young roes that are twins.' What utter pabulum! It's even worse than the poetry he's written for me."

"Thank you, Madam," answered Elishat. She bowed her gray head. "The king appears to be turning increasingly to the pen in order to please his Hebrew paramour. You can expect more copies of royal love-letters to be forthcoming."

"Keep up the good work." Nodding her head in approval to the polished bronze mirror which had been proffered to her, Jezebel rose from her dressing table. Looking resplendent in her scarlet dress whose fabric trailed three feet behind her, she exited her bedroom and went to meet Ahab and her siblings.

As soon as the royal party was assembled, they quitted the palace and, surrounded by a troupe of servants, strolled down the paved lane to the neighboring residence. There they were greeted by the master of the house, Naboth the Jezreëlite, and the sumptuous banquet which he had prepared for them. Jezebel and the others feasted upon oily duck, roasted chicken, mutton, sirloin steaks, and a colorful variety of fruits and nuts. To wash down this feast, they drank sweet red wine that had been grown in Naboth's own prized vineyard.

It was to this very vineyard that Jezebel and the others retreated after having their fill of meat and drink. Not into it, exactly, but rather to the adjacent patio that served as a bridge between the vineyard itself and the house. Lined with bricks, this patio was enclosed by a two-foot high limestone wall upon which soft velvet cushions had been placed for the guests. In front of where they were bade to sit, several servants manned a confectionary cart overflowing with sweets, which Naboth kept stocked exclusively for when entertaining his royal neighbors.

Baal-Eser, sloshing wine from his cup as he strode over to Jezebel and Ahab who were sitting together on the wall, declared, "Your neighbor certainly makes good wine!"

"Oh, yes, it most certainly is." Turning his still-nodding head towards his wife, Ahab said, "Don't you agree, Jezebel?"

"What?" murmured Jezebel, only half paying attention to what they were saying.

Her eyes were instead focused on the other end of the patio, specifically on the fire pit located there. This fire pit was being attended to by several members of Naboth's household. Among the men who were turning the sizzling, meat-heavy spits above the open fire was Naboth's son. He was a tall, broad-shouldered youth. His skin was without blemish and tanned the color of ochre. Wearing only linen breeches that stretched from his waist to his knees, the youth's muscular arms rippled and glistened with sweat as they turned the spit in a most pleasing and rhythmic fashion.

"Don't you approve of the quality of Naboth's wine?"

"The fruit of these vines leaves something to be desired," answered Jezebel, licking her red lips while she silently counted the seven dark downy hairs sprouting out of the youthful chest. "But the soil here has good drainage, and would probably make for an excellent herb garden."

Glugging down the last of his wine that had not ended up in his beard during his prior slugs, Baal-Eser roared, "Well, I like this wine! Come, Ahab, let's go refill these cups!"

As her brother led her husband away, repeatedly thumping him on his back much to his chagrin, Jezebel was left sitting by herself for no more than a minute before she was approached by her sister Ummashtart.

"Good evening, Jezebel."

"Yes, it is," replied Jezebel reservedly. Her polished nails digging into her palm, she suppressed a scowl when her sister sat down beside her.

"I admit, Sister, that before coming here I had not expected to find so glorious a court. It's almost like being back in Tyre."

"You should have seen what barbarous crudities I found when I first moved to Israel," said Jezebel with a smirk. "It took years, but I've managed to transplant a modicum of civilization into this backward land."

Ummashtart patted Jezebel's manicured hand. "And you've done splendidly. Even that mangy band of rustics, who attempted to burn your palace down, could not detract from your exalted state."

"Of course," mumbled Jezebel, her right cheek twitching. "Certain backwater peasants may chafe at my reforms, but there's scarcely anything they can do. Anyone who wishes to be anything must needs adapt to our Phoenician way of life. I've eliminated all dissidents from positions of power, wealth, or status."

Tilting her head to the side, Ummashtart frowned and said, "All of them?"

"*All.*" There was a note of agitation in Jezebel's voice; she clenched her right fist beneath her left hand in an attempt to suppress any expression of what she was really feeling.

"Sister, dear," whispered Ummashtart, leaning close to her ear, "I don't doubt you sincerely believe all persons with power support you—and I do hate to have to tell you this—but..." She glanced over at Ahab conspicuously enough to draw Jezebel's attention to him. "Earlier today, I walked in on your husband. He was with his Hebrew concubine and (though it might surprise you to learn) one of those Hebrew priests. The three of them quite clearly had just finished performing some rite of the Hebrews when I entered. Ahab did not deny it when I confronted him. So, my darling sister, while you may have succeeded in ensuring your subalterns are loyal to your program of reforms, the king himself evidently eludes your persuasion."

*That bastard son of a whore performed Hebrew rites?!* Jezebel's flesh heated with rage and she barely restrained herself from digging her sharp claws into her thighs. She drew in a deep breath and exhaled. "Oh, that's nothing: he's not at all serious about it," she chuckled, crinkling her aquiline nose and feigning an amused countenance. She positioned her blazing and bulbous eyes to transfix her sister's. Struggling not to pant from furious exasperation, she added, "He always puts on a little show for his whores. His latest one is a worshipper of the Hebrew God, so of course he'd act out a pretend sacrifice or whatever those people do. In a few days, like always, he'll tire of her and move on to the next one. And who knows what he'll do for that one? He might even dress in drag and do a belly dance."

"Really? Just an act?" Ummashtart narrowed her eyes and frowned. "Despite your words, I sense you are deeply disturbed by this."

"What's there to be disturbed about?"

"You aren't afraid your husband is relapsing into his native religion? Or that his concubine has acquired... a great influence over him, perhaps even exceeding yours in certain areas? This would not be the first time a king preferred his concubine."

"Of course not!" hissed Jezebel. "Do you think for a moment that a whore—and a slave-whore at that—could inveigle my Ahab? Nonsense! Don't judge my husband with that same disposition you used in judging Hasdrubal! Ahab would never betray me the way you betrayed your husband."

Her nostrils flaring and her eyes snapping wide, Ummashtart nevertheless managed to speak with a steady tone. "I never betrayed Hasdrubal. I am deeply offended that you would say that."

"Of course you did! Everyone knows what you did to your first man—pardon me, your first *husband*. (You doubtlessly had many men before him.) Hasdrubal was your lawfully-wedded husband, your lord, your world. And like some treacherous daughter of a goatherd, you betrayed not only his bed but also his person into the bloodstained hands of the executioner. Though I suppose the quickness of the axe spared him from the messiness of divorcing his king's sister."

"A lesser woman would think you were deliberately distorting what happened, Sister dearest. Yet I know it was not your will when Father exiled you to this far off land, lying beyond the limits of Truth but not of ignorant Rumor. I don't know what sort of malicious gossip from the parlors of Tyre may have made their way to you. So let me set you straight. I respected Hasdrubal as any wife should, obeying his commands and faithfully assisting him. Yet despite my domestic fidelity, I had no say over what treasonous plots he concocted outside the home. A woman owes allegiance to her husband, yes, but each of us owes a greater allegiance to our sovereign lord. When I learned of Hasdrubal's conspiracy, should I have supported him against our brother and my king? No! Acting merely as a loyal subject (let alone a faithful sister), I warned my king, who rewarded my errant husband according to his works."

"And he rewarded you by making you his queen." Jezebel curled her lip and glared. "Now who's distorting the truth? You made the calculating choice to trade in your petty lord for a king."

"No! You're wrong. There was no conspiracy on my part. Baal-Eser and I, we did not fall in love until after Hasdrubal's punishment."

"Is that what women of your ilk call it? 'Fall in love'?" Jezebel laughed.

"Why these incessant jabs? For as long as I can remember, you have always spread the most malicious gossip behind my back and uttered the most hurtful things to my face. Even as a young girl, I can still see my elder sister crouching in the corridors, whispering lies about me to the palace's lowliest servants." Ummashtart grasped Jezebel's wrist. Her voice cracking and a teary trickle escaping her mascaraed eyes, she said, "Why have you always hated me?"

Jezebel brushed her hand away. "Stop being so melodramatic. I have nothing personal against you; for your information, I don't even rate you high enough to be worth slandering. You're simply imagining things if you believe otherwise."

"No, Baal-Eser told me what you said about me being a whore."

Jezebel grinded her teeth. *Well, if he was foolish enough to marry you, I'm not surprised he betrayed my confidence... so long as that's all he betrayed.* "So what? I merely spoke the truth."

"Why have you always hated me? Was it because Mother left us?"

"Don't call her 'Mother'!" Slamming her fist down on the cold limestone, Jezebel spat, "She was *my* mother, not yours! And a far better mother than that sow which spawned you!"

"You have no right to attack my mother."

"Why not?" Jezebel's breathing became faster and her skin's temperature rose as though she had exchanged places with the meat on the spits. "Your mother was a conniving whore who seduced our venerable father; and as though being a concubine would not have been subversive enough, that bitch bewitched him into making her a full wife and second queen. Two wives cannot subsist in one household. Nor can two queens coëxist within a single realm. Your mother's conduct was typical for her kind: once she had installed herself within the palace, like some spotted hyena lording it over her clan, she hastily worked to wrest supremacy of position from my mother, our father's lawful wife. Then, boiling over with arrogance—bitch that she was!—she turned against my mother and drove her out of her own home."

Ummashtart merely shook her head. "That's not true."

"By Baal's balls, it *is* true!" Forming a fist which she slammed across her chest, ruffling her dress, Jezebel shut her eyes and made a single sniffle. "I loved my mother and she loved me. She was a great woman: shrewd, educated, pious towards Baal, of great assistance to Father in his quest to ascend the throne... After all that, she did not deserve to be undone by your whorish mother—to be deprived of her husband, her children, everything!" Her hate-filled eyes shot open and she soared to her feet. Pointing accusingly at Ummashtart, her finger jutting out so fast that it almost hit her sister's nose, she whispered, "You asked if I hate you? Yes, yes, I *do* hate you! I hate you more than any other woman alive: for you are nothing but the fetid residue of that disgraceful union and a reminder more painful than childbirth of my mother's persecution."

There was silence. As Jezebel, crossing her arms and scowling, towered ominously over her sister, Ummashtart calmly sat motionless. Finally, after drawing in several deep breaths, she unflinchingly met the hostile eyes.

"You say you want the truth? Fine. Then let me tell you what you must surely already know. Your mother wasn't driven out by my mother or by anyone: she ran off with a lover after their affair was discovered by our venerable father. You can hate me for a lie if you want. I don't care. Yet if you're expecting me to respond to your unjustified hatred with my own, I'll have to disappoint you. For far from hating you, Jezebel, I can only pity you. To hear you spew such cockamamie smears against my mother with perfect earnestness—which earnestness I do not doubt any less than I doubt that you truly loved your mother—leads me to conclude that the pain of losing your mother forced you to invent this yarn. Invent it so as to repress the limb-gnawing truth that you are apparently not strong enough to accept. And from what I've gathered since I've been here, your characterization and passionate abhorrence of another woman usurping the first wife's place seems, far from being an imagined childhood trauma, more accurately to reflect your present angst that Ahab will replace you with a more congenial wife—not because you love him but because he's your gateway to the power you have always craved. So I fully understand where you are coming from. However..."

Ummashtart calmly stood up and pressed herself against Jezebel, allowing her hot breath to wash over her sister's scowling, reddened face. "...I will not sit idly by while you slander me with your wicked tongue. Your words are doubly wicked: for you hypocritically judge me when you are doing the very thing you accuse me of. No matter how much you preen yourself in public (and especially around your clueless husband) as though you were some paragon of chastity and feminine modesty, you and I both know what kind of woman you are. Do you see shadows cast by paramours? Look no further than your bedchamber for the shadows' owners—or should I say Baal's temple? You deplore marital betrayal? I wonder what Ahab would think if his ignorance of your sordid trysts and manipulative habits were cured. YOU are the whore, Jezebel, *you*! Like mother like daughter, so are your vile deeds."

Having spoken her mind, Ummashtart turned her back on Jezebel and marched across the patio to return inside the house. Jezebel, her mouth agape and dry eyes unblinking, merely stood where she was. As her pounding heart died down and color returned to her blanched face, she clenched her vein-bulging fists. Her whole body quaked.

*That lying whore thinks she knows all! She presumes to read my mind, discern my motives, blame me for having fears instead of those creating them? Bah!* She shook her head. *Not even the gods know what secrets simmer at the bottom of my heart!*

She leapt up and headed straight for Ahab, who was merrily raising a glass of wine to Naboth's hilarious tale. She grasped his hand from behind and whispered through clenched teeth, "Come with me."

Yelping with surprise as her cold skin touched his, he spun around. "Jezebel! You startled me!" he exclaimed as she repeated her demand more insistently. "Yes, yes, I'm coming."

Jezebel led him away from their fellow guests, going a hundred paces out into the vineyard. After scanning the moonlit field for eavesdroppers, she turned to him and said:

"I know what you and your Hebrew harlot did this afternoon. My brother's wife told me everything."

Despite the darkness of the night, the look of horror on his face—the pale skin, the arched eyebrows, the constricting pupils, the quivering lips around the gasping mouth, the foul-smelling stream of sweat gushing forth from his clean-shaven sideburns—was as perceptible as if it were high noon on the summer solstice.

"Je-Je-Jezebel!" squealed Ahab with a voice higher and more strident than usual. "I c-c-can ex-explain!"

"Explain what?! That you have turned your back on our lord Baal and embraced the Hebrew heresy?" *Which isn't the only noxious Hebrew thing you're embracing...*

Ahab waved his hands and his head violently shook back and forth like a lamb in a wolf's jaws. "No, no, no, my dear, not at all! I don't know what your sister—*half*-sister," he hastily corrected himself when she grunted, "but she didn't understand what she saw."

"So her eyes deceived her?" asked Jezebel, stepping closer to Ahab. She cocked her head and put her arms akimbo. "You *weren't* offering up sacrifices to the natives' God?"

"No, no, no... It wasn't a sacrifice," he said, twiddling his thumbs. "It was more like singing hymns..."

"To the Hebrew God?"

"Well, uh... yes."

"So you admit you denied Baal."

"But I wasn't denying Baal! Do we deny him when we sacrifice to Astartë, to Aglibol, to Manuzi? There are so many gods and goddesses in the world: offering up a prayer to one more harms no one. Perhaps it could even benefit us, to have another god on our side."

"Wow, what a profound philosophical insight! Yet you never previously exhibited any desire to propitiate the God of the Hebrews... then again, you never previously had a Hebrew harlot coaxing you with wheedling words to engage in forbidden actions behind your queen's back."

"No, it wasn't her." Ahab tentatively reached out and placed his shaky hand on her shoulder. "She didn't ask me to do it: I thought of it all on my own."

*Oh, so now she's got you doing such things of your own accord...* Jezebel concentrated her bulbous eyes on him and snapped, "Why? To please her?!"

"Well, um... yes," murmured Ahab. "I mean, I do love—"

Flinging his hand off her, she spun around and refused to look at him. "Then it's even worse than I thought!" Making the snuffling sound that accompanies weeping but without actually shedding any tears, she sighed, "You don't love me anymore." Then she started staggering back towards the patio, ignoring his pleas to stop.

"Don't say such an evil thing!" cried Ahab, sprinting to get ahead of her. He stopped her and, panting, protested, "I love you! I really do!"

"And is this how you show it? By doing the *one* thing that you know I cannot stand? I am the daughter of a priest of Astartë, nourishing his religion in this once-heathenish land, and yet you mock me and all that I hold dear by worshipping a foreign god in my own home. You do all that—*just to please your whore*. How can I believe you love me?"

"Of course I love you! I love you more than anyone else! What is a few syllables worth of hymns in comparison to one's own flesh and blood? Yet to soothe your concerns for our regal sons and heirs, I commanded that the sons born to my concubines be raised elsewhere, all seventy of them. Would I have exiled my own children from my palace unless I loved you?"

She snorted. "That just proves my point! If you can so easily send your own blood and flesh away, then there's no reason why you can't dismiss some slave-whore whom you barely know. Not, that is, unless you prefer her to your lawful wife."

"What are you saying?" said Ahab, his lower jaw quivering.

"I want you," said Jezebel, pressing herself so close to him that their noses touched, "to confirm these mighty words of yours with deeds. Prove your love for me! Cast out that bondwoman! Get rid of her! Use your other concubines or, if you need new flesh to slake your lust, just buy another one, buy a whole crowd of them for all I care—so long as it's anyone other than *her* who's the worst of them all. Do that and then I'll know you love me."

Her words left him dumbstruck. Shifting his weight back and forth between his legs, Ahab stared blankly at her. The seconds, each one more awkward than the one before, dragged on and on in silence. Finally, taking a deep breath, he rested his fist over his heart and looked down at the weed-infested dirt.

"Jezebel, I love you and I think I've done more than what's reasonable to prove that I do. If you can't appreciate that, well, I can't do anything about that. *I* know I love you. How could I not? For you're not only my queen, and the wife of my youth, and the mother of my children... but you're also the light of my life, my other half, my soul's destined match. But that does not mean you're the only woman I can love. Nava, I love her too. Not the same way as I do you; no one else could ever make me feel the way you do. But Nava, she makes me feel, well, special when I'm around her—like I'm the only man in the world. She's such a sweet girl, so kind and innocent. Though I could never love her as much as I love you, I do love her, very much in fact, more than my other concubines. I realize you won't like this, but I'm sorry, I won't send her away. You'll just have to learn to live with it."

Jezebel stopped blinking as she stared at him. Her left cheek twitched. *He's refusing me? ME?! He's never refused me!* "How can you possibly 'love' two women?!" she screeched, yanking on the garment around his shoulder. "You profane the word! There's only room in your heart for one!"

"You're wrong!" Ahab stayed still as she tugged on his clothing. Looking into her eyes, he placed his hand on her cheek and said, "Unlike women, we men have room in our hearts for many loves."

"And yet you'll jumble your love for me with your unbridled lust for her!"

"That is where you are mistaken. I can keep my feelings for the two of you separate: it is an easy thing for a man to do. Just as a baker keeps his flour in one jar, his salt in another, the yeast in yet another, and so on for all his ingredients—each one in isolation from the others but all equally at the baker's fingertips—so too do we men separate our feelings for our women. You should know that. Just look at your father, whom you're always extolling and holding up as a model I should strive to emulate. Ithobaal was famous for his love of women, almost rivaling King Solomon. No husband could relax in whatever town your father visited. Yet I pride myself on prancing only with my own fillies, and by no means would countenance adulterous liaisons as your father did. Be that as it may, I am certain that he would never have let any wife of his dictate whom he might and might not approach. And I agree with him on that. So you will have to learn to live with my decision. For I am the king of this land and it is my word that is law."

Watching him, his head held high as he marched across the vineyard, Jezebel felt her knees buckle and collapsed onto the earth.

*Great gods! What has happened to my husband? The one time he withstands a pressure that would normally snap his feeble spine in two, tells off an implacable adversary staring him down... and he has to choose* me *to rebuff? ME?! The woman whom yesterday he would have given both his eyes for?*

She gazed up at the starlit sky, her mouth open and her jaw quivering.

*He's even further under the spell of that Hebrew witch than I thought. She has warped his mind into an unrecognizable mess. O Baal, help me or we're both undone!*

# CHAPTER FOURTEEN

A S THE SUN ROSE higher over the horizon, its warm rays
filled the palace courtyard and caressed Jezebel's skin, who
loosened the cloak about her neck. She gazed approvingly as the
priest, standing at the marble altar specially erected for the Festival
of Dagon, raised the knife into the air. The sharp metal gleamed
in the sun as it ascended; but the victim could not see it on account of the two acolytes who were holding its head down in the
opposite direction. Then, with the signal given by the queen, the
priest plunged the knife into the ram's neck. Jugulated before the
creature had time to howl, its lifeblood sprayed in every direction
as the acolytes held a jug to catch the pooling blood.

*Such a beautiful sight*, thought Jezebel as her eyes tracked the
trickling blood which shimmered in the sun. Turning around, she
came face to face with Ahab.

"That was a splendid sacrifice to start the spring," he said, venturing to lay his forefinger on the back of her right hand. "Of
course, not as splendid as you are looking this morning."

"So it was." She pulled her hand away from him and covered it
within the sleeve of her other arm. Casually glancing at the other
faces moving around the courtyard, she asked dryly, "Where's your
little Hebrew woman?"

"You know she never attends one of these events."

*Oh, yes. Your precious whore is far too coy to prostitute her heart to more than one god.* Jezebel snorted. "Are our expeditionary forces ready?"

Ahab nodded vigorously. "The army will be prepared for departure tomorrow. Won't they be surprised when we reveal what their mission will be?"

"Excellent. As soon as Ben-Hadad is vanquished..."

"So, Jezebel, the strategy is truly as good as it sounds?"

"Of course!" She rolled her eyes. "How many times have I gone over it with you?"

"I know, I know, it's just the Aramaic army, with its reputation and all, and all the forces at Ben-Hadad's disposal, not to mention his allies..."

Jezebel sighed in relief as the king's meandering train of thought was mercifully interrupted by the approach of the priest.

"Your Majesties," he said, bowing his grizzled head to them. "I trust that the sacerdotal performance was acceptable to you."

"It was as I thought it would be," answered Jezebel. She blinked her eyelashes serenely while condescending to allow the old man to kiss her right hand.

"Well, I thought it was the best one I'd ever seen," said Ahab, patting the priest on his back. "Your execution was masterful and without a flaw. I'm so thankful Baal-Eser sent you to us. Your brother, Jezebel, is really quite generous."

*Well,* thought Jezebel while scowling crossly, *it's not as though he did it for nothing...*

"For twenty-eight years I officiated at Dagon's Festival in Tyre."

"And I guess this is your first year doing it in Israel," remarked Ahab. He stroked his stubbly chin. "Did the change in venue seem strange as you were sacrificing, or is that too mundane a thing to concern so venerable a priest as you?"

"No, Your Majesty. After a lifetime of performing this rite, I could do it anywhere, even perform it while dancing on my head. The location does not matter in the least bit: the gods are all around us. I did, however, consider it a treat to once again propitiate the gods on the original day of the festival. My spirit felt as though it were in its prime again." With a haughty laugh, he added, "Now if only my knees and back felt the same!"

Disregarding his laughter, Jezebel's ears twitched from what he had said before. "Are you daft, old man? What's this 'original day of the festival' nonsense? The Festival of Dagon has always fallen on the third day from the spring equinox."

"Pardon me, my lady," replied the priest, his long gray whiskers hitting the courtyard's stone as he bowed to her. "I forgot that the reform wasn't implemented until two years after your departure to Israel, to wed your wonderful husband whom I'm now pleased to call my—"

"Yes, yes, whatever," interposed Jezebel, snapping her fingers beside his head. "Tell me about this reform."

"Well, back when you were still Tyre's plucky princess, the Festival of Dagon did indeed fall on the third day from the equinox—the third day *after* the equinox. Then, for reasons which slip my mind, it was decided that the festival should thenceforth be celebrated on the third day *before* the equinox. So, you see, if I'd wished it, I could have gotten a fast steed and travelled back to Tyre to celebrate the festival there and then return in time to celebrate it here! Though that's just one of the many passing fancies I entertain in my old age." When he received no response, he added, "I know you youngsters wouldn't understand, so I'll leave you both to your royal duties."

The priest departed without waiting for any farewell, having wasted his last several sentences too. For both Jezebel and Ahab beside her had frozen when they heard about the modification of the festival's date. Their faces were white, their mouths agape, their eyes unblinking and wide. As the last of the attendees streamed past them, the king and queen, as motionless as sepulchral statues, remained in the lifeless courtyard.

"Jezebel," murmured Ahab at last, the strident syllables catching in his throat as he struggled to swallow, "when your brother said that he would set out with his army the day after the Festival of Dagon, did he mean the day after the Tyrian festival or did he mean after the one in Israel?"

"He must've... he had to... I mean... such a small thing... there's no way... oh god, no!" Pulling up the lower hem of her dress, she darted towards the palace. *Surely the gods wouldn't allow that bastard to do... to me...*

"Wait up, dear!" cried Ahab, wheezing as he sought to catch up with her.

Yet before either of them could enter the palace, they were greeted by a wild-eyed messenger. "Your Majesty, Your Majesty!" he shrieked, cutting his face when he stumbled on the ground during his sprint towards them.

"Yyyyeeeeesss..." said Jezebel, articulating the word slowly as though to protract the time. Her heart was beating like that of a lamb beholding the butcher's mallet.

"It's WAR!" screeched the official, waving his arms. "Baal-Eser crossed the border and made war on Aram five days ago. Ben-Hadad just routed the Tyrian army yesterday. Now he, and the thirty-two kings who call him lord, plus all their men and chariots, the whole combined force, is marching towards Samaria! He says he'll destroy us! He claims we're part of a conspiracy against him! He'll arrive in less than two days! The gods help us!" Not waiting to be dismissed, the dismayed official rushed back inside the palace, falling twice more in his haste.

*This isn't only a setback: it's a disaster! If his whole forces are arrayed against Samaria, our army will...* She stood where she was, resting her cheek on her hand and trying to appraise everything that she had been told.

Suddenly Ahab's trembling hand grabbed her upper arm and shook her from her thinking. His eyes were huge and gazed anxiously at her.

"Jezebel, what are we to do?"

"We get to Samaria before him—force march the troops! That's what we do."

"But the plan is ruined! Ben-Hadad has the advantage! We're going to have to face the Arameans all by ourselves."

"Our army is well-trained, precisely for a day like this. We'll make our stand..."

# CHAPTER FIFTEEN

*O*H, THINGS LIKE THIS *never happened during my father's reign...* Stifling a groan, Ahab shifted uncomfortably in his throne of state, crossing and uncrossing his legs while rubbing his gurgling stomach. *Why did the stars have to align against us when I was king?*

He unconsciously looked up at the ceiling. Unlike the plain marble in the throne room at the residence he had constructed in Jezreël, where he had spent most of his reign, gilded stars dotted the ceiling of the Samarian throne hall; the golden twinkles were arranged with mathematical precision so as to reproduce those constellations visible to the naked eye on the day of the summer solstice. He had been in the official capital of Israel for less than three hours—not enough time even to reacquaint himself with the city's officials—before he had to confront the reason for his homecoming. And this reason was personified in the three Aramaic messengers now standing halfway down the path leading up to the royal throne. With a grimace engulfing his fat, chapped lips, Ahab waved for them to approach.

The first Aramean was young, with large muscles exposed from under his tunic's sleeves, and on his face he wore an arrogant smirk as he eyeballed the king. The second man, wearing the same smirk but with a rotund belly in lieu of rippling muscles, crossed his arms contemptuously and whispered something to the third man. This man whose beard, unkempt and gray, reached down to his navel, was the one who stepped forwards.

"Our lord," said the elder, "King Ben-Hadad of Aram Damascene, is greatly angered by your treacherous, underhanded, and villainous plot against him and his kingdom."

"No, no, there's a misunderstanding. We never—"

"Silence!" yelled the young Aramean. He made a fist at Ahab and shook it threateningly.

The eldest messenger touched his younger companion's arm to calm him before returning his gaze to Ahab. "Do not try to escape your destiny with words. Our master, and the thirty-two kings who call him lord, is at this moment readying his troops to take this city by storm. If he does, then not even two bricks will be left next to each other! Place no vain hope in your paltry soldiers. Victory on the battlefield is beyond you. Yet fear not: he is a kind and merciful master, and thus sends you an offer that, if you are prudent enough to accept, will spare both you and your subjects from needless pain, bloodshed, and agonizing deaths."

Ahab gulped as a streak of sweat rolled down his left temple. "T-tell me h-his message."

The three messengers glanced at each other. Then, as though reciting their carefully choreographed rôles in a chorus, they declared in unison, with an almost chant-like quality to their voices, the following demand: "Thus says King Ben-Hadad: 'Your silver and your gold are mine. Your women and your children, even the best of them, are mine also.'"

*O gods above! This is terrible!* Ahab's hands involuntarily clenched his stomach. *Oh, my... Am I gonna... I hope not. Oh, no...*

"What's your answer?" demanded the young Aramean, raising his right eyebrow.

As a throbbing pain rippled through his stomach, Ahab tottered down his throne's steps and mumbled, "Give me a minute to consider."

He scurried across the room towards the east chamber and re-treated into the empty room. No sooner had the porter drawn the doors shut than the king, having managed to travel only nine feet inside, fell to his knees and heaved up the bitter, chunky, foul-smelling, mucusy contents of the royal stomach all over the sparkling marble floor.

"O my lord, no!" came a voice through the opening door.

Ahab feebly propped himself up on his elbows and glanced over his shoulder. Nava rushed over to him, knelt beside him, and threw her warm arms around his back while she began making soothing sounds.

"Don't tell me you've vomited again," huffed Jezebel, entering the room several seconds after Nava.

Wiping the acidic taste in his mouth on his gold-fringed sleeve, Ahab murmured, "I know you're right, dear, and I apologize for not being able to control my nerves better."

She glared scornfully at him. "In this dark hour, Israel needs its ruler to have the stomach of a king, not that of a sickly, choleric infant incapable of doing anything but shitting itself."

"What a horrible thing to say! Don't you see that our lord is in distress?!" said Nava with a forceful note in her voice. Her nostrils began to flare.

"He's just being a baby."

After helping Ahab to his feet, Nava turned to face Jezebel. "How can you of all people not want to come to his aid?" She dug her nails into the clothing about her thighs. "You are his *wife*."

"Yes, *I* am." Jezebel, narrowing her bulbous eyes to slits, marched over and loomed over the concubine. "That's what gives me such insight into my husband's inner state. An insight only a *wife* could perceive."

*Oh, how I hate seeing them fight!* Ahab shut his eyes and shook his head. *Why can't they just get along?* Brushing the dust off his garments, he cried, "Stop it, stop it, both of you!"

As when two stags, which have been sparring over the ownership of the herd, thrusting their heads against one another while emitting the most brutal groans, hear the hunter's voice and the hunting dogs' bark afar off and, now in terror for their lives, give up their struggle, disentangle their antlers, and flee whithersoever their legs will carry them, so too did Ahab's wife and concubine unlock their gazes from each other. Then they turned to look at him.

"There's an army outside that wants to destroy my kingdom! The last thing I need is for you two to be fighting inside!"

Nava scampered over to him and pressed her soft warm hand delicately on his cheek. "Forgive me, my lord," she begged as Jezebel, without even the smallest muscle in her body appearing to move, glared coldly at them both. "You deserve so much more than this."

"Now, I've come in here for a reason," he said, "and that's to consider Ben-Hadad's proposal." A great shiver jogged up his spinal discs when he mentioned the Aramean's name. *What would my father have done?*

"Yes, a decision must be made." Jezebel approached him on his left side and, with a scowl directed towards Nava standing on his right side, asserted, "There's only one viable choice to make: defy the Aramean! Meet him on the battlefield! If he hungers to devour our kingdom, he must not be allowed to get it without getting the most severe bout of indigestion any man ever had."

"While there's a certain dignity in your tenacity, I think—"

"Are you insane?" said Nava, interrupting Ahab. She pointed her finger straight at Jezebel, who remained visibly unfazed. "How can you order our king to do his own undoing? Have you not seen the hordes of soldiers outside the city's gates?"

"And we've got our army inside the city's gates! The men are ready for war. It would be a waste not to use them to make a heroic last stand against the enemy."

"Are men merely pawns to you, to be lined up, shuffled about, and sent to their deaths without the slightest concern for them? Do you realize how many young lives would be sacrificed under your plan? And for *what*? For your pride? For your inability to admit defeat?"

Her nose crinkling and her upper lip rising in disgust, Jezebel hissed, "Don't ever address me this way, slave! I am your queen!"

"And what an unqueenly queen you make!"

*Oh, Father Jacob, did your women ever squabble like this?* He sighed. Then, stamping his foot twice, he bellowed, "Both of you, CUT IT OUT!"

Nava leapt back, cupping her mouth with her shaking hands; Jezebel, in contrast, simply snorted while rolling her eyes.

"I appreciate both of your concerns and your desire to help. Yet I think I already knew the answer before I came in here." Taking a deep breath, Ahab turned to his wife. "Nava is correct about the inferiority of our strength. Despite raising this army to make war on Ben-Hadad, we were never supposed to face him alone. Yet, owing to the vicissitudes of fate, Baal-Eser's army has already been defeated, leaving us alone to meet the Arameans and their allies. I therefore rule that we accept the terms offered us."

"You're making a terrible mistake!" exclaimed Jezebel. "You'll destroy everything we've worked for!"

Rushing over and planting a great kiss on his stubbly cheek, Nava murmured, "A most merciful decision, my lord, although I'd support any decision you made."

*How you instill such confidence in my heart!* thought Ahab, fondling her breast. Ignoring Jezebel's ongoing criticism, he turned towards the doors and clapped his hands. When the porter opened them, the king held his head high and marched back over to his throne.

The murmurings which had occupied the room since his abrupt departure stopped the moment he ascended his throne. Then, signaling the Aramaic messengers to approach him, Ahab declared:

"Heralds of Ben-Hadad, return to your master and relay to him my decision. For thus says Ahab: 'I accept your demand, my lord, O King. I am yours and all that I have.'"

# CHAPTER SIXTEEN

"T HAT DAMNED IDIOT!"

First the glass vase atop the dressing table shattered on the floor, followed by the explosion of the ceramic platter formerly decorated with painted roses, and ending with the ornately-carved cedar nightstand bleeding splinters of Lebanon as a hard kick pierced its side like a javelin through a man's lower intestines. Looming over the carnage, her flanks heaving, heart pounding, vision narrowed to a tunnel, and a spatter of spittle coating the sides of her open mouth, Jezebel exclaimed, "That bastard's sold me out!"

Sitting at the foot of her mistress's bed, Elishat kept her gaze focused on the littered floor. "It is most unfortunate he accepted the Aramean's ultimatum."

"*Unfortunate*? It's more than *unfortunate*! It's regal malpractice!" The veins on Jezebel's forehead bulged as she thrashed her fists against her breasts. "After all the years he heeded my counsels on foreign relations and accepted my guidance, one might have supposed some of it would have rubbed off on him—that by now he'd have a modicum of awareness when it came to negotiation. But, no! He's got no more perceptiveness, no more shrewdness, no more forethought than, than—his hole-filled mind retains words of wisdom like a leaking chamber pot holds its steaming piss!"

"Yes, Madam."

Jezebel snatched up a small porcelain jar full of myrrh and smashed it against the wall; a sweet aroma quickly filled the bedroom. "What doesn't he understand about an adversary's first demands? Ben-Hadad demands all our country's treasure? Every invader accepts whatever is at hand. He claims ownership of Ahab's wife, children, and concubines? No self-respecting king not yet crushed beneath the victor's fungus-infected heel would stomach such rhetoric. Of course the Aramean makes a giant opening demand! That's what all invaders do! They don't actually expect to get it all—that know that even trying to get it all would require such sustained fighting that the costs would far outweigh the benefits!—but they nevertheless invent the highest figure they can think of, forcing the other side to take a mental inventory of just how much they possess, so that in so doing the value of the subsequent agreed-upon ransom seems but a trifle when compared to the prospect of losing everything. If Ben-Hadad were an idiotic negotiator like my husband, he'd have simply demanded three copper shekels and a toothless hag! He knows the way the game is played. Whereas my Ahab... Ahab! I've no doubt, if he were a commoner, that, whenever he went down to the bazaar, he would pay the first price the vendor proffered without the slightest thought of haggling. He'd quickly become a marked man. The hucksters would eagerly await him like wolves lying in wait for their lamby lunch, mercilessly fleece the fool for all he's worth, and then, as soon as he's departed with his worthless trinkets, burst their lungs and crack their ribs from all the laughing they'd have at his expense! Oh, Baal, how I hate *that man!*"

After making an end to her venting, mostly from lack of breath than from emotional catharsis, Jezebel staggered over and collapsed facedown onto her bed, which smelled strongly of myrrh and cinnamon. She pounded her pillow and sadly wondered, *Why, Father, why did you ever yoke me to that man? I'd rather be married to a peasant's stout-hearted slave, confidently swinging his long pointed pitchfork about, than to a royal baby constantly soiling his marshmallow of a throne!*

She passed several minutes thus in her tear-filled melancholy until suddenly there arose a knocking upon the door.

Not bothering even to lift her head off her wetted pillow, Jezebel commanded with a muffled voice, "Tell whoever it is to go away."

Elishat answered the door with a brisk demeanor; her crisp imperatives, however, quickly turned into a protracted back-and-forth.

*Ugh, I told her to get rid of them. What's she doing?* thought Jezebel, craning her neck aloft and looking up just as Elishat was racing over to her.

"Madam," she said, "I'm informed that Ben-Hadad's messengers just returned and the word going around is that he's rejecting Ahab's acceptance of his prior terms in order to pile even heavier burdens onto our king's back."

With twin fists soaring towards the ceiling, Jezebel's upper body leapt forwards in the bed while her neck hurled backwards. She let out a raucous, "YEEEAAAAAHHH!"

"My lady!" gasped Elishat. She reached out with her swift-moving arms to help her mistress out of bed; but they proved too slow for Jezebel, whose feet had already slammed upon the floor.

"This is excellent news!"

"It is?"

"Of course it is!" Jezebel rushed over to her dressing-table and, leaning her head sideways to view herself in the bronze mirror, grabbed a few bottles of cosmetics and hurriedly began reworking her patchy, mascara-bleeding face. "The gods have given me a second opportunity to return Ahab to my side and to extricate myself from my husband's disgrace."

Having applied a final dash of carmine lipstick to her lips, she darted out of her room, with Elishat following closely on her heels. *If I do this correctly,* she thought, wringing her hands, *then I'll get this dispute with Ben-Hadad settled not by feebleness and defeatist appeasement but by the final argument of kings...* Her green eyes shot wildly back and forth in her head as she foresaw every step of her plan; but the one step she did not see was that by which her feet were taking her. For lost amid her labyrinthine cogitations, she was oblivious to her surroundings in the palace and had to be stopped by Elishat from going past the throne hall.

"Madam, we're here."

Wordlessly Jezebel entered the throne hall. The scene was almost a replica of its rehearsal earlier in the day. Courtiers mulled around the room beneath the starry ceiling. The same three Arameans, even the eldest of them brandishing a smirk upon his face, stood at the foot of the throne. Ahab sat upon it. His face was pale and his breathing only a modicum below what would qualify as hyperventilation. His weary, bloodshot eyes met his wife's briefly before he turned them all over the room, glimpsing at this corner and then at that group of personages, clearly searching for someone in particular. Jezebel looked around herself and the corner of her reddened lip rose.

The king's Hebrew concubine was nowhere to be seen.

*Once again he seeks the bewitching Hebrew... But in defeat she is too ashamed to show her foul face. All the better for me to make my move...*

At last, clutching his gurgling stomach with one hand, Ahab signaled with the other for the heralds to deliver their message.

"Thus speaks Ben-Hadad, saying, 'Although I have sent my messengers to you, saying, "You shall surrender to me your silver and your gold, and your women and children," yet I will send my servants to you tomorrow about this time, and they shall make a thorough search of your house, and the houses of your servants. And it shall be that, whatsoever is pleasant in your eyes, they shall put in their hand and take it away.'"

Gulping with his Adam's apple nervously contracting, Ahab focused his almond eyes on Jezebel, who was standing ahead of the courtiers a mere ten feet away from the throne. With his lower lip quivering, two rivulets of sweat leisurely drifting down his stubbly cheeks, he stared at her for many seconds, not venturing to blink once. His pupils were constricted and undulated within his brown irises like a whole mouse in a snake's digestive tract, gazing pitifully towards her as if to beg her to approach and calm them.

Jezebel did not budge from her spot.

With a deep sigh, Ahab declared: "Tell Ben-Hadad that I must consult with the elders of Israel and will reflect on his proposal. I will give my response to him tomorrow."

The Arameans consented to the delay. As soon as they had quitted the room, Ahab leapt down from his throne and hurried over to the queen.

"Jezebel, Jezebel," he said, his voice shrill and nasally, "did you hear what happened?"

"I saw everything," she replied nonchalantly.

"Why is this happening?" asked Ahab, his shoulders sagging along with his intonation. "I agreed to every single one of Ben-Hadad's demands. But instead of being appeased, he's now demanding even more of me! What did I do wrong? What?"

She gently touched his cheek with her hand. "Ahab, Ahab, Ahab. How many times have I stressed the importance of appearances to you? When you meekly nodded along to everything he sought, not challenging even the least whit of his insane demands, you appeared cowardly and base in the Aramean's eyes. Now you must fight him! Show the world that you too are a king."

"Your words sound good to the ear, but... our inferior strength and position relative to the Aramaic army is still the same as before. I'll hear what our lords say tomorrow. Maybe they'll agree with you. I just don't know what to do... If we fight them..." Bending over, Ahab clutched his stomach and garbled, "Excuse me," before racing out of the room.

Rolling her bulbous eyes, Jezebel turned to Elishat. "Come, we have much work to do tonight. While I believe, after Ben-Hadad's reneging, that most of the lords will freely take my side, I know several whose stubbornness, avarice, or indifference will cloud their better judgment. We must neutralize them lest their hostile influence mislead Ahab."

"If the majority already supports you, are a few dissenting voices truly that threatening?"

"A single insipid word can just as easily be seized upon by a fool to his own destruction as can the collective vocabulary of nine languages." Jezebel narrowed her eyes and rubbed her hands together. "The fate of my kingdom hangs in the balance! I cannot afford even the smallest chance that one of them dissuades him."

"But should Ahab prove so inconstant that even a single dissenting elder could sway him, what if even the unanimity of the elders fails to persuade him? Then what will you do?"

"I hope it should not come to this. But, if necessary," said Jezebel, pausing as her aquiline nose wrinkled in disgust and her red lips puckered as though tasting the bitterest of lemons, "I will resort to even the most loathsome means of persuasion..."

# CHAPTER SEVENTEEN

---

A S THE LAST OF the elders filtered into the throne hall, Jezebel scrutinized them. Her eyes passed quickly over those standing closest to the throne: they were the right-thinking elders, sagacious, prudent, and not in need of supervision. Instead, her eyes were drawn to those who were congregating in the rear of the room.

There was Zev, his chubby fingers twirling the golden, diamond-encrusted necklace that Elishat had slipped to him the prior night. Beside him stood Ilan as unmoving and expressionless as a tree; no one could guess from his face the sort of ecstasy he had experienced a few short hours ago with one of Jezebel's handmaidens. Hillel, whose unrelenting tongue was accustomed to flog others' intelligence by beating their eardrums bloody, remained uncharacteristically mute—his booming baritone of a voice overwhelmed by the guilt and refreshed memory of having laced his late stepson's wine with poison. Finally, pressing his sweat-lined body up against the very wall, was Abihu. Abihu...

Unlike the others, Abihu was kind, gregarious, conscientious. He never absented himself from even the least crowded sessions of the Council, never unduly pressured anyone to adopt his line of reasoning, never offered advice calculated to satisfy his own private benefit... He was also a good father and it was concern for his sons and their fellow soldiers that had led him to refuse Elishat's appeal to support her mistress's cause. When told of his obstinacy, Jezebel herself had to intervene, summoning him out of his bed to share a midnight snack with her in the palatial kitchen.

Abihu had arrived still wearing his bedclothes, his grizzled hair disheveled by his recent slumber. He told Jezebel upfront that he was unwilling to reconsider his opinion: he would advise the king that they not engage the Arameans in battle. She replied that for such a shrewd counselor he had gravely misjudged the situation. She would not dream of discussing politics with him at that most ungodly hour; all she desired was to share a snack with a man well-noted for his conversational excellence. Snapping her fingers, a kitchen maid brought forth a box which she set before him. There were three young roosters in the box. Through a coïncidence of fate, the roosters bore the exact same names as Abihu's three sons. Jezebel, after blurting out this ominous fluke, bade him choose one for a snack; but Abihu, blanching and finding it hard to swallow, merely shook his head whilst staring helplessly at her. Without any vacillation, Jezebel grabbed a rooster and, as Abihu stood watching with his wide unblinking eyes, she coldly wringed Gershem, Oren, and Caleb's necks in turn, addressing each bird by name and wishing each one perpetual peace in death.

Licking her smirking lips, Jezebel held her gaze on Abihu for several moments before turning to Elishat and whispering, "How did Ahab look when you last saw him?"

"He appeared as melancholic and timorous as yesterday, Madam."

Jezebel rested her chin on her long, finely manicured index finger. *Let's see how he looks afterwards...*

Suddenly the throne hall doors were thrown open and, with everyone observing him, Ahab slinked through the crowd and crawled up onto the throne. He repeatedly licked his fat chapped lips, adjusted his sitting position, and rubbed his moist palms together. Finally, ending the murmurings with a rising hand, Ahab addressed the elders.

"Elders of Israel, counselors to your king, I have summoned you to give me your advice. As you know, the army of Ben-Hadad is besieging our city. It is larger than ours and therefore I agreed to the terms which he demanded in exchange for peace. Despite my compliance, he reneged on his own proposal and is now demanding the complete denuding of the kingdom and the right to seize whatsoever he wishes. Should I accept his latest demands, or should we fight despite our weaker position?"

The crowd broke up into several whispery groups but quickly coalesced. One long-bearded elder stepped forwards and announced: "This foreign man speaks wickedly and his word cannot be trusted. Do not listen to him nor consent!"

Jezebel nodded approvingly. *Yes, we must fight. Show Ben-Hadad and the world that Israel is a force to be reckoned with...*

Ahab, his face expressionless, asked, "Is Samuel's pronouncement the will of you all?"

Her bulging eyes quickly spearing everyone with their glimpse, Jezebel was about to smile at the unanimity but clenched her teeth and her fists when Abihu began to inch forwards. *Don't you dare defy me, you filthy pig, or I will...* She relaxed when he abruptly turned around. *Yes, yes, that's right... Keep going.*

With his head and shoulders sinking, Ahab said, "I will consider this advice. You are dismissed."

"Elishat," whispered Jezebel as they sidestepped the retreating elders, "do you really think it possible that Ahab has yet to put his foot into his little whore's shoe?"

"That rumor took hold of the palace servants, Madam, after the beginning of their dalliance, and its strength persists to this day. Neither he nor she has ever corrected that perception; her vague words even hint that it's true."

Jezebel's soft-angled eyebrows scrunched and her teeth nibbled her lip. *Then this should especially sway him...* She bade Elishat adieu and confronted Ahab as he was descending from his throne. "How fares the king?"

His forehead flexed with wrinkles, his almond eyes were bloodshot and heavy, his arms wobbled feebly beside him, and his sluggish gait nearly caused him to stumble down the throne's steps. Sighing heavily, with his shoulders sagging, Ahab said, "Not well, Jezebel, not well. This crisis is draining me... Never has my crown weighed down so heavily on my head."

*A head so ill-suited for regal deliberation...* "Yet I trust that you now recognize the course you must take."

"Oh, Jezebel, not now... Please don't rehash your argument; I already know your position. I'll decide what to..." He yawned. "I just want to sleep. My agitated mind warded off sleep's sweet embrace from me all last night."

When he began to walk away, his feet shuffling past her, she leapt in front of him like a lioness pursuing a gazelle. "Ahab," she exclaimed as she pressed herself up against his body, her serpentine arm curling around his thick neck, "discussing politics and war is the last thing I want to do with you."

"Je-Jezebel... wh-what are you...?"

"I want to reënergize my sleepy husband through sleepless sleeping." Her tongue slithering across his blushing cheek, moistening the flaky skin, she nuzzled up close to his ear and, while nibbling it, whispered in detail all the many things that she would do.

Ahab gulped with difficulty. His pupils dilated and he forgot how to blink. His beating heart vigorously pounded on her chest like a boxer's punches. His breath quickening, its hot pants caressing her face as her free hand stroked his limb, he garbled, "You truly are a goddess among women...!"

***

T HE CROWING OF THE cock heralded the rebirth of day. As the first rays of light trickled through the balcony, Jezebel grunted and blinded her disgusted eyes with the pillow.

Next to her on the bed, sitting straight up and shooting out his arms just as though he had finished first in a footrace against a host of worthy competitors, Ahab was grinning. He put his big hand around her waist and murmured, "Alas, my darling, the dawn has come far too soon. Of all days in the year, I wish she would have lingered in her bed today."

*She's probably, as those Greek barbarians might say, hastening to escape the vomit-inducing sight of her shriveled old decrepit husband...*

"O goddess Dawn, why such haste when you are so unwelcome to all? I love having my beautiful wife by my side; the air is cool and the clear-voiced birdies sing from their slender throats. Why did night have to yield to you, why did the stars retreat before your merciless face? If only a storm had broken your axle or your horses fallen through the clouds! Have you never dallied with your lovers? Heaven is filled with the names of those with whom you played behind your husband's back. So why do you begrudge my wife more time with her lawful husband? Look, Jezebel, look!" He pointed out the window to the reddish light on the horizon. "She's blushing with shame! And yet the day rises as usual, not a whit slower."

Jezebel swallowed the acid rising in her throat.

"Sadly, my dear, I'll have to leave you now so that I can rouse the men for war."

"Yes..." said Jezebel slowly as she set herself upright. "You have a battle to wage today. I pray to Baal that he makes your nerves as strong as iron and grant you victory in this war. Are you ready to fight, dear husband?"

"Am I ready?" Ahab threw off the bedspread and leapt onto the floor. Pounding his chest, he exclaimed, "I feel as though I were a new man! Newfound energy courses through my veins as if I were struck by lightning! I've never felt more alive than I do now! And I owe it all to you," he added, stooping over her so as to brush her silky black hair and inhale its aroma. "For it was your most gracious favors which made me feel this way. If I prevail in battle today, sweet Jezebel, it will be entirely because of you. You're the kindliest woman I've ever known. Remember that."

She narrowed her eyes. "Kindlier than even your mother?"

"Well, apart from her. She's done everything for me... everything except of course what you and I just... I mean obviously she and I've never... because that would be just so... well, that's to say, uh, you know..."

Jezebel bit her lip to stop a smirk. With a gentle nod, she said, "I understand. Now go, dear husband, go!" She pointed towards the door. "And do not return without Aramaic spoils."

"I shan't disappoint you, dearest wife!" Ahab bent over and kissed her forehead with his wet lips before turning around to charge out of the room like a puppy freshly loosed from its kennel.

As soon as he was gone Jezebel collapsed facedown onto her pillow with a great sigh. For several minutes she lay there, her whole body shivering with disgust as a foul taste seeped up into her mouth and her mind kept regurgitating thoughts of the previous night.

At last Elishat announced herself. "Good morning, Madam." She approached the bed.

"What's so good about it?" groused Jezebel.

"Did your labors not prevail against the king?"

"Oh, they prevailed alright." She started stirring herself. "Like a common harlot, I yielded up my body to that man and in exchange clinched his resolution. Even now he's off preparing for an all-out fight against the Aramean."

While helping her mistress to don her clothes, Elishat said, "I regret that interests of state left you no other choice than that."

"And what's most vexing," said Jezebel, pausing to push her head through the dress's top, "is that I had to permit him to sow me on the new moon. From experience, I now know that that's the day on which my seedbed is most fertile. So, unless the gods

145

deign to be merciful, I'm now condemned to have a little Ahab sprouting up within me."

"You wish me to fetch a pessary and have the cure on standby?" said Elishat, asking the question as casually as if she were inquiring what color to paint her mistress's eyes.

"Not this time. Ignoring the unpleasantness of it and the week-long weariness that follows, it may prove beneficial to produce another fruit. For if the drudgery of a single night can make Ahab as pliant as I found him this morning, then giving him another offspring should cement his devotion to me. Don't you remember how he was during the last two?"

Not bothering to stifle her chuckle, Elishat remarked, "He seemed then as obedient as the most perfectly trained puppy."

"Yes..." As Jezebel gazed into her mirror so as to arrange her golden necklace just so, she thought, *Let that whore strut around like a queen while she can. For as soon as I give him more royal offspring, he'll forget all about his slavish lusts...*

"So now that the king has agreed to fight Ben-Hadad, do you think, Madam, our forces can win the day?"

Jezebel threw her head backwards. "How should I know?" Crossing her arms, she remarked, "Our forces are outnumbered more than two-to-one by the Arameans. That's to their advantage. Yet they are fighting on strange ground whereas our men know this land like the back of their hand. That's to our advantage. Nevertheless, the Arameans are led by Ben-Hadad, who in a few short years has demonstrated exemplary military prowess—a truly genius tactician—while our men are cursed to be led by Ahab... Only the gods know how this battle will turn out."

"I've already sacrificed three cocks to Baal. I pray fervently he spare us in this war."

"Yes. But regardless of the outcome, we must strive with all we've got. For it would be intolerable to keel over and allow the Arameans to conquer us without resistance. And, of course, we might still win." She shut her green eyes and clenched her teeth; her forehead scrunched with wrinkles. *But if I had to guess, Ahab will most likely preside over a catastrophic defeat.*

Handing the queen her final adornment, Elishat said, "Did I hear correctly that the king himself is leading our troops?"

"He is. Like my father, my brother, or the Aramean, Ahab will command our forces in the field, like a real king."

"I did not think warfare was your husband's forte."

"No, but after last night he has the passion one would like to see in a general. His captains and lieutenants, obviously, will be the ones plotting the strategy and overseeing battle deployments. Yet Ahab's presence amid our troops might just possibly inspire them." *Most of them are peasants and have never laid eyes upon him; they could be deluded for at least a day...*

"Pardon me for my bluntness, Mistress, but isn't it risky to permit him to put himself in harm's way like this? What if he should die in battle? What would happen then, to us?"

Jezebel, carefully examining herself as she applied ruby lipstick, paused from her labors. "Well," she mused, "that would depend on the battle's outcome. If we should prevail against the Arameans, and maintain our independence, then Ahab's death, while regrettable, would not impair us in our kingdom: my son Ahaziah would inherit the throne, which I'd help him safeguard. But if Ahab should die along with our freedom, and Ben-Hadad make Israel his latest conquest and add us to his burgeoning empire, then... we would have to seriously reëvaluate our options."

Gnawing her freshly reddened lips, she thought, *I suppose Ben-Hadad could always use another queen in his harem. It's inconceivable that any of his current wives can adequately advise so great a king as he....*

# CHAPTER EIGHTEEN

"AND YOU SHOULD HAVE seen the looks on their faces when I said it! You could tell they had expected me to submit to Ben-Hadad's perfidy a second time. Especially that arrogant young Aramean. He had the sort of cocksure look you see on youths who are in over their heads but way too stupid to realize it. But then I ascended my throne and, bellowing down to them like Baal in a tempest, I told them, 'Tell my lord king, "All that you did send to your servant at the first I will do. But this thing I may not do."' They were so dumbstruck they couldn't utter a single syllable—they just dashed out of the room like I had rained fire down on them! It was amazing! I felt such a thrill run up my leg when I forced them out of my presence. And I'll force their master out of my realm too!"

While recounting the events of the morning, enthusiastically gesturing with his arms to emphasize both the key moments and the inconsequential, slapping his thighs and upper left arm, clapping his hands, and finding it difficult to maintain a steady tone of voice, Ahab had the rays of the sun radiating behind his head in such a way that he appeared to sport a golden aura. Yet the thickness of his skull blocked the sunlight from reaching Nava's face, which was overshadowed by his.

Seeing her gloomy countenance as she pressed her body up against the shadowy colonnade, Ahab took her delicate hand and pressed it against his chest. "Forgive me for rambling on, my sweet little pomegranate. I was so taken in by my own masterful performance that I haven't even asked you how you feel."

"My lord," replied Nava softly, shifting her foot while keeping her round brown eyes fixed on the ground, "I am still saddened at Ben-Hadad's betrayal. You did everything he asked for and yet that was still not enough for him."

Ahab formed a fist. "Many men are liars and cheats, never content with what they have but always envying others for what they have; lamentably, politics intensifies these ambitions."

"Your wife seemed to have recognized these facts." She sniffled, and a lone tear escaped her dour eye. "I feel so foolish now for my naïveté, for counseling you to take the course you did... I'm just a stupid slave. What do I know of politics?"

Gasping, Ahab grabbed her face by the sandy locks of her hair and directed her eyes towards his. "Don't say that, don't ever say that! What you said, you said out of sympathy for our soldiers; needless slaughter would not help anyone. Never apologize for being merciful. Jezebel is an expert politician, consummate diplomat, and brilliant strategist. She knows precisely where she wants to go and how to get there; but too often lost in her calculus is the human cost." He pulled her close and smacked his chapped lips against her moist mouth. "You're a sweet girl, Nava, a thoughtful, considerate, and loving girl. And going forwards, as I confront this threat menacing my whole kingdom, I will need you by my side: for you give me the kind of help which Jezebel cannot offer."

"Oh, my lord, I-I'm blushing." She nuzzled her warm cheek against his face. Swallowing determinedly, she murmured, "You are such a good man and noble king. I promise you, in the sight of God, that I will cling steadfast to you as you face your ordeal. I pray that God bless you and save His people Israel from the Aramaic horde."

Ahab smiled and rubbed her soft, delicate button nose. *I'm so lucky to have you...*

The clanging of synchronized feet interrupted their embrace. Turning around, Ahab frowned. Escorted by armed guards, and still wearing his defiant expression, came the young Aramean envoy. "You again?" said the king sarcastically. "I thought I made my answer clear to you. Do Ben-Hadad's messengers lack memory, or do you simply wish to receive another rejection?"

The Aramean sniffed and his face scrunched up into a yellow tooth-revealing scowl. "If I were allowed to approach, I could give Israel the greetings my master sends."

*Insufferable prick...* Putting his arm around Nava's waist and pulling her against his flank, Ahab signaled his guards to let the Aramean approach.

Keeping his hate-filled eyes locked on the king as he stepped forwards, the Aramean spat upon the ground in front of Ahab's feet and then ground the spittle beneath his sandal. "Thus says Ben-Hadad: 'The gods do so unto me, and more also, if the dust of Samaria shall suffice for handfuls for all the people that follow me.'"

"Don't let this arrogant insult go unanswered," whispered Nava into his ear.

"I won't." Ahab, curling his fat lips, glanced down at the Aramean and snorted from his upturned nose. "The hunchbacked shouldn't boast as though he were an upright man. Now, guards, get him out of here. I do not wish to see another Aramean unless it's on the battlefield where I shall defend my crown and realm."

Once the guards had departed with the envoy, Nava threw her arms around Ahab's thick neck which she proceeded to cover with warm, moist kisses. "My lord, you spoke so forcefully to that rascally heathen, so decisive. I love watching you rear your righteous fury against the wicked."

Ahab, beaming, let out a chuckle and said, "And I love having you by my side to see it."

"Simply exercise your righteous powers and put a stop to this evildoing, O King, and I have complete faith that the God of our forefathers will reward you with victory over the impious Arameans."

# CHAPTER NINETEEN

---

"**H**OW SOON BEFORE YOU think Ben-Hadad attacks?"

"Well, his final messenger departed the city right at nine o'clock," began the commander, rubbing his chin. His bushy eyebrows were squeezed together in thought. "It should have taken about twenty minutes for him to reach the Aramaic camp. By now Ben-Hadad is probably readying his troops. He could give them their marching orders anytime now."

Ahab glanced at the sundial located in the center of the palace pavilion. It was a large slab of red granite, roughly twelve feet in diameter, which had been skillfully carved into a dodecagon. The sides had been cut so sharply that the edges posed the danger of minor laceration to any bare foot careless enough to brush up against it; the surrounding moat filled with polished white pebbles that glistened in the sun, however, proved to be a sufficient safeguard for unthinking extremities. Rising from the center of the granite was the gnomon made of black marble whose triangular blade cast a shadow across the mark for eleven o'clock. "And are our troops ready?"

"Nearly so, my lord. A few platoons quartered in the western part of the city are still *en route* to the Asherah Gate."

"Very well. You may leave now."

With a respectful salute, the commander left his king with his thoughts. Ahab ambled over to a granite bench and sat down beneath the lofty ghaf tree overshadowing it. Resting his head in his sweaty hands, a deep sigh escaped his regal lungs.

*Oh, what am I to do? Only a few hours ago I felt so confident and vigorous. Thoughts of Ben-Hadad's defeat, my kingdom's salvation, the warm embrace of Nava, finally winning Jezebel's approval... all came easily to my impatient mind. But now, as the hour of battle approaches, I find it difficult to muster hope, let alone courage to face it. We are so badly outnumbered.*

A great shiver went up his spine.

*Oh, why didn't I just submit to Ben-Hadad's second request? He probably would have demanded more like before... But what if he didn't? What if he would have accepted it? I could've salvaged something of my realm instead of losing it all. It's too late now. Or is it? What if—if I could send an envoy before the battle begins, and make Ben-Hadad an offer of...*

"Why has your countenance fallen, O King?"

The rasping voice, piercing his concentration as a gadfly does a cow, awakened Ahab from his introspection. Jolting up with surprise, he looked towards the pavilion's entrance. An elderly gentleman dressed in moth-eaten sackcloth, the ragged hairs of his beard clumping in discreet greasy tufts, was moseying in his direction with the aid of a scraggy cane.

"Who are you?"

"The better question is: who are you?"

"I'm the king of Israel!"

The elderly man shook his leathery finger. "Then why do you sit here in unkingly angst? A king is not a potted plant: a king is the active part of his kingdom's soul, the director of all its movements. Be not passive in the face of heathen hordes but rouse yourself and fight like a man in defense of his home."

"That's easy for you to say, old man," huffed Ahab. He grated his teeth and glared at the ground. "Your age spares you from the horrors of battle; but I and the younger men must expose ourselves to premature death."

"All men are mortal; death is the common end allotted to us all. Why then do you fear this absolute certainty? Fear not those who can kill the body; rather fear Him who can kill the soul."

Ahab's wrinkly forehead rose while his mouth fell. "Are you one of the worshippers of the Hebrew God?"

The elderly man rested his body weight on his cane and cocked his head. "You address Him as though He were foreign to you. It ill befits an Israelite's lips so to speak. But yes, I am a worshipper of the God of Abraham, of Isaac and Jacob—and a prophet too."

"A prophet? Like Elijah? Are you one of his followers?"

"I am not of Elijah's company although both I and my brother are sent from a common Father."

"Why have you come?"

"Yahweh loves His people even in spite of their inveterate disobedience. He wills that you and your people may come to know His power and renounce the idols of your hearts. For this reason He is sending you a sign."

Ahab licked his chapped lips and gulped. "Tell me His sign."

Throwing his head back, the prophet drew in a gust of air and bellowed, "Thus says Yahweh: 'Hast thou seen all this great multitude? Behold, I will deliver it into thine hand this day; and thou shalt know that I am Yahweh.'"

Ahab asked, "By whom will the Arameans be vanquished?"

"Thus says Yahweh: 'By the young men of the princes of the provinces.'"

"Who shall order the battle?"

Leaning forwards, his hot rancid breath enfolding the king's face, the prophet answered, "Thou."

Ahab shut his eyes and, clenching his fists crosswise across his chest, stared blindly skywards. *O God of my fathers, is what this man says true? Are You really able to give me victory over my foe?* Opening his eyes, he said, "Tell me everything that—"

The prophet was gone.

"What?" Ahab blinked. At his feet lay the old man's staff. He picked it up and handled the gnarly wood. *Where'd he go? Oh, well.*

Casting the staff to the ground, Ahab raced out of the pavilion, flagged down a chariot, and proceeded to the Asherah Gate whose blue glazed bricks were noticeable from afar. The street leading up to it was clogged with soldiers. Bypassing the men, Ahab arrived in front of the immense gate where his commanders were in the midst of planning the coming battle.

"Hold everything!" shouted Ahab as he leapt down from the chariot. Ignoring their startled looks, Ahab breathlessly began giving his commands. "Tell the princes of the provinces to assemble their young men. Number the rest of our troops and ready them for battle."

A couple commanders left to execute the orders. The princes sent two hundred and thirty-two young men, born in aristocratic houses, to the king. To these, Ahab committed the seven thousand soldiers who were congregating in the streets of Samaria; invoking

Baal and the other gods to favor them in their endeavor, Ahab instructed them to attack Ben-Hadad. After the army went out of the city gate just as the sun was reaching its zenith, Ahab retreated to the fortified tower on the eastern wall from where he could best oversee the organization of the battle.

"Have they met the enemy yet?" asked Ahab, shielding his eyes from the sun as he sought to catch sight of the battle.

A senior commander, his unblinking eyes fixed on the clouds of dust in the distance, said, "It appears they're just about to—yes! Our front ranks made contact! The battle is begun!"

*I sure hope that prophet was right*, thought Ahab as he concealed his fingernails between his double rows of teeth. "How long do you think it will last?"

"The gods only know. Every battle is predicated on different factors."

Ahab stepped away from his position by the wall's edge and began marching up and down the wall. His feet repeatedly crossed the bricks, advancing twenty feet before yielding back the trodden territory. Lost in thought and oblivious to how much time had passed, Ahab had to be physically accosted by his aids to hear the news.

"Sire, Sire," shouted the officer, waving his hand in front of the king's face, "one of our soldiers has returned with news!"

"He has? Where is he?"

"Here, Sire." A young man with a still-bleeding cut on his left cheek knelt before him. Resting his forearm on his breastplate that was wet with others' blood, he announced, "We've routed the Arameans! Despite their greater numbers, their king and his commanders failed to marshal their forces into unified lines of battle. They kept giving orders that were either flawed or too sluggish to be of use. Frankly, they acted as though they were drunk! Now Ben-Hadad is in full retreat."

Ahab slapped his thighs and leapt upwards. "Excellent, my boy, excellent! We've saved Israel! Quick!" He turned to one of his attendants. "Prepare my chariot! I'll finish those churls off myself."

\*\*\*

AHAB HAD QUICKLY MADE his appearance on the battlefield although the point of major fighting was by then well past. The bulk of the Arameans had already fled eastwards but there were stragglers still in the vicinity, wounded men unfit to move, and others who had been trapped beneath their chariots or the bodies of either their horses or fallen comrades.

When the blood-red sun was setting in the sky, Ahab's chariot wheeled into Samaria. A great smile was painted on his face. His hand rested smugly on the handle of the gory sword which had cut down thirteen men and hamstrung seven horses. *What a wonderful day...*

Passing through the gateway, Ahab spotted the elderly prophet.

"You were right, old man!" he called to him, waving his sword. "God gave me the victory today. Our kingdom is secure."

The prophet, not taking his unblinking eyes off of Ahab's, shook his head. "You may rightly rejoice this day, O King, for the God of Israel has seen fit to show mercy; but do not put your faith in past victories. The Arameans are chastened but not crushed.

Go, strengthen yourself, and mark, and see what you do. For at the return of the year the king of Aram will come up against you."

# CHAPTER TWENTY

E IGHT MONTHS HAD ELAPSED since Israel's victory at the Battle of Samaria. Apart from a few minor skirmishes on the frontier and some localized unrest on the part of Hebrew worshippers, Israel enjoyed peace both at home and abroad. During this interregnum Ben-Hadad licked his wounds, rebuilding his army and biding his time. Ahab, too, did not pass this time in idleness. He toured his kingdom, taking stock of Israel's defenses, recruiting new soldiers to bolster his forces, overseeing the output of the armories, and confirming the strength of his governors in their provinces. He did not entrust such crucial cares to his advisers as had been his wont but, abandoning his formerly lackadaisical approach to governance, spent his days personally in the field with his army.

"Nava, dear," said Ahab as he approached her tent. When he reached out to pull the leathery flaps of her tent aside, he tugged too hard and accidentally ripped them off. Looking at the tattered material dangling limply in his hands, he mumbled, "Sorry."

"That's okay." She placed her soft hands on his right arm and rubbed them up and down the large biceps that he had acquired in the intervening months. "You're still not used to this strength."

Ahab's skin grew warm at her touch and his cheeks flushed, although his bushy beard concealed most of the sudden redness. "You're right," he agreed, wrapping his muscular arm around her thin waist. "I understand now why my father preferred leading his armies to remaining at home. Serving alongside my men, sharing in their toils and rations, and forsaking the enervating delicacies of palace cuisine has made me into a new man. I feel stronger and better than I've ever felt before!" On a whim he lifted her up, twirled her once around, and then gently set her down with a kiss. "But having you by my side matters more than all of that. Exercise and nutritious food can make a body sound but they are powerless to strengthen the spirit. Without your support, I wouldn't be able to face Ben-Hadad, let alone defeat him."

"Please, my lord, you're making me blush," she murmured, resting her pallid cheek against his brown beard. "Don't undercut yourself. *You* are the one who's doing everything. And I know, God-willing, that you will defeat the Arameans when they return. How far out are they?"

"Our scouts estimate that they're three days out."

"How many men does Ben-Hadad have?"

"That's what is most frightening. The Arameans are said to number in the tens of thousands. Despite the increases in our army's size, it is still significantly smaller than what Ben-Hadad is said to have. If only Israel were larger or Ben-Hadad's domain less extensive!"

"Then let us pray together."

Falling to their knees, they knelt on the dusty ground and clasped their hands together, interlocking the fingers. With her eyes tight shut, Nava began the prayer. "O God of our father

Abraham, You Who overthrew the army of Pharaoh in the Red Sea, please hear me and grant my request. Grant Your people Israel and their noble king victory over the Arameans who dare to blaspheme Your holy name. Save us, O Yahweh, and confound the heathen. Amen."

"Amen," concurred Ahab, bowing his head. *O God of my fathers, you already gave me one victory over a superior force. Please, grant me another! If not for me, then for her...*

Rising to her feet, Nava hugged him and asked, "Would you like some lunch?" She pointed to trays of apples, cucumbers, and figs in the corner of the tent.

"Sorry, but I must officiate at the sacrifice to Baal."

She rolled her round brown eyes and huffed, "Why do you continue to propitiate those foreign gods? Do you not believe in our God?" She crinkled her button nose.

"It's not that at all," replied Ahab, resting his hand on her agitated cheek. "I do believe in Him. But you must remember that most of my soldiers worship Baal and seek his favor. And I need to keep up their morale ahead of the coming conflict; to ignore their beliefs would demoralize them."

"If their king were to be open about his convictions," she said, blinking her dilated eyes as she stared intently at him, "many soldiers would convert to the religion of their commander-in-chief. The example of a king, whether it be for good or ill, always proves most potent with the masses."

"Now's not the time for stirring internal conflict over gods. Once the enemy is defeated and sent back home, their bodies whipped and bloodied, then we can discuss affairs of the spirit."

Giving her one final kiss, Ahab quitted the tent and made his way across the loud, crowded camp to the blood-stained altar that had been erected to Baal. As he approached it, he thought to himself, *I know Nava would hate to hear this, but this isn't just for my men's sake. The more gods I can get on my side can only help me. (And I need all the divine assistance there is!) If there were any ritual by which I might induce Ben-Hadad's gods to abandon him and transfer their backing to my side, I would perform it in a heartbeat—even if the ritual required the offering up of one of my concubines' sons.*

\*\*\*

T HE SHARP EDGE OF the knife glinted in the sun when Ahab raised it high. Clasping it between both his hands, his arms forming an isosceles triangle, the king brought the metal down hard. The muddy sow, squirming on the stone altar, let out a plaintive screech which was as high-pitched as it was short-lived. Blood splattered everywhere as Ahab violently dragged the knife across the beast's throat. It was a big pig. Warm blood kept pouring out of its carcass, soaking Ahab's wrists and sleeves and pooling around his sandal-clad feet.

Raising the bloody knife, Ahab looked to the sky and cried out, "Hear me, Baal, and accept this sow's lifeblood in token of our devotion to you. Grant us victory in our fight and smite our enemies with blows of death!"

The mass of soldiers, who had been watching this sacrifice with blank stares and hushed solemnity, suddenly erupted in roars of approval.

Ahab looked them over and smiled. *What wonderful young men I've been blessed with... I've no doubt they've got what it takes to humble Ben-Hadad, if only they are given a fair chance. If the gods grant me victory...*

A sacrificial assistant handed Ahab a linen rag. He used it first to wipe the droplets of blood that had hit his wrinkly forehead before proceeding to wipe his bloodstained hands while he headed back towards his tent. The now discolored rag was still soaking up blood when, next to the clanging tent housing the camp's blacksmith, Ahab was confronted by a grisly, prematurely graying man who could not have been much older than himself.

Before the king could reäct, this unknown man snatched the bloody rag out of his hands and hoisted it over the king's head as though it were a crown.

*What the—!* The visible portion of his cheeks turning almost as red as the rag and his nostrils flaring, Ahab stamped his foot and yelled, "You fool! Do you KNOW who I am?" He reflexively took a step back when the man, responding to his outburst with a good-natured smile, revealed a mouth missing half its teeth while the half that remained were marred by black spots. His eyes were bulbous, crusted yellow, and the right one appeared cloudy with blindness.

"Know you? Who does not know you? You are the king of Israel, scion of Abraham, Isaac, and Jacob, who forsakes the God of his forefathers by serving strange gods, defiling himself with the blood of pigs." The gentleman waved the rag over Ahab's head, allowing drops of blood to roll off onto his face like tears. "You can't believe how sorely you have disappointed your ancestors."

*This man is either insane or he's...* A cold chill went up Ahab's spine. "Tell me who you are. For you do not speak like other men."

"I am no one, merely dust and ashes walking up and down the earth. Yesterday I was not, and tomorrow I will not be, but today I am honored to convey the will of the One greater than us all."

"Are you a prophet?" asked Ahab, cocking his neck while his eyes became wide.

The man bowed his head. "Yes, I am a prophet—a prophet of Yahweh, if you need me to so specify. And I had better specify. For you consort with the worshippers of Baal, and their priests and soothsayers; and I would not wish you, in your ignorance, to reckon me among the impious."

"Forgive me for my intemperate comments," began Ahab, bowing his head. "I did not realize you were a prophet of our God."

"*Our* God?" The prophet paused to glance over the king. "Do you profess to worship the God of Israel?"

"Oh, yes, yes, yes," said Ahab, vigorously nodding his head at each affirmation. "Just a little while ago, my concubine and I fell to our knees in worship of God. He knows that I am His."

"Then why do you give sovereign honor unto Baal, proclaiming to the world that you are *his*?"

"You misunderstand. That was for the benefit of my men. It didn't mean anything. It was just a pig! What has that to do with my allegiance?"

The prophet, shaking his head, said, "And what if one of your subject's were to hail Ben-Hadad as his king, or volunteer to serve in his army? Would you view him as still loyal to you?"

"Those are entirely different things. There are countless gods worshipped among the nations."

"There are many kings among the nations, too."

"Yet a man can only serve one king in this world while acknowledging the power of many gods. Yes, I occasionally worship Baal, but I am still a Hebrew by race and therefore I will worship the God of the Hebrews. And I do pray fervently unto Him that He will grant His people salvation from His enemies. Ben-Hadad and his sacrilegious army are quickly approaching, intent on desecrating the land promised to our father Abraham, and we need our God's blessing to avoid that calamity."

The prophet shut his eyes and sighed. He murmured, "God will grant the victory you desire."

"Oh, thank you, thank you," said Ahab, dropping to his knee and kissing the prophet's bony hand. "You don't know how happy your news makes me! I knew God would look favorably upon my good works, and the prayers I have chanted, and the many fatted calves—the best in my flocks—that I have offered up to Him. Yes, and after my victory God can expect to receive from me the greatest—"

"FOOL!" Suddenly the prophet snatched his hand out of Ahab's clutch. His nostrils flaring, his eyes snapped open and angrily glared at the kneeling king. "The sacrifices and incense of a backslider are by no means pleasing unto Yahweh!" he howled, spittle flying onto Ahab's face.

Ahab, his heart skipping a beat, stared blankly up at him.

"Do not boast of your 'good works' and pat yourself on your back for worshipping Yahweh while you are covered in the blood of animals offered up unto heathen gods! You seek to mingle oil with water, hoping to combine the benefits of each; but oil and water can no more mix than can the worship of God and idols. Yahweh will not grant you victory on account of your own merits. For you must yet do more, much more, to repent of your many sins."

Struggling to rise, his legs wobbly from the shock of the prophet's words, Ahab mumbled, "But, but, I-I thought you said I would be victorious?"

"You shall be."

"But you just said God wouldn't reward me with victory."

"He shall not."

"I don't understand."

"Then stop your prattling and listen!" bellowed the prophet. "Thus says Yahweh: 'Because the Arameans have said, "Yahweh is God of the hills but He is not God of the valleys," therefore will I deliver all this great multitude into thine hand, and thou shalt know that I am Yahweh!'"

Wringing his hands, Ahab ventured, "Then I still will be victorious?"

The prophet narrowed his eyes and huffed. "Yes, O King, you will have the victory which you crave even more than you value your soul. Although you do not deserve it, God will nonetheless grant it to you for the sake of punishing the Arameans, whose sins are even more grievous than your own. Go, kill the Arameans! And as you do, reflect that you are worthy of the same fate."

"I thank you, you holy man of God. Please tell Yahweh that I thank Him for His promise of victory. I truly want to serve Him. I really do! I've even read all the holy writings of Moses to find out what I should do. But it is hard to know what God wants! I know what a Levite should do to cure leprosy, but I still don't understand what God expects of me. Only tell me what I should do and I will do it."

Turning his back on Ahab, the prophet raised his foot to go; and as he went, he snorted, "If, having read the Scriptures, you must still be told how to act religiously, then you are in a worse condition than you would have been in had you never read them at all!"

# CHAPTER TWENTY-ONE

"Ugghh..." moaned Jezebel, pressing her head back into her moist pillow. "This heat is killing me!"

She snapped her fingers. Instantly the eunuch standing beside her, a sweaty river streaming down his forehead before branching off into distributaries along his cheeks and chin, let out a tired pant; despite his evident exhaustion, he boosted the frequency with which he waved his peacock feather fan.

From across the royal veranda, dimly lit on account of the black translucent tapestries that had been carefully hung to limit the fierce sun, Elishat rose from her seat and approached the queen. "Would you say it's mostly the heat of the day or your pregnancy that is discomforting you?"

Jezebel grinded her teeth and dug her nails into the couch on which she was sprawled most uncomfortably. "It's from the white-hot rage I have for that bastard! What's he up to now?"

"The king's army was last reported to have encamped outside Aphek six days ago. The Arameans have also mustered their forces at Aphek. It's only a matter of time before they meet in what is expected to be an epic battle."

"Bully for them! The more dead, the more verses the poets can compose." Jezebel snorted. "At least I still have you, Elishat. *Someone* to tell me what's going on in the world."

She bowed her head. "My only wish is to serve you, Madam. I will always be at your complete disposal."

*I can remember when* he *said those exact words...* "I appreciate the work you do. Your intelligence gathering is excellent as always. Though, by all rights, I shouldn't have to depend on your skills alone. *I* should be there, with *him*, when the climax of this war is about to be decided. But where am I instead? Here! He's confined me in Jezreël! Oh, how I know he hates me..."

"Despite his incalculable faults, Madam," said Elishat, resting her hand on Jezebel's tensed knee, "the king is right that the battlefront is no place for you."

"What about *her*? He allows *her* to join him on the front."

Elishat shook her head. "But the Hebrew woman is not in your condition, Madam."

"So she's still in the clear after all this time? What's her secret? Rue tea?"

"The latest report is the same as the first. The king's concubine still successfully resists performing the chief duty of a concubine."

*Yeah, right*, thought Jezebel, covering her perspiring face with her sleeve. *How long will a dog put up with the scent of a juicy steak dangling before its jaws without attacking it? Am I expected to believe Ahab hasn't laid his grimy hands on her? In all likelihood, she's probably just naturally barren, just like that insipid, childless God she worships... Maybe some bloodlustful Arameans will break through the supply lines, penetrate her bordello, and—oh, yes, Baal!—wipe that smarmily chaste smile off her face...*

"Do you wish me to withdraw, Madam?"

"No, no, no. I'm just, so, damned, hot!" Jezebel snarled and slammed her fist into the eunuch's empty groin. "Fan harder, you worthless slave! Or would you rather toil in the millhouse?"

The chastised slave momentarily reeled from her blow before resuming, with forced gusto, his assigned task.

Sighing, Jezebel exclaimed, "Just look at what that man did to me!" She raked her swollen hands down her colossal abdomen. "This is the longest, worst pregnancy I've ever had!"

"By the gods' mercy, it'll be over any day now."

"Yeah, probably right after my husband loses the war because I wasn't there."

"It's out of your hands, Madam," said Elishat soothingly, sitting back down in her chair. "You must remain at home where it is safe."

"*Safe*? Really?" Jezebel threw her head back and let out a raucous laugh. "I'm in far greater danger *here* than I would be *there*. You've never had children, Elishat, so I'll pardon you for your ignorance. But I have. And from experience, I'd far rather be at Aphek, fighting in the thickest part of battle three times than give birth just once!"

Elishat bowed her head in silence.

"If I were at Aphek, I'd right all his idiotic mistakes, devise the appropriate military strategy, and make sure he didn't fu—aar-rgghhh!" Jezebel doubled over from a jolt of intense pain and clenched her abdomen.

"Madam!" exclaimed Elishat, jumping up. "Should I fetch the midwives?"

Clenching her teeth, Jezebel spat, "NO! It's not time yet. By Baal I wish it were, but it's not." A single tear rolled down her cheek. "This is just pain from the bastard's betrayal of me."

"Is there anything I can get you?"

*How about a new husband?* She sighed, waved her hand dismissively, and relaxed her body. "No. What I need right now... I need to stop that Hebrew whore from turning him against me anymore than she already has." *I must first stop the bleeding—then the real battle can begin...*

"Be calm, Madam." Elishat leaned over and gingerly rubbed Jezebel's swollen wrist. "You have been the king's wife for twenty years—longer than the concubine has been alive—and in all that length of time he has adored you. Everyone who's observed him can see that he loves you. Despite this protracted dalliance with the Hebrew woman, which in truth is only a blink of the eye in comparison with the hallowed age of your marriage, you remain foremost in his heart."

"Appearances are deceptive," sneered Jezebel, folding her arms across her chest. "Don't be like the naïve women who accept a man at face value. I'm Ahab's wife: I know him down to the lowest, most fetid crevices of his soul. He's a ship without a helmsman, a chariot without a driver. Of course he adores me: I'm the first woman he ever had. I made the strongest impression on him, which I've carefully reïnforced over the years. When we were first married, anytime we were separated—even for the briefest of times—he would write me multiple times a day. He still wrote me at least once a day before that whore pushed her way into our lives. But now..."

She snapped her fingers and a servant brought her a silver platter, on which was the latest letter Ahab had sent to her.

"It's been seventeen days since he last wrote me. And he's been encamped at Aphex for six days, so what's hindering him from writing to me? *Her.*" The taste of blood hit her mouth after she had been chewing her lips. Jezebel spat upon the floor in front of her fanning eunuch. "The frequency of his letters has been declining this whole past year, ever since he left on his 'oversight tour' around the kingdom. Don't tell me he doesn't want me with him because of the war: he didn't want me accompanying him during peacetime either. He wants to enjoy his whore and she wants to keep him away from me. The less he sees of me, the weaker my hold on him becomes; the more she has him all to herself, the deeper into her beguiling swamp he sinks. Ahab's weak. Always has been. He has no personality of his own. He listens to whoever last spoke to him. That quality has served me well all these years when I could control whom he consulted, but now it's become a great liability. For now another woman, a Hebrew slave no less, an infidel, has wrapped him around her heathen fingers. Having sidelined me, she's gained a monopoly on access to him and can work in peace at turning him against me. And if she should succeed..." *I'll be deposed, banished from my home, exiled with my gods while that whore exalts her heathen religion. Oh, I should have had her poisoned the moment I learned she was a Hebrew, before Ahab had grown so attached to her!*

"She cannot succeed, Madam," vowed Elishat, forming a defiant fist. "A woman of that background can in no way triumph against a daughter of Tyre's royal house. You are a born queen and a woman of far greater intellect and ability than that ill-bred, provincial whore."

"You're damned right I am!" said Jezebel, rising from the couch. Her cheeks flushed with blood newly pumped from her hastening heart as she approached one of the tapestries shading the veranda. Ripping the nearest one down, she glared at the horizon with her bulbous eyes while menacingly inhaling the warm afternoon breeze. "By Baal, I will not lose everything I've spent a lifetime building. Israel shall be a new Tyre, glorious, and without the stench of the heathens. That Hebrew whore may dream of stopping me, but she'll soon learn what an adversary she's up against. I never relent until I win!"

*But I've got to act quickly before it's too late...*

# CHAPTER TWENTY-TWO

"**Y**AAA-HOOOO!" EXCLAIMED AHAB, LEANING over his chariot's side and stabbing the downed Aramaic warrior with his spear.

The Aramean howled in agony when the spear pierced the flesh beneath his left lung. A cloud of blood erupted from the wound when the spear withdrew and blew several feet backwards in the wind kicked up by the chariot's departing wheels.

Ahab rested his arm on the back of his chariot and looked back with a gleeful smile at the fresh corpse which he had left lying in the dust. "This is my fifth kill of the day," he boasted to his charioteer. *And I've never felt more alive!*

The sun had reached its mid-afternoon position amid a battle that had been raging since midmorning when Ahab gave the order to attack the Arameans' ranks. A breakdown in communications had paralyzed Ben-Hadad's army, resulting in his army's various formations to be stationed haphazardly across the field of battle and unable effectively to coöperate in battle. Hence, despite the Arameans fielding a larger number of soldiers, Israel's army quickly gained the upper hand and ground. A large scale slaughter ensued when Ahab's forces smashed through Ben-Hadad's ranks. The surviving portion of the Aramaic army retreated pell-mell inside the walls of Aphek, against which Ahab's troops were now preparing to lay a siege.

As the chariot's wheel screeched to a stop in front of several of his officers, Ahab called out, "How goes your forces?"

"Excellent, Sire," answered the ranking captain. "We've got the enemy completely on the run. All that's left is to take the town."

"And are we well-positioned to do so?"

"Yes, we could starve them out within a week. But that may prove unnecessary." The captain called to several of his underlings who promptly led five men over to Ahab. These men were naked apart from sackcloth around their waists and bristly ropes tied around their necks.

"Who are these men?" said Ahab, cocking his head.

"These men are counselors of Ben-Hadad."

"Why are they dressed like this?"

"We have shed our royal apparel," answered one of the Arameans, "to demonstrate our abject state." He and his companions simultaneously dropped to their knees and bowed their heads as though offering them to the executioner's blade. "We know that the kings of the House of Israel are merciful and we entrust our lives to your clemency."

*Interesting... Could Ben-Hadad be looking to sue for peace?* Licking his lips and rubbing his hands together, Ahab said, "Do you speak only for yourselves or for your king, too?"

"We are messengers of him who once held sway over the four corners of the earth. Your slave, Ben-Hadad, says, 'I beg you to let me live.'"

Ahab rattled his spear against his chariot's bronze railing. "Is he still alive? Then I wish him to be my brother."

"Your brother, Ben-Hadad?" echoed the messenger. He and the others silently looked over Ahab.

"Yes," replied Ahab, leisurely stroking his brown beard. "Despite your king's previous acts of arrogance, I am merciful, as you say, and I will be gracious in victory. Go, bring him here."

The Aramaic messengers departed to retrieve their king while Ahab pondered the day's developments.

*I am supremely fortunate... I have overcome the odds and vanquished the greatest king in the world. (I guess that title now goes to me...) With victory in sight, I can cement a lasting peace, establish Israel's defenses, and show the nations of the earth that we are not to be underestimated... Nava will be so proud of me... and Jezebel.*

"Sire, the Arameans return."

The captain's shout awakened Ahab from his thoughts. A figure appeared a hundred feet away. Dismounting slowly from his stallion, Ben-Hadad ambled over to Ahab's chariot. His face was dour: his forehead was marred with creases, his eyes sunk into his head, and his mouth agape. Reaching the conqueror's chariot, he awkwardly knelt down in what was clearly an unaccustomed gesture.

"I am yours, O king of Israel."

Stretching his arm out, Ahab said, "Come up here, Brother."

Ben-Hadad stared without blinking at the offered hand for several moments before he finally took it and accepted the assistance in climbing up into the chariot.

"Well, I can honestly say that I did not expect this would be the outcome of the day."

"Who of us can foreknow what the gods have decreed for us?" said Ahab pensively. He placed a hand on Ben-Hadad's shoulder.

"They have watched two generations of our families shed royal blood under heaven. Now, I believe, they wish that we make peace and end the enmity. As friends, and not enemies, our kingdoms can jointly prosper and grow greater than ever before. That is what my heart tells me should be so. Will you share this vision with me?"

Ben-Hadad sighed and bowed his head. "You have devastated my forces, scattered my allies... I have little choice but to relent."

"Then what do you propose as a settlement?" Ahab locked his gaze onto Ben-Hadad's, who stood his ground without blinking or flinching.

"The cities, which my father took from your father, I will restore to Israel; and you may collect tolls in the streets of Damascus, as my father collected tolls in Samaria. Is this acceptable to the king of Israel?"

Ahab delayed in answering as visions of the lost cities—Ijon, Dan, Abel-beth-maächah, and all Kinnereth with the land of Naphtali—raced through his mind. These cities on Israel's northern frontier had been conquered several years before Ahab was born. His father Omri was not yet the king of Israel but still served as a general under King Baäsha. Omri was a good general and had already won several battles, for which reason he was put in charge of guarding Israel's northern border. Yet despite his military excellence, there was little he could do when Ben-Hadad the Elder swooped down from Aram because he had been left with few soldiers under his command. The bulk of Omri's soldiers had been reässigned to the army of Baäsha, who at the time was besieging Jerusalem and fortifying Ramah in Benjamin. The reässignment initially seemed innocuous since no attack from the north was expected: Baäsha had a treaty of alliance with Aram. But then Asa the king of Judah sent all the silver and gold from Solomon's Temple to Ben-Hadad the Elder so as to bribe him to switch sides and to free Jerusalem from its devastating siege. Consequently, when the Arameans attacked Israel, Omri proved unable to repel them. He fought vigorously, even postponing the fall of Abel-beth-maächah by three days through a daring tactical maneuver in front of the Tanur Waterfall that reddened the Iyyon River with the blood of Arameans. Nonetheless his army was far too outnumbered to do anything in the end but lose. Despite retaining his military reputation undiminished, which soon led Baäsha to promote him to commander-in-chief of all the kingdom's land forces, Omri was broken by the devastating defeat not only in three ribs but also in spirit. The loss of these cities thereafter always proved a sore spot with him; his inability to retake them in either of the two futile attempts made during his reign further tormented him and distressed those of his household who had to witness his anguish.

"Is this acceptable to the king of Israel?" repeated Ben-Hadad.

Snapping back to the present, Ahab clapped his bearded cheek. "Your words please my heart. On the basis of this treaty I will set you free."

***

A s soon as the kings had come to an understanding, the fighting quickly ended. The battlefield, which had moved so vigorously amidst blows and punctures, now was animated by both sides' searching the heaps of bodies for men yet living.

With the setting sun bathing the bloodied earth with reddish light, Ahab was somberly inspecting his forces and commending men for particular acts of bravery. This man had slain an enemy commander, and this one had stopped an Aramaic chariot from crushing a dozen Israelite men; this one had killed two Arameans with the same thrust of his long spear, and this one had leapt onto an Aramaic chariot's horse while it was mid gallop and caused it to crash. Individually these feats were notable but not pivotal; collectively they made all the difference and personified why Ahab's army had prevailed against the forces of Ben-Hadad.

"Excellent work, men, excellent work," said Ahab, patting each man on the shoulder as he walked down the row of soldiers lining up to be looked over by their king.

When the king reached the middle of the row, he passed a certain man whose eyes were bandaged and his face covered in ashes. Suddenly the man started shouting.

"What's the matter?" asked Ahab, spinning around to face the bandaged man. "Do you need a physician to examine your eyes?"

"My eyes are covered not only from injury but also out of shame," murmured the bandaged man, holding his head low. "Listen, and I will tell you my dismay. I, your humble servant, went out into the midst of the raging battle; and, you see, suddenly a warrior turned aside and brought a man to me, and said, 'Guard this man for me. If he should be missing when I return, then your life shall go for his life, or else you shall pay me a talent of silver.' And as your servant was busy here and there, he was gone."

"You were distracted from guarding some man's ransom by fighting my enemies?" Ahab put his arms akimbo and let out a haughty laugh. *What concern is that of mine?* "You have destroyed snares set for me. That is a far more valuable deed than if one of my subjects can claim a ransom for himself. Do not fear the other man's retribution. And don't feel ashamed." He placed his fingers around the man's bandage and tenderly peeled them back.

Ahab gasped.

"You!"

With the bandage removed, the bulbous, crusted eyes stood out. Although the right one showed the cloudiness of blindness, the left eye, which was bloody and blue, focused on Ahab with a white hot intensity. Opening his mouth to chuckle, his grin revealed disfigured teeth.

*This is the prophet who accosted me while I was performing my sacrifice to Baal!*

"I see you recognize me. Good. Then you know I am a messenger of God. And thus says Yahweh: 'Because thou hast let go out of thy hand a man whom I appointed to utter destruction, therefore thy life shall go for his life, and thy people for his people.'"

# CHAPTER TWENTY-THREE

C URLED UP ON HIS tent's cot, submerged in the blackness of the evening, Ahab sighed.

The tent's flaps stirred and a familiar voice called out, "Sire, why is it so dark in here?"

The gloomy darkness fled the tent as soon as Nava went over to the table beside his cot and lit the oil lamp. Sitting down at the foot of the cot, she started rubbing Ahab's back.

"My dearest king, why do you appear crestfallen? I should have thought this day's astounding victory would have elated you beyond all men."

With a heavy sigh Ahab took her warm hand into his. Stroking it, he muttered, "I did rejoice, sweetheart, at my victory today. After concluding peace with Ben-Hadad, which promises the restoration of the cities my father lost, I felt so proud at succeeding where my father failed. All my life men compared me to my father who, as founder of our dynasty, continues to cast a long shadow. He ended the civil war with Tibni and reunited Israel after Zimri's treachery plunged the kingdom into chaos. To celebrate this victory, he founded Samaria and transferred the capital from Tirzah to it. And he conquered the Moäbites and made them our tribute-paying vassals to this day. If you want to truly understand my father's importance, just ponder this fact: I am told that the Assyrians even refer to Israel on their maps as the Land of Omri. Everything my family has was built by my father, or at least used the resources he amassed. Above all, I owe my crown to him. Never before today had I any great accomplishments of my own to point to, that would make men say, 'Ahab did this' instead of viewing me merely as 'Omri's son.' And that gnawed at my soul. It is painful for a man to reside in his father's shadow. But this day changed all that. Finally, I had proven my worth as a king. I not only scored a decisive victory against a foreign foe but I also reversed the one major failure of my father's life which grieved him to no end—avenging my father's defeat, as it were. I had at last emerged from my father's shadow, even surpassed him. And I was so happy..."

"Oh, Sire," said Nava, planting a kiss on his cheek. "I never knew you felt that way about your father."

"This is not the kind of thing that is easy for a man to talk about, kings least of all. For we are constantly before the public gaze and every man scrutinizes us for the slightest sign of weakness. Although we exceed all other men in power, we are like the highest cedar in the forest: when a thunderstorm comes in, it is the highest cedar that the lightning first attacks. Hence kings are forced to brood over our deepest fears and insecurities by ourselves lest, revealing them, an enemy use them against us. That is the burden that royalty must bear. But when I am with you—you make me feel so secure, so cherished, that my most inward thoughts easily spring forth."

"Stop it... you're making me blush."

"But it's true! I've never felt comfortable to speak of this with anyone—not even with my wife or mother." Ahab embraced her cheeks with his palms and kissed her forehead. "Whoever heard of a king confessing his heart's secrets to a concubine?"

"What's so strange about that?" she asked modestly. "We concubines are our masters' most intimate of confidants, laying bear to them all the nooks and crannies of our existence, and yielding ourselves without holding anything of ours back: for what is ours is yours."

"You speak with such a great wisdom that few men would believe a concubine could possess."

"Some men, despite their legal freedom, lead slavish lives; whereas other men, although enslaved, comport themselves with the dignity of freemen. So, too, do we bondwomen not uncommonly exceed in insight those high and mighty freewomen who overlook us (amid so many other things that escape their lofty notice)."

Ahab hugged her tightly to his chest and inhaled the sweet scent of her hair. "Your counsel is as excellent as your approachability... That's why I can tell you what made my heart sink amidst this joyous day. It's all because of that prophet."

"What prophet?"

"Do you remember when I told you of that prophet who confronted me after I performed a sacrifice, the one with the hideous teeth and eyes? Well, that same prophet accosted me while I was congratulating the troops after the battle. Claiming the authority of God, he pontificated that my life shall be destroyed because I negotiated peace with Ben-Hadad rather than destroy him utterly. Apparently I was meant to continue the slaughter." He sighed and shut his almond eyes while his fat lips trembled. "That is why I feel despair."

Nava wrinkled her forehead and, frowning, said, "This cannot be. He predicts doom for *that*? Are you certain that you understood him properly? Prophets' words are often obscure."

"Yes: he plainly said God will punish me for sparing the Arameans."

"I think that 'prophet,' as he calls himself, presumes too much to know the will of God," said Nava. She wrapped her arms around his chest and embraced his hairy cheeks with hers. "Had he censured the sacrifices to the pagan gods which you insist on performing despite my repeated admonitions to the contrary, then I would be willing to incline my ears to him. But for him to accuse your noble-hearted clemency and call down evil on you for simply being the good man that I know you are—it's preposterous!"

With his eyes widening like famished eyes do when they behold a sumptuous meal, Ahab said, "You believe his prophecy is wrong?"

"Of course it is," she insisted, tapping her breast twice with a clenched fist. "Why would God want to destroy you for showing mercy? For God is merciful and 'His mercy endureth forever,' as the Psalmist says. No matter what this so-called prophet may say—and say in order to undermine the ongoing renewal of your worship of God—there is no way on earth that the God of my fathers would strike you down for that. And after you've made such great strides in returning to His fold."

"I am so glad to hear you say that. I had suspected as much, but I didn't trust my knowledge of things divine enough to be sure."

"Don't undercut yourself: you're a Hebrew." She rested her soft hand on his chest which vibrated from his heart beating more rapidly. "You *did* know. In your heart."

"My dearest Nava, you are the warm sun who has dried up the rain of my sadness and anguish. You always do." Ahab sniffed as a couple tears trickled down his left cheek. "My whole life, I've looked for a woman with whom I could share not only the high points of life but even the ruts and ditches we encounter along the way. Someone special who would be there to console me and comfort me like no one else can. But until I met you, I'd never experienced such a woman."

"No, don't let that be so," murmured Nava, nuzzling his cheek with her soft skin. "Surely you, a veritable king among men, must have known at least *one* woman who would give you her shoulder to cry on?"

"I'm afraid not... Isn't that pathetic?" *I know it's pathetic... Oh, God, give me strength...* Drawing in a deep breath, he took her hand in his and said, "I've had many concubines before you, but I never truly knew them beyond how Adam knew Eve (as Moses put it). Those were merely indulgences of the flesh, not like the spiritual union that subsists between us. None of them ever made me feel like I could confide my whole soul to them the way I can to you."

"And what of the queen?"

"Je-Jezebel, well, she..." Ahab let go of her hand and turned his torso away from her. He took a deep breath and then exhaled. "She has been my wife for twenty years, borne me two sons so far (if that number has not already risen), and offered me the most prudent advice concerning matters of state. I truly love her and value everything she has done for me. But when it comes to the human element of a marriage, of being 'willing and able to console one's spouse' as the priest who officiated at our wedding put it... Well, as hard as I've tried, I've never been able to get more than a modicum of that from her."

"Although I know nothing of your early years with her, the picture your words paint match up with the contemporary Jezebel I have seen. I still remember, with indignation, the day Ben-Hadad's messengers delivered his first ultimatum. In spite of your self-evident distress, the queen callously chose supporting her own preconceived agenda over stooping to give you the consolation you deserved."

"Don't get me wrong. I do love her very much. It's not her fault: it's simply who she is. Far be it from me to try to change her. But the ability to offer consolation, consolation of the moving, intimate variety, is sadly not something she was gifted with." Ahab took Nava's hand again and stared deeply into her round brown eyes. "That is where you come in. Despite your common background and inferior status as a concubine, you royally demonstrate your ability to console me, to support me, to make me feel like the man I've always wanted to be..."

Casting her eyes downwards, their lashes bashfully blinking, she answered, "It is true that I am only a concubine, not a wife; but I can, with wifely affection, perform a wife's duties better than your current wife has deigned to do."

"And you perform them so praiseworthily!"

"If only," sighed Nava, "people were permitted to recognize that. Sadly, they hear the name of 'concubine' and cannot imagine wifely behavior."

"What's in a name? You already do all things save one that a wife ought to do."

"And were I your wife," she murmured, rubbing her face against his cheek and whispering in his ear, "even that one exception I would do (and with the greatest of joy too)."

His heart beating like the hooves of a racehorse and a cold sweat running down both his temples, Ahab leapt to his feet and exclaimed, "Then how about I make you my wife?"

She stared at him with a blank expression and quickly caught her falling jaw. "Would you really consider doing it?"

"Would I?" He grabbed her by the hand and raised her to his feet. Clasping her to his chest, he stroked her cheek and declared, "Hell, I'll make you the queen of Israel too!"

Nava's pupils dilated wide and, her whole body quivering, she stuttered, "B-but would Jezebel approve of your decision?"

"Forget Jezebel! Am I not the king of Israel? Am I not the one who sits on the throne? Then I get to make the laws; and the laws are whatever pleases me. And it pleases me, Nava, daughter of Ichabod, hereby to grant you your freedom, to make you my full wife, and, in the sight of God and all men, to declare you to be the second queen of Israel!"

"Oh, Ahab, my love!" Her voice broke with emotion and she could utter not another sound. She wrapped her arms around him and locked her lips onto his, making such forceful contact that they both fell backwards onto the cot.

# Chapter Twenty-Four

A CACOPHONY OF STRESSED shouts and shuffling feet filled the corridors and halls of the palace in Jezreël as everyone sought to have everything in perfect order when the king and his entourage returned. Servants fluffed pillows, mopped the floors, and topped off goblets of sweet wine. The bustling kitchen emanated the scent of smoked hams, mutton, duck, cherries, and honeyed cakes. The courtyards and surrounding grounds were cleansed and weeded. In every direction one might look, droplets of sweat were flying as panting people were rushing about.

Jezebel, however, lingered calmly around her bedchamber, decked in red. She wore a scarlet dress, a ruby choker, and a tiara studded with garnets; even her long sharp nails were painted red.

"Hand me the mirror," she commanded the eunuch stationed beside her. He held up the five foot long sheet of metal. After gazing at herself in the polished bronze, moving her body this way and that, Jezebel commented to Elishat, "You wouldn't believe how great it feels to have dislodged that great burden," while she ran her hands across her recently thinned waist. *Still have some pockets of fat to work off here and here, but I've done it before...*

"It pleases me to see you in higher spirits," answered Elishat.

"I am." *At least until Ahab and his whore arrive...* Jezebel glanced at the afternoon sun streaming through the window. "When will they arrive? I am not in the habit of waiting around for that man."

"The messenger reported that the king intended to stay at Samaria for only two days before proceeding here. Assuming there were no delays, he should be arriving any—"

The sudden blasts of trumpets emanating from the front courtyard cut off Elishat as she was speaking.

"Finally," murmured Jezebel exasperatedly while exiting her room. She strutted down the hallway and turned the corner.

More trumpeters lined the entrance that was being thronged with spectators ready to herald the arrival of their king. With the palace servants and courtiers chanting in unison "Long live the king!" while stretching out their arms in order to have the privilege of feeling his flowing indigo apparel as it passed, Ahab made his way through the crowd like a clownfish swimming through a tentacular canopy of sea anemones. Jezebel, however, kept herself aloof at the rear of the corridor from which vantage point she glowered at her husband.

"Thank you for this spirited greeting, my subjects," said Ahab, raising his hand and his voice so that he could be heard over the din. "It's good to be home again, and with victory achieved!"

"The king appears quite animated, don't you think?" whispered Elishat.

Jezebel nodded with a frown. "Yes," she said, eyeing Ahab sharply. His almond eyes glistened with vivacity, his bushy brown beard gleamed with oil of myrrh, his biceps and quadriceps rippled visibly beneath his robes with every movement he took, and he interacted with the crowd as comfortably as an expert impresario. "His months on campaign seem to have rejuvenated him. He's in better physical shape than he's been in years; one might even dare say he's not unattractive to the eye."

When Ahab had made his way halfway down the packed corridor, Jezebel made her move. Snapping her fingers to her train of followers, they cleared a path for her to approach the king.

"Greetings, Ahab."

"Jezebel!" said Ahab. Spinning around at the sound of her voice, he gave her a quick hug. "It's so good to see you again. It's been so long."

"Yes, it has been." *Is that the* best *greeting he can muster?* She gestured to one of her handmaids who presented a baby to Ahab.

"Is this our child?" he asked, rubbing his finger beneath the infant's chin.

"This is our newest son," answered Jezebel.

Ahab took the baby into his hands and gently lifted him up.

"Another son, excellent," muttered Ahab. He playfully popped the bubble forming around the child's mouth. "This is every father's dream."

Jezebel glanced at all the faces in the crowd. Someone was missing. A minute smirk unrolled around the edge of her reddened lip. "Where is that companion of yours, Ahab? Did she finally wear out your lust?"

"Where is Nava?" He handed the baby back to the handmaid and spun his head from side to side. The look of jubilant light-heartedness had now morphed into concern. "She was behind me when we exited the carriage."

Jezebel glared at the back of his head as he walked away from her and waded through the crowd.

*So your little whore is more important to you than your wife and newborn son. You wretched bastard...*

Snapping at her handmaid to take the child back to the nursery, Jezebel huddled with Elishat at the end of the corridor. Pacing vigorously in a tight circle and emphasizing her agitation with her flailing arms, her voice cracked as she began to gripe.

"Did you see what a lukewarm greeting he gave me? When we were newlyweds, he would have smothered me to death from white hot passion! Oh, how he's degenerated!"

"I know, Madam. This is truly a great indignity to you. And he barely even glanced at the infant before casting him off to look for his paramour."

"We are still losing Ahab's affections to that shameless harlot. We must do something to staunch the bleeding or else. For who knows what he'll next do for—"

Suddenly the corridor roared with exclamations of astonishment.

Jezebel spun her head around to see what had elicited the gasp from the crowd. Her bulging eyes constricted their pupils and revealed the whites above their green irises when they spotted the abomination. It was *HER*.

Nava, wearing the fakest of humble expressions and Ahab's arm around her waist, overawed the crowd with the sparkles radiating from the diamond-and-pearl-encrusted crown around her perfidious forehead.

"A crown?!" hissed Jezebel. Her eyes blinking rapidly, she turned to Elishat with a snarl. "He's honored a concubine's ignoble head with a royal crown? The *s-a-a-cr-i-i-i-le-e-e-g-e*! Why doesn't he just pillage the treasury and cast all the royal jewels into the swine's mire while he's at it?"

"I sympathize, Madam. The Hebrew has raised herself far beyond her station."

Jezebel clenched her fists and would have stormed over and accosted the concubine, rescuing the dishonored crown from the usurper's head, had not Ahab raised his hand to calm the crowd and begun to speak.

"Friends and kinsmen," he said, smiling as he glanced at everyone there, "it pleases me to inform you of an act that delights my soul. For this woman"—he hugged Nava tight and kissed her cheek—"has been my constant companion this past year on my campaign against the Arameans. Her unwavering support carried me through the hardships of war; her kind demeanor and humanity has been a source of inspiration for me and kept my mind focused on the grand plan; her affability and approachability has blessed me with the ability to confront and deal with my most sensitive thoughts."

*Am I imagining this, or has he become an even larger blowhard than before?* wondered Jezebel with a scowl.

Ahab continued with several more strains of praise for Nava, who submissively gazed up at him between her bouts of blushing. At long last Ahab reached the conclusion.

"Although some might reduce a concubine simply to her sensual allure and be incapable of entertaining any nobler thoughts of her, they would be mistaken. For what I and my precious Nava have experienced was not the mere indulgence of the flesh but a holy union of souls—an intimate understanding of one another which most men can only idly dream of. Notwithstanding her humble birth and subsequent servile status, she has transcended all that by her praiseworthy character and nobility of spirit and has daily proven herself worthy of the highest of honors. Therefore, bowing to the dictates of both justice and mercy, I have not only freed her from the slavery which was most cruelly thrust upon her (thereby raising her status to that of full wife), but also, out of my magnanimity, and in recognition of her undeniable merit, I crowned her in Samaria yesterday as Queen of Israel. Behold, my second queen and your queen!"

*NOOOOO! He couldn't! He wouldn't! I never thought he would go this far!*

As the courtiers and servants clapped loudly and gleefully expressed their approval as ignorant crowds are often wont to do to gratify the latest caprice of their tyrants, Jezebel swooned and was caught by Elishat without anyone else noticing her attack. Her heart racing and a chill engulfing her whole body, she gasped, "Did he really say he crowned her?"

"I'm sorry, Madam. You heard correctly."

"My god! She's sold her virginity for a crown. The conniving whore!"

\*\*\*

A S EVENING DREW ON, the grand banquet proceeded with much fanfare and much more sparks beneath the surface. Between the seven courses of succulent delicacies, Ahab regaled his guests with tales of his exploits fighting the Arameans. He described his gallant actions in battle, how he comported himself in his chariot and slew many men, and recounted Ben-Hadad's submission to him. Ahab mentioned how he made a detour through the formerly lost cities of Ijon and Abel-beth-maächah—the first time in years that a king of Israel had set foot in them—and was triumphantly hailed by the inhabitants. He also recounted how he was able to parade victoriously through the streets of Damascus, accompanied by a chastened Ben-Hadad; the inhabitants lined the streets in astonishment that their once glorious king could have been defeated. As he narrated each event, his eyes twinkling and face engulfed with glee, the courtiers were mesmerized by him and hung on his every word, none more so than Nava whose round eyes could not be pried from him. Everyone, that is, except the king's first wife.

Throughout the banquet Jezebel discreetly glared at her husband and his new wife while neatly tearing up napkins beneath the table. Every time Nava leaned over to whisper some sweet nothing into Ahab's ear, or he skinned a grape and gently placed it between her lips, Jezebel snatched another napkin from the desperate eunuch struggling to replenish her supply and to prevent a linen mountain from growing beneath the table.

After the final course of dessert had been consumed and the dishes removed by the servants, a bard was summoned to sing for the guests. He was an old man with grisly gray hair; dressed in threadbare apparel, he walked unsteadily with a cane on account of his dimness of eyes. Yet despite his outward decrepitude, his powerful voice had retained the vivacity of youth.

"What would Your Majesty like to hear?"

Ahab, looking longingly at Nava as he spoke, replied, "Sing us *The Tale of the Abandoned Shepherd Boy and Girl*."

"A classic of romantics," murmured the bard dispassionately. Clearing his throat, his baritone voice boomed through the hall as he recounted how, once upon a time, a boy and then a girl were each abandoned at birth in a far-off glen. A shepherd found the boy; later another shepherd found the girl; and each raised his foundling as his own. The youths grew in age and beauty, becoming shepherds themselves. While tending their respective flocks, they often would encounter one another on the breezy plains. As the seasons changed, their feelings for each other likewise changed: they fell in love but, being young, did not know what was happening. A wise old cowherd enlightened them and explained that the only cure for their aching hearts was kissing. Warm embraces, however, soon turned to cold dread when bandits rode off with the girl. The boy suppressed his fear and went in search of his beloved. He found the bandits' camp and in the night slew the guard. With hearts a-racing, the boy led the girl out of the camp without detection and they escaped to the nearby city. There they were taken in by a kindly merchant whose tearful eyes soon spotted the golden clasp upon the boy's tunic and the dagger with an ivory handle on his belt—the same tokens he had left with his newborn son when he abandoned him all those years ago. Reunited with his son, the merchant called all his friends to come to a great banquet. At this banquet was an elderly gentleman who nearly fainted when he saw the girl wearing a cap interwoven with gold, gilded shoes, and gold-embroidered anklets: for he had last seen those very tokens when he placed them beside his daughter in a glen years ago. The boy and girl were thus each reunited with their families, prosperous and powerful; and being wedded amid the pomp of the city, they returned to the countryside to live well, raise happy children, and grow old in peace.

With the song concluded, the room erupted with applause at the bard's performance and glasses of wine were raised in his honor by everyone. Everyone, that is, except Jezebel.

*Saccharine gibberish*, she thought. Glancing at Ahab putting his paws around Nava's bosom, she scratched her nails against the underside of the table.

"That was an excellent rendition, my good man," said Ahab, toasting the bard. Hiccoughing a little, he added, "And now I should like the next song to be selected by a lady most dear to my heart."

Jezebel reflexively clenched her jaws when Ahab's roving eyes fell on her. Swallowing the bile that had been pooling in her throat, she opened her mouth to speak. But before the first syllable could escape its dental barrier, Ahab turned to Nava and proclaimed:

"Sweetie, command the bard to sing a song. For that is the privilege of royalty."

"O my lord, I would be honored."

Jezebel ground her teeth and glared unblinkingly at the lovers. *You filthy spawn of lust... How* dare *you disgrace our table with your paramour!*

It had been pursuant to protocol for the king to make the first request of the bard. But ever since she had been sent to Israel by her father, Ahab had always given Jezebel first choice after him at all their banquets. Never had he given away her precedence to anyone else, much less to a woman already encroaching upon her queenly estate. That made Jezebel's flesh burn and itch with rage.

"And what may I sing for you, my queen?" asked the bard.

Jezebel's right index finger's nail broke on the table's underside when the word "queen" was pronounced.

Gazing sheepishly at Ahab, Nava said softly, "Please sing to us about *The Maiden of Jerusalem*. It's a song my father always used to sing to my mother."

Nodding his head, the bard concurred. "Yes, 'tis a song made for lovers." He cleared his throat and sang about a beautiful maiden whose cruel stepbrothers forced her to till their vineyard under the burning sun until her snowy skin was deeply tanned and had become as dark as the tents of Kedar. One day the wise king of Israel was passing by her vineyard and his eye caught sight of her. Even sweaty and dirtied from toil, her voluptuous beauty shone through and enthralled the king. He took her aside to an apple tree and she lay under it with him. They exchanged kisses sweeter than the dripping honeycomb and the king brought her back with him to Jerusalem. No longer did the maiden toil in another's vineyard; now she had a garden filled with pomegranates and spikenard that she kept enclosed and allowed not anyone to enter. The king went off to his palace, and the maiden yearned for his return. Desperate to hold him in the flesh and not only in the phantasms of her dreams, she went around the streets of the great city. The watchmen accosted her in the night, but she would not be deterred. At last the morning came and so did the king. He returned in glory to her and escorted her to her new home. Surrounded by the pageantries of the court, he wed her and crowned her queen. The king then brought her into his chambers and laid all night betwixt her breasts. And their love was sweeter than wine.

Whooping and hollows filled the air along with several wine glasses when the bard finished. Ahab, embracing Nava, kept muttering, "Light of my life," while the other guests turned to their own beloveds and mingled their wine with tears. Besides the bard who, on account of his age and professional demeanor, kept a stern and unmoved face, there was not a single person in the room who was not physically moved by the song. Not a single person, that is, except Jezebel who remained glowering in her seat, gnashing her teeth, and ripping up more napkins than a pack of dogs set loose upon an unsuspecting kitchen.

When the outpouring of emotion had subsided and it was possible for one to be heard, Jezebel thudded her goblet three times on the table. "If it would not be presumptuous of me," she said, locking her unblinking gaze on Ahab's eyes, "I would like to select a song."

Ahab, gulping, said, "Yes, yes, of course, Jezebel. I was just about to ask you. Bard, sing whatever my wife desires."

With a sardonic smirk tickling her ruby lips, she said, "Sing to us about *The Abduction of the Daughters of Shilo.*"

As soon as she had made her request, several of the guests flashed looks at each other and whispered quiet comments to each other. It was an old song, well-known, but one more commonly sung at soldiers' drinking bouts than at a posh party in the palace. Ahab blushed and looked awkwardly at the floor while Nava screwed up her face as though she were tasting month-old milk. Despite the general lack of enthusiasm for her selection, Jezebel did have one person express positive interest.

"Ooooh," exclaimed the bard, his old eyes squinting greedily while his liver-spotted hands rubbed up against each other, "that's a good one!" He reared back his head, inhaled deeply, and thundered:

"*Come, my brothers, come, my friends! We must do what must be done! The other tribes seek our ruin; the other tribes plot our hurt. Exclude us from our rightful place, consign us to extinction? We men of Benjamin, though never in numbers greatest, yet were a worthy number to make our fathers glad. Now we, only thirty score, hardly more than boys, need wives to avert our tribe's doom. Yet what do the other tribes do? Having slain our sisters all, they've sworn not a daughter to give, not one of theirs to save Benjamin.*

"*Come, my brothers, come, my friends! We must do what must be done! In Shiloh there's a festival where the virgins come to dance. Let us to the vineyards go and wait for them to come; then may each man grab whosoever his eyes delights. Lo, here come the maidens galore, singing and dancing in chorus. Arise, sons of Benjamin, and do what must be done!*

"*Now they flee, pale with fear: not one appears as she did before. Some tear their hair; others cry for their mother. This one tarries while that one scurries. But our captives they all become. And if any denies her lover, then clasp her to your heart and say, 'Why stain your cheeks with tears? As your father was to your mother, so shall I be to you!'*

"*Go, my brothers, go, my friends! We have done what had to be done! Now let us enjoy our joyous prize. We have gotten the necessary brides. On them fear itself looks fitting. From them shall we gain some sons for Benjamin, perpetuate our fathers' race, and bequeath to history this warning: Squeeze the juice of your neighbor's vine only if you are sure that it holds no poison!*"

Dead silence greeted the end of the song. A few of the older guests, remembering the boisterous days of Ahab's father's court, grinned and cast knowing glances at one another. This was a song which Omri would regularly enjoy. The younger guests, however, who had come of age under Ahab's more refined reign, looked awkwardly at each other and shifted in their seats; a few even blushed. The song's subject matter was not one which had hitherto graced the table at any of Ahab's prior banquets. How were they to respond? Praise the bard's eloquent delivery but condemn the lyrics? Applaud a work of prior generations? Or say nothing lest they say something amiss? Silence, indeed, seemed the safer course; and as the moments passed, silence held sway in the room.

Yet at last silence's hold on them ceased.

"What a horrid song," muttered Nava, clasping Ahab as he held her in his arms and was briskly stroking the back of her head.

"I know, I know. It's not one I would have chosen." He cast a quizzical glance at Jezebel.

She glared back at him and chuckled under her breath.

# CHAPTER TWENTY-FIVE

---

"THE CANCER IS REACHING lethal levels," murmured Jezebel darkly as she paced the floor of the nursery. She had retreated here immediately after the banquet. "I never thought Ahab would go so far as to crown his precious whore. All the times he told me I was the only woman he could ever love—lies, utter lies! He prefers a whore to his lawful wife!"

"The depths of men's betrayal should never be underestimated," said Elishat, entering the room and conversation. She placed her hand gently on Jezebel's shoulder.

"Forget about him. He's a fool—what else is new?! It's that scheming whore's fault." Jezebel's neck veins bulged as she clenched her fists. "She's had him all to herself for months—to turn him against me! That was her plan all along. For there was no reason, before the resumption of war with Aram, that he had to tour our kingdom continuously. She knew that he would easily fall victim to her undue influence if he was out of my protection. Don't you think it's telling that Ahab hastily crowned her *before* returning here? That's because she egged him on to do it away from me, knowing that if I had access to him I would have prevented her from gaining a crown. She's had months to work on him, to identify his weakest spots and find the thumbscrews with which to twist him, without me being able to do a damn thing about it. For I could have stopped her... I would have, too... if I hadn't been laid up here by—"

At that moment, as if to finish his mother's sentence more forcefully than any words of hers could, the infant let out a bellicose wail.

Glaring at the cause of the noise, Jezebel snapped her fingers and called, "Tanith!" and the royal wet nurse dashed over to offer her breast to the infant.

*I will not allow one whore—and a* Hebrew *whore at that—to undo everything I've worked my whole life for...* Turning to Elishat, Jezebel inquired, "Did you find the item I described?"

"Yes, Madam." She took a thin silver case out of her sleeve.

"I thought so." Jezebel removed a gleaming knife from the case, whose golden handle was formed in the shape of a lion's mouth with twin emeralds affixed therein for eyes. Its silver blade protruded like a tongue from the handle. "This is the exact same design as the knife the whore was using during dinner. Even the rivets reveal the common pattern."

"So the king duplicated one of your wedding presents for his lover?"

Jezebel snorted. "I doubt he even remembered giving this. He'd said he had it designed after one of the images he so frequently sees in his dreams. I'm sure he made the second knife completely oblivious to the fact he had given me an identical one already." She put the leonine utensil back inside its case and slid the case up her thick sleeve.

"My queen, my queen!" came a voice from the hallway.

*What now?* Jezebel turned to the doorway just as one of her handmaids burst in.

"My queen," gasped the handmaid, dropping to her knees before her, "the king's female companion is on her way here."

"*Here?*" Jezebel turned to Elishat. "She really is a presumptuous woman, no?"

"What do you wish us to do, Madam?"

Staring at the doorway as the faint sounds of footsteps echoed from the hall, Jezebel crinkled her aquiline nose and, putting her arms akimbo, said, "Let her come. It's time we have a frank conversation about our situation."

The other women in the room looked nervously at each other in the silent seconds that elapsed until Nava arrived. When she entered, she slowly glanced around the room. Her squinting eyes and frowning face bore the same apprehensive expression that appears on a novice soldier who, separated from his comrades, has strayed into enemy-held territory in which every rock, every blade of grass, even his own shadow, potentially conceals an enemy thirsting for his blood. Approaching Jezebel, she neither bowed, nor hailed the queen, nor performed any of the other rituals that pious subjects perform. Instead she lifted her taut chin high and bluntly said, "Jezebel, I want a word with you."

Digging her nails into her palms, Jezebel, without taking her unblinking eyes off Nava, said to the others, "Leave us."

The others left without a murmur although not without darting frenetic eyeballs from queen to queen. As she closed the creaking door behind her, Elishat, peering through the closing gap, rested her beady eyes on Jezebel, and the cradle, and then Jezebel again before the door had shut.

Several seconds passed awkwardly in silence. Then Jezebel snapped, "Speak! Don't think you'll earn a higher fee the more time you spend with me. I am not one of your usual clients. I am your queen!"

"Jezebel, Jezebel," murmured Nava as she slowly shook her head, her long sandy hair held tightly in place by her crown. "It doesn't take much for you to lash your tongue."

"It's not my custom to welcome burglars and interlopers with pies and kisses."

Nava rested her forefinger on the rim of her crown. "Our husband gave me this crown of his own free and gracious will. I would have thought someone with your reputation for shrewdness would understand." She narrowed her brown round eyes and smirked. "I guess I was mistaken."

"Don't presume to correct me! *My* husband's will was just as incapacitated by lust as if he were toiling under the influence of a belly drowning in beer."

"Don't confuse Ahab's lofty motives with your sordid views of life."

*Arrogant peasant!* Jezebel growled and inched closer to her enemy. "Just tell me why you came and skip the pleasantries. Ahab isn't here, so you can speak plainly."

"I sensed intense hatred during dinner. While I am under no misapprehension as to the chasm that exists between us," remarked Nava, walking circularly around Jezebel while gazing at her out of the corner of her eye, "and sincerely doubt if we could ever bridge it, I should rather hope that we can, at the very least, agree to erect certain guardrails so that we do not end up causing ourselves to plunge headfirst into the deadly stalagmites below."

Jezebel's left eyebrow rose. *She seeks a non-aggression pact so she can have time to establish her position unmolested... But once established....* Jezebel smacked her lips and asked, "Just what do you propose?"

"That we delineate our respective places, both in the palace's apartments and in our royal functions, lest we step on each other's toes."

*As though I would nourish a viper at my breast, providing it with refuge until it was strong enough to bite me...* She put her left arm akimbo while shaking her right hand vigorously. "What you propose is impossible. Two women cannot dwell under the same roof and share a husband without igniting sparks that would make the fires of hell seem lukewarm in comparison."

"It's a shame you feel that way. I would have preferred it if we could have gone a few inches past the threshold of the new era before locking horns with each other." Narrowing her eyes and flaring her nostrils, she added, "But if not, I should warn you against underestimating me. My father—before you killed him—was a Levitical priest faithful to his God. As such, he not only had to practice rites of religion but, of necessity, to master the art of organized resistance to your persecutions. To outsmart your goons, to divine friend from foe, to persuade others to join him in his holy cause—all this I watched him do from my earliest memories. From him I learned how to be a fox to avoid the snares and a lion to overwhelm the wolves. So don't dismiss me as some silly bumpkin. For I promise you this: dare to tangle with me, and you will find me a worthy opponent."

*And thus the veil is dropped!* Clenching her fists, Jezebel spat, "Whatever happened to that docile lass whose charm and girlish innocence mesmerized my husband to no end? Would he even recognize this woman of threats who now accosts me in the nursery?"

"Ahab recognizes that I seek only the best for him and his immortal soul. And under my righteous influence, his eyes are beginning to open to the magnitude of your wickedness and your followers. I will not allow you to manipulate my husband for your own, selfish ambitions any longer."

"It didn't take long for this mild lamb to cast off her sheep's clothing and reveal the she-wolf within," murmured Jezebel, sizing Nava up. She pressed forwards into her space. With less than an inch separating their faces, Nava's warm breath hitting her cheeks, Jezebel stared into her eyes and snarled, "Was that saccharine demeanor of yours—which disgusted me as much as it perversely pleased *my* husband—as bogus as your vaunted chastity?"

"If I am not meek like a lamb, it is only because your evil handiwork has forced me to steel my heart and cultivate the cunning capable of first surviving and then confronting your degradations. For I was a naïve girl once, merrily picking the flowers of the field without a care in the world. I loved my family and they loved me; there was so much love in our house, that the hatred lurking just outside was inconceivable to me. But because of *you*, Jezebel, in one moment I lost my family, my freedom, and my innocence too."

Jezebel cackled. "Oh, yes," she smirked, flinging her silky black hair back affectedly as she swaggered across the room, "*every*thing's my fault. As though I haven't heard that from your countrymen already! If it doesn't rain, blame Jezebel. If the earth shakes, blame Jezebel. If your tipsy aunt Abigail falls down the well, blame Jezebel. If you get a hangnail from your hummus, blame Jezebel. Be it however great or small, you Hebrew dogs make me the bogeyman responsible for all. (I'm shocked you haven't accused me of nailing your God to a tree. At least that would explain His conspicuous absence.)"

"Vile blasphemer!" shouted Nava, pointing her finger at her. "Don't try denying it! You are responsible for persecuting the worshippers of Yahweh! That is why we hate you!"

Jezebel snorted. "What exactly have I done? What cult images have I smashed? You Hebrews abjure iconography. What temples have I destroyed? You say only Jerusalem can have a Hebrew temple, so there's none in our kingdom. What animals do I forbid to be sacrificed? I permit you to sacrifice goats, and lambs, and all the other animals your Moses said to use—and pigs, crocodiles, and every other creature under the heavens too! So you see, unlike you Hebrews—who arrogantly assume you can dictate others' beliefs, burn their temples, shit on their altars, melt their household gods, *murder* the holiest of Baal's holy men—I am quite permissive in matters religious."

"You lying bitch!" screamed Nava, the foamy saliva erupting like a geyser from her mouth. "You murdered my father and brothers with your evil persecutions! I was a Levitical priest's daughter, the sister of Aaronic priests, the most worshipful men alive. Until the day your goons showed up! On your orders, they slit my father's throat and disemboweled my brothers upon our dinner table and forced me to watch them die. I was but a child and I had to see those horrors! How do you answer?"

"Your kinsmen were rebels who obstinately defied the royal decrees. They deserved their fate."

"They were fulfilling the commandments of their forefathers' God and the dictates of their consciences!"

"When moths try to gnaw upon my wardrobe, I crush them. Why should their moral reflections and motivations interest me? Their vandalism is palpable. Self-defense is my only course."

"You're an evil, heartless woman," said Nava, shaking her fist. "You complain that your subjects hate you? Maybe if you did not despise them like bugs you wouldn't incur so much hatred. But by your repeated cruelties, you've proven yourself congenitally incapable of displaying the slightest humanity."

Jezebel pursed her lips. "I have no kindness for rats and cockroaches. They ought to be exterminated."

"Did you really think you could eliminate all of us worshippers of God?"

"Of course I did! And I had nearly wiped them all out before you came." *And had I succeeded, I could have prevented Elijah from killing my priests...*

"You will never defeat God," insisted Nava, raising her hands heavenwards and gazing upwards. "By His grace, I have found favor in Ahab's eyes and am steadily winning him over to the cause of God. So you can forget about 'cleansing' this land of pious worshippers. He will no longer put up with your persecution."

"As his wife of twenty years, I know firsthand that only a fool places his trust in Ahab."

"Such contempt for our husband! He has already promised to issue an edict of tolerance for my people, allowing all Hebrews to worship our God openly and without harassment; and I know that his word is true."

"What Ahab whispers into his lover's ears ought to be written on the breeze or in rapid waters."

"Does it grate you to realize you have slipped from your zenith and are plummeting to the nadir of your influence? By as much as you promoted your foul idolatry, I will doubly promote the worship of the true God! I will strip your idolaters of their privileges and redirect the full support of the royal treasury to my fellow Levites."

Her facial skin flushing with heat, Jezebel said, "You arrogantly speak as if the future were foreordained. Yet as the Ishmaelites say, 'Don't set out the milk pails before the camels calf.' Many a concubine has attracted *my* Ahab's eye over the years; he always loses interest in them eventually."

"Yet how many did he crown queen?"

"You contemptible whore," hissed Jezebel. Her right hand, concealed within her left sleeve, fiddled with the knife case therein. "I don't care if he crowns you queen of queens! By Baal, I swear I'll turn him against you and drive your peasant stench out of my house. No matter what it takes, I will NEVER let you win!"

Nava sneered and rubbed her belly. "You should not hurl such threats at me. You'll not be rid of me that easily. If you think Ahab heeds me too much now, just wait until I present him with regal offspring."

"Give birth to a hundred bastards for all I care," snapped Jezebel. "All his other bastards have been banished; I'll banish yours too."

"I am now a queen," huffed Nava, her upper lip rising on the right side, "and your equal, Jezebel. You cast out the concubines' sons but mine will be firmly planted here. God-willing, I am even now carrying royal seed within me which soon will blossom into a lush branch of Ahab's dynasty."

"Are you saying what I think you're saying...?"

"Only that you should not presume to control Ahab's will or 'place milk pails before the camels calf.' Remember the example of King David: he bequeathed his throne to a son of one of his later wives."

*First she steals my husband and now she plans to snatch my children's inheritance!* Through gritted teeth Jezebel replied, "My sons will inherit their father's throne, not your bastard spawn." *Or else I'm no daughter of Ithobaal!*

"Just keep repeating that," answered Nava darkly as she turned to go, puffing up her chest, "like the heathen repeat their prayers. Maybe your repetition will be more fertile than that of the babbling idolaters."

"I will see you in hell first!" hissed Jezebel.

Suddenly the baby, who had lain quietly in his cradle during the entirety of their tête-à-tête, let out a whiny howl.

Nava glanced back at the cradle and then at Jezebel. "Why don't you tend to your own child?" she asked. A smirk suddenly appeared on her face and through squinted eyes she stared intensely at Jezebel. "Look at your little son over there. Although born from an idolatrous womb, he will grow up in the court of a pious king. Despite the heathen poison he'll imbibe in your milk, his father and I, by giving him the Bread of Life to consume, may yet make a good Hebrew out of him."

Jezebel leapt over to the cradle and, grabbing the baby and pressing him against her bosom, spun around to face Nava. She was panting heavily, like a lion which, outrunning a trio of hunters, has taken refuge in a cave that has no other exit than past the hunters. "You'll never turn my flesh and blood into a Hebrew!"

"But just imagine it! A son of Jezebel worshipping Yahweh, demolishing heathen temples, following the laws ordained by Moses... He might even be circumcised!" Without waiting to hear Jezebel's retort, she sauntered out of the room and let the door clank loudly behind her.

Jezebel stood as still as a statue. Her unblinking eyes glared at the shut door while her heart beat at as high a rate as war drums in the thick of battle.

At last she thrust her neck back and let out a screech.

"DAMN her!" she yelled, causing the baby to squeal. Her nostrils flaring, and drops of cold sweat running down her forehead, Jezebel adjusted her grip on the baby and pressed him closer to her as she began pacing around the nursery.

"The Hebrew bitch thinks she has me beat. She's plotting to create a heathen dynasty. She even dreams of turning my own children against me..." She lifted the infant up and, scrutinizing him with the intensity of a diamond merchant inspecting his wares, sniffed, "There's no way you're going to turn against me." *I didn't birth you to go against my interests...*

Jezebel set the baby back in his cradle. Clasping her hands behind her back, her neck, inclining stiffly downwards, she fixed her bulbous eyes on the floor. Then she resumed pacing, going counterclockwise around the room. Her agitated feet made loud clinks as they struck the floor.

*I should have killed the whore when I first discovered her Hebrew sympathies... Oh, Baal, what madness stopped me? Had I killed her then, I wouldn't be on the edge of desolation... Did pity make me forbear from killing her?*

She wrinkled her nose and spat upon the floor.

*Mercy has no place in the world. No, it's not my fault. How could I have known Ahab would become enslaved to her witchery? He'd ploughed many a concubine before. Yet his deviant lust for her lasted beyond the typical duration of his flare-ups. I should have stopped it... But I was distracted by her compatriot Elijah's rebellion—I had no time to monitor what fields he was sowing... This is all* his *fault! He's betrayed me, he's marginalized me, he's brought my replacement into my own house, and even now he is planning to reward the murderers of my priests.* "Oh, Pygmalion..."

She ceased from her pacing. A lone tear trickling down her cheek, she shut her eyes and clenched her fists.

*Ahab's idiotic conceits of statecraft led you to that deadly ambush. Now his lust-driven egotism, selfishness, obstinacy—puffed up to an unprecedented height of insanity thanks to the self-serving flatteries of that whore, he is leading me to my doom. How much longer before his so-called wife manipulates him into casting me out of my own home? It's like what happened to Mother all over again... Oh, Baal, no!*

Grinding her teeth, Jezebel folded her arms across her chest and resumed pacing. *I should have killed that whore then but now it's too late. She has brainwashed Ahab to her way of thinking, made herself a goddess in his eyes. A direct, open attack on her would rebound against me, just as if Father had attempted to raise an army against King Phelles rather than slay him in his bath... No, that won't do. So first I must destroy her image in my Ahab's eyes before I can destroy her in the flesh. But how? A lesser woman, a lesser queen, would rack her brain so long, lose her nerve, be completely undone by the enemy... But not me! I am the daughter of Ithobaal! Defeat is not in my blood!*

Jezebel gracefully turned around and stared off in the direction of Tyre. "Oh, Father, I know what you would do."

Steepling her fingers together in front of her middle abdomen, she walked slowly over to the cradle. There lay the baby, his little hands fondling a blue blanket embroidered with white lambs. With her heart beating calmly and her breathing relaxed, Jezebel lifted him up and gazed at her son. He let out a little squeak when his mother first picked him up. His mouth began bubbling heavily, spouting seven streams of saliva rolling gently down his cheeks like the distributaries of the Nile. Meanwhile his eyes were wandering around the room in every direction, focusing on the lamp on the table, then the velvet cushion lying against the wall, and then the bundle of swaddling clothes which the nurse had left neatly folded beside the cradle—focusing on absolutely everything but his mother. After this, swaying in his mother's arms, he started jerking his legs; his warm foot gently tapped his mother's cheek.

Her nose crinkled.

Setting him back down in the cradle, Jezebel rested her chin on her thumb and chewed her lower lip. After only a few moments of contemplation, she muttered, "What the hell—it'd probably just grow up to be like its father anyway."

She reached into her sleeve and pulled out the knifecase. Removing the knife, she held it upright before her face, whose grave and stiff expression was reflected back at her in the blade's sharply glistening metal. She reversed the knife's direction in her hand while simultaneously raising it. Then she plunged the blade down dead-center into the baby's windpipe. Her blow was so swift that her child expired before he could even utter the faintest protestation. Yet despite his silence in life, his death reverberated with the sound of ripping flesh and metal hitting the wood of the cradle. There was also the liquid noise of his blood gushing out of his throat; pooling around his limp head, the blood turned the scant tufts of whispery hair gracing his tiny head into a strange looking hue and made him an accidental redhead.

Laying the knife beside its victim, Jezebel ambled away from the cradle. She held up her arms and carefully looked them over. There was only a single drop of blood marring her left sleeve: the rest of her body was clean of any bloodshed. She licked her thumb and scrubbed the blood off. When she reached the door, she meticulously ruffled her hair until it frayed. She fixed her sharp nails into her cheeks just an inch below the eyes and tenderly guided them downwards, making bloody tears in her flesh. As a final detail, she thrust her hand into one of her pockets and drew out a small flask of peppermint oil. She squeezed a few drops out onto her index finger and rubbed it under her eyes. Even without direct contact, the proximity was enough to cause her eyes promptly to being watering.

Straightening up, Jezebel drew in a deep breath and exhaled. Then, after opening the door, she staggered out into the hallway and let out a piercing howl:

"MMUURRRRRR-DDEERRRR! Murderer! My baby's been murdered!"

# CHAPTER TWENTY-SIX

"T HAT WAS A MAGNIFICENT feast," burped Ahab as he waved his hand to the servant to take away his twenty plates of various sizes and states of half-eatenness. "Tell the chef he outdid himself." Reclining back on his couch, he glanced around the room.

After the bard's recitations and the subsequent pleasantries of acrobats, the women had retired while the male banqueters remained. Ethan, the steward of the palace, was sipping his drink now and again but he was paying much more attention to the king. Ira, the newly appointed governor of Ijon, was on his seventh goblet of wine; in between gulps, he brandished a giant smile and was toasting his fellow guests and their chairs in turn. Uriel, the chief commander of the cavalry, was rambunctiously slamming his goblet on the table and ordering the servants about as though they were soldiers under his command. Hiram, the governor of Jezreël, had drunk himself into a stupor; his head was slumped down onto the table, lying in the pool of wine from his spilled cup beside him. Asher, the master of the king's wardrobe, was holding his liquor better than some others.

"My lord," said Ethan, "tell us again about how you slew Hezion of Damascus."

"Well," began Ahab, taking in a deep breath as a preface to his narration, "I first commanded my charioteer to—"

Suddenly a troubled clamor wafted in from the hallway.

*What could that be?*

As the dinner guests who were still conscious turned to one another with quizzical expressions on their faces, the noise increased in sound. Ahab rose from the table. "Come, men. Let's find out what's provoked this noise." *I haven't heard this much clamoring in the palace since the night of the riot...*

Entering the hallway, Ahab pulled aside a wild-eyed courtier and demanded, "What's happening?"

"Your Majesty," said the courtier, dropping to his knee and not daring to look up at Ahab, "it's horrible! Your newborn son has been murdered in the nursery! Queen Jezebel is inconsolable!"

"WHAT?" gasped Ahab. His mouth, so recently wet with wine now quickly becoming dry, dropped along with the thudding cup which was still in his hand. His pupils constricted within his almond eyes and his heart began to race almost as much as the thudding of a horse at full gallop. Ahab rushed past the courtier and hurtled down the palace corridors towards the nursery, outrunning his companions and ignoring the aghast-looking persons whom he encountered along the way. *Oh, God, what has happened?*

At last Ahab reached the scene of the atrocity. Jezebel stood outside the nursery doorway, the wall barely propping her body up in its agony. Her twitching cheeks were bleeding from the grief-marks carved in her flesh; torrential tears were making wet spots on her dress. She was lashing her fraying hair from side to side while screeching curses and profanities from her foaming mouth. Congregating around her were Elishat, the wet nurse, and Jezebel's handmaids, desperately throwing their arms around her and uttering gentle words to try, in vain, to calm her. Further down the hallway, drawn by the sounds of mourning, a steadily growing crowd lingered and watched in silence.

Shoving past the onlookers, Ahab raced to embrace his wife.

"Jezebel, Jezebel," he gasped, taking her in his arms and staring into her convulsing eyes, "tell me it isn't true! Tell me I've been misinformed."

"You've been informed correctly," replied Jezebel. After initially going limp in his arms, she managed to raise a shaky arm and pointed into the nursery at the cradle. "There, there! Our son is dead! Murdered!"

*No! No!* His heart beating rapidly, Ahab muttered, "I can't believe it. Who could murder our child?"

"SHE DID!" Jezebel thrust Ahab's arms off her and, snarling fiercely, reared onto her own feet. With her sanpaku eyes radiating hatred sharper than a two-pronged spear, she pointed into the crowd.

Clenching his fists and baring his teeth, Ahab spun his head around to confront the murderer of his child. But following the line pointed out by Jezebel's accusatory finger, instead of beholding a filthy rogue exuding his child-killing evil, Ahab's eyes came to a rest on someone else. He gasped and his heart momentarily fainted from the shock. Wading through the crowd and about to reach the row closest to the nursery was none other than Nava!

*Great God in heaven! What in the hell does this mean?!*

His mouth hanging so low that a trickle of spit started flowing out, Ahab stood entirely motionless apart from his eyes glancing back and forth repeatedly between Jezebel's finger and Nava. She was definitively pointing at her.

"She did it! She's the one!" Jezebel tugged hard at Ahab's sleeve, her nails digging into his skin, while continuing to point with her other hand. "She murdered our child!"

"Ahab," said Nava, approaching him with a mystified look on her face, "what on earth is happening?"

"Someone killed my little boy," mumbled Ahab blankly while staring into the distance.

"God's saints! That's horrible!"

Grabbing Nava by her sandy hair, Jezebel screeched, "Stop the hypocrisy, you lying whore! You've murdered my child!"

When Nava let out a blood-curdling screech, Ahab shook his head and then stepped between them. Taking Jezebel's hands and holding them away from their victim, he said, "Stop it, Jezebel! You're hysterical. You don't know what you're saying."

"Did she really just accuse me of murder?" panted Nava, patting her ruffled hair. She narrowed her round eyes and spit flew from her mouth as she yelled, "You audacious bitch, don't you DARE try to frame me for this!"

"You've slashed and shed my flesh and blood!"

"If I wanted to shed your blood, it would be *your* blood and yours alone!"

"May all the gods strike you down, heretic!"

"God damn you, heathen scum!"

*Oh, my God! Oh, my God! What am I to do? What am I to do? This is worse than war!* "Stop it, both of you, just stop it!" His heart was flying and his head was becoming light from his hyperventilating lungs. Placing his moist arms around Nava's waist to calm her, he said, "Please, darling, don't respond to her outbursts. Maternal grief has consumed her wits. She's not in her right mind."

"You're siding with her against me?!" screeched Jezebel. She slapped his face hard. "I'm your wife!"

The veins bulging on his clenched fist, Ahab stepped back from her and yelled, "Damn it, I love you, Jezebel! But I can't believe she's capable of such a horrific crime."

"Do you want proof?" said Jezebel darkly, glaring at him. "I'll show you proof!" She whipped around and zipped into the nursery. Returning with a blanket-wrapped bundle in her arms, she held it up so that all could see the infant, his little throat slashed and his blood still fresh on the blanket. "Look at your son, Ahab! Just look at him! And then look at the murder weapon!"

Ahab's arm slipped off of Nava when Jezebel took the knife out of the bundle.

*No, it can't be. Is that—is that what I think it is?*

A smirk spreading across her face, Jezebel snorted and said, "I see you recognize it."

Ahab wearily lifted his hand and received the knife from Jezebel into his palm. He concentrated his dry, unblinking eyes on the bloodied blade. With his other hand he gently ran his fingers along the handle. "This is..." He turned to Nava and garbled, "This is the knife I gave you during your coronation ceremony. You can tell by the distinctive design and layout of the jewels, which the craftsman skillfully arranged according to my precise instructions."

"No, it's not. It can't be!" protested Nava. Her eyes, blinking apace, were wide and her mouth agape as she reached out to clutch Ahab's arm. "You know I'd never harm you or your children! We understand each other like no one else can. Don't listen to these lies! She's lying, I tell you, lying! Jezebel's trying to frame me!"

"I-I... I want to believe you," said Ahab, patting her cheek with his other hand. He sniffled as a couple of tears rolled down his face. "You're so sweet."

"Is this some sort of cruel joke?" Jezebel's warm palm smacked him on his cheek and flattened his beard. "You hold the murder weapon in your hands and yet you still side with the murderer!"

He pressed a shaky finger onto his quivering lower lip. "No, no I'm not. There has to be some logical explanation for this..."

"There is! You brought a murderous she-wolf into our house, her fangs bared against me and my child and against all that is holy. You betrayed us just like you betrayed the gods, offering us up on the altar of her depravity. You sacrilegious bastard!"

"No, no!" Ahab vigorously shook his head. "I never betrayed any of you! All I ever did was to perform a few Hebrew rites." *What was so wrong with that?*

"You want Hebrew rites, huh?! You want them so badly?! Then how about the biggest Hebrew rite of all!"

Dropping the baby out of her arms, Jezebel snatched the knife out of Ahab's limp hand. She stooped down and ripped away the blanket and clothes. The dead child flopped face down onto the naked floor. Flipping him over, she performed the ultimate circumcision: hacking at its base, she severed altogether the life-giving organ from her dead son's body. Then she picked up the amputated penis and threw it against Ahab's face.

"There! I hope your Hebrew whore is happy! Our son will be one of hers in death!"

Ahab did not make the slightest gasp at her action nor did he make a reply. He had neither winced nor even blinked when his son's little member hit his wrinkly forehead and rolled down his face. The trail of blood dripping down his cheeks proved quite visible against the blanching background. He stood as though paralyzed.

Finally, Ahab raised his trembling hand and touched his cheek. His fingers reddened with blood. Holding them less than three inches in front of his watering eyes, he stared at the blood which swayed on his hand or else it was his eyes which were swaying. He continued staring as if his bloodied fingers were the only sights in the world; and as he stared, a gurgling sound arose. He forced his eyes to glance around to determine where the noise was coming from. But before he could find it, it made itself known. With his hands involuntarily clutching his stomach, Ahab keeled over and disgorged, in large putrid chunks, all the rich food and sweet wine that he had consumed during and after his dinner.

Once his stomach had stopped burning with pain, he straightened up, spun around, and started running. Forgetting that there had been an audience present this whole time, Ahab crashed into several people when he began his retreat. He shoved past them and flew down the halls, alternating between coughing up bitter flecks of vomit and spitting free-flouring tears out of his mouth.

When he reached his bedchamber, he darted inside and locked the door behind him. Howling and being unable to stop himself, Ahab staggered over to a table on which were assorted glass vases, ceramic dishes, and ivory decorations. He violently swung his arms all across it, knocking all the objects onto the floor which resounded with their breaking. He kicked the table across the room, stepped over the shards from the smashed objects, and headed directly to the waist-high cupboard beside his bed.

With his hands pulling the handle so hard that the drawer came off, he grabbed a bottle of wine from inside, used his teeth to tear away the oil-soaked rag stuffed into the bottle's neck, slunk onto the floor, and began glugging down less alcohol than that which spilled down his front. Ahab smashed the bottle against the wall while it was still a quarter full; clutching a new bottle and pressing it to his fat lips, he held his knees up against his torso with his other hand and struggled to escape the events of the night.

*Oh, Yahweh, Baal, any god in heaven or hell who'll hear me—what did I do to deserve this?*

# Chapter Twenty-Seven

"Hurry, Elishat," said Jezebel as she briskly flew down the hallway. "When you have the wolf by the ears, you can neither safely hold it nor let it go: your only escape is to bash its skull in!"

"I will do all I can for you, Madam," replied Elishat from two steps behind her. "But is this the right move? Although the king is currently indisposed, how will he reäct when he hears of this?"

Jezebel glanced back at both Elishat and the two handmaidens with her. "The king's reäction will mold itself according to who prevails on the field of battle. As ducklings swim in a row behind their mother, so too will Ahab fall in line behind me when I am again his sole wife."

When Jezebel and her squad turned around the corner, they encountered two soldiers stationed outside Nava's bedchamber who instantly arched their shoulders. Standing abreast in order to block the door, the soldiers raised their swords in front of one another and clanked them together in an X-formation.

"Stand aside and let us pass," commanded Jezebel.

One of them, a young man, gulped. "W-we're under orders not to let you pass."

"By whose authority?"

"By Queen Nava's," answered his comrade, a middle aged man whose shuddering hand almost broke the swords' formation.

Leaning into his face, her breath visibly causing his skin to crawl, she declared, "*I* am Ahab's queen, his first queen, his true queen, the queen you'll have to deal with for all the years to come... not that murderous imposter. Stand aside!"

"W-we're under orders not to let you pass."

Jezebel placed her flat palm on the spot where the two swords crisscrossed each other and gently pushed the metal forwards so that the swords' broadsides were pushed uncomfortably against the guards' chests. Cocking her head, she said dryly, "Then you'll have to put these swords to use. But first ask yourself: are you prepared to murder the king's wife to safeguard the murderer of the king's child?"

The guards cast nervous glances at each other. Without a word needing to be uttered between them, they simultaneously lowered their swords and their heads. Then, stepping aside with a sigh to let Jezebel and her entourage through, they slunk away down the corridor.

Nava was inside, sitting at a round table with her back to them. Her hands, which were held up in prayer, quickly slammed down on the wooden surface as she shot upwards and spun her neck around at the sound of their arrival.

"I see not even soldiers can stop you. Did they forsake me, or did you dispatch them like you dispatched your own child?"

"Don't speak of my child, whore!" shouted Jezebel. "All Jezreël is talking of your treacherous infanticide."

"Except I am innocent." Nava's hand snatched an object on the table and raised it so that all could see. "Look here!" she demanded, furrowing her forehead and pursing her lips. "This is the knife Ahab gave me: the one you claimed I used to kill your child. But here it is, un-bloodied and nowhere near the crime scene. God knows which one of us is guilty of this sin."

Jezebel's expression did not change one whit. She folded her arms and coolly said, "Restrain her."

As the handmaidens in tandem each grabbed one of her flailing arms and Elishat picked up the knife that had fallen from her hand during the scuffle, Nava looked at them and shrieked, "Can any of you honestly tell me you believe her lies?! She clearly killed her own child in order to frame me! It's plain as day!"

"We are Queen Jezebel's faithful eyes, ears, and hands," answered the one before the other added, "We would not presume to judge her."

Nava glared at Jezebel and bared her teeth. "Your henchwomen's reply does not surprise me. No honest person could remain long in your service: for they would either spit out the first drop of your wickedness and be saved, or else they would be corrupted by it and become wicked like you."

Jezebel approached her and slapped her face; her nails drew blood from Nava's cheeks. "Hebrew scum! My Tyrian aides are unquestionably loyal to me. That is their honesty, the best which any queen could count upon. But your kind wouldn't understand loyalty. You Hebrews have always been a rebellious race, treacherous to kings, hostile to all mankind. No wonder your God forsook you: even He couldn't stand you any longer."

"God is not mocked by your blasphemy!" Her nostrils flaring and her eyes fluttering, Nava declared, "He will avenge me and my people."

Jezebel smiled smugly and chortled. "You leap right to vengeance—what, no begging me to spare your life? You've already given up?"

"I'm not so foolish as to hope for mercy from you nor am I disposed to grant you the pleasure of watching me beg." Nava held her head high and murmured, "Blessed are You, O Lord God of our fathers: your name is worthy to be praised and glorified forevermore…"

"Cease your irreligious gibberish, infidel, harlot, maggot! Only my husband could derive pleasure from your loathsome self," muttered Jezebel through gritted teeth. She glared fiercely at her. "It will please me sufficiently to cleanse the land of your filth—both you and your compatriots. Was it really less than an hour ago that you were boasting how you would corrupt the country with your Hebrew heathenism? The gods of Phoenicia have always looked favorably on my family. You never stood a chance. For I am the daughter of Ithobaal of Tyre."

"And a murderer, just like him! He killed a man to gain his crown."

"And I'll kill thousands to avoid losing mine!"

Before Nava could utter a retort, Jezebel had stabbed her in the heart with her own knife which was un-bloodied no longer. She let out a brief gasp as the blade came out of her body, splattering blood in every direction that covered Jezebel's front and hit both handmaids in the face. Nava's head had flown backwards from the blow's suddenness, lying limp over one shoulder just as does a garden poppy which, having burst into full bloom, bends and droops its red head to one side under the combined weight of its seeds and a sudden spring downpour.

Even after she was dead, Jezebel continued to stab the corpse; her arms strained their muscles as they repetitively drove the tip of the blade through mangled flesh towards Nava's backside. Panting, she at last let go of the handle and commanded her handmaids to drop the body which they were still supporting.

"Elishat, see to it that this, this *thing* is suitably disposed of. Maybe the pigsty could use more material for its floor."

"At once, Madam. How do you feel?"

Jezebel snorted, "Frankly, I don't feel anything at all." *One might have thought I would feel pleased to eliminate my rival; but she was far too inferior to provide serious mirth, as though a trained athlete should boast about outrunning a crippled old man.* She glanced at the disfigured corpse. *Nonetheless, it is good to claim the victory.*

Elishat bowed her head. "Thank the gods, it is finished."

"No, it's only half finished," replied Jezebel as she headed to the doorway. "Just as the milkmaid has to muster strength to churn her butter after she has milked the cow, so do I still have to deal with Ahab."

\*\*\*

MIDNIGHT HAD NEARLY OVERTAKEN the sleepless palace. Whispers were still passing from hall to hall and room to room as the night's two murders were talked about.

Jezebel was alone in her room. Seated with her legs crossed, she was resting her eyes and her head on a downy pillow on the back of her chair as she awaited the looming confrontation. Her senses functioning perfectly, she gently turned her head towards the door when the thud of stumbling feet arose and grew steadily louder.

"Jjjj-eeezz-eee-bbbbeeel," came Ahab's raspy voice.

Cupping her hands on her lap, Jezebel snapped open her bulbous eyes and nonchalantly gazed at the doorway.

Only Ahab's hand, firmly grasping the doorpost, had thus far entered her room; but after a few more huffs and the continued rasping of her name, he managed to heave his whole body through the door. He looked worse than the lone survivor of a shipwreck cast adrift for days on end. His almond eyes were bloodshot and stared blankly, his oily brown hair unkempt, his drooling mouth agape, and his beard caked in wine that had made it start clumping here and there. All his clothes reeked of alcohol and were coated with it in addition to several prominent patches of chunky vomit over his legs and abdomen; he had somehow even succeeded in coating the fabric over his buttocks with vomit.

*My, oh my...*

While still holding onto the wall, Ahab raised his shaky hand and pointed at Jezebel. "Jezebel, they tell me you killed Nava. Is that true?"

Jezebel, without blinking, looked him in the eye and nonchalantly replied, "Yes, I did."

"But, but I loved that woman..."

"So I had gathered. I am not an idiot."

"How could you do it?"

"With the same knife she used to kill our son."

Ahab, after belching foul-smelling air which caused him to stumble onto his knee from the force of the burp, recovered and started lurching in her direction. "How do you know she was guilty? She denied it! There was no trial. No way to prove it. How can you know?"

"Trials exist to determine guilt when the truth is doubtful. Everybody knew she was guilty. A trial would have been superfluous in her case. Justice demanded her death and the majesty of the throne requires that all its enemies be swiftly punished."

"You shouldn't have taken it upon yourself to make this decision. I'm the king!" He stamped his foot hard on the ground, or rather, as hard as he could muster in his current condition. Despite it not being that hard of a stomp, the intemperate movement of Ahab's leg unbalanced him and he fell onto all fours. "It was my decision to make. Mine!"

Jezebel's narrowed eyes glanced down at her husband. "Ahab, it was better that I spared you from having to make that decision. For we both know how intimately linked you were with that woman, how dominated by your emotions rather than using reason to think clearly. It was that very heedless intimacy of yours that led you to bring her into our house, where she had full access to everything, even the nursery..."

"I loved that woman," insisted Ahab as he crawled towards her on his knees. With his face grimacing and tears rolling down his cheeks, he spoke into the floor and said, "She encouraged me, comforted me, made me feel so good every time I was around her that I wanted to do everything for her."

"Yes, she expertly manipulated you for her own gain, flattering your ego so as to blind you to her perfidy."

"She was always beside me, speaking of kingship as though she truly grasped the sorts of burdens that we kings bear."

"Rummaging your pockets, grasping all the royal jewels you're burdened with."

"But no matter what she'd done, I could never have brought myself to kill her, to harm even one hair on her sweet, sweet head…"

"Which is why I freed you from your impossible situation."

Jezebel braced her teeth but otherwise kept her body motionless when he grasped her thigh. He looked up at her. His eyebrows were lowered and his bloodshot eyes burned with anger.

"Jezebel, I, I, I…"

His hand slipped from her thigh and he collapsed onto the floor. Snuggling his face against her foot and clasping her dress in his hands, he wept piteously and moaned, "I'm sorry. I'm so sorry! Oh, Jezebel, I was such a fool…" Globs of snot ran down his mouth as he babbled, "I thought she was someone I could rely on, could trust with my most intimate thoughts. But it is as you say: she was only using me."

"Don't beat yourself up too much. You're only a man. You couldn't resist that lying har—that perfidious woman's wheedling and ever-saccharine, self-effacing dissimulation."

"But our son is dead because of me," whined Ahab. He wiped his sleeve across his face and smeared saliva and snot everywhere. "If I hadn't brought her here, our son would still be alive."

Jezebel licked her lips. "Well, that is a terrible lesson that you will have to live with. But if it helps you not to fall for any other scheming concubines in future, then perhaps it was worth it."

"How can it be worth it?" He gazed up at her through tear-soaked eyes and sniffled. "You gave me a son… you carried him in your holy womb all those months, underwent the pains and labor of childbirth, all that—for nothing. It was all for nothing because of me..."

"Yes, yes it was."

"Jezebel, Jezebel... Oh, I'm so vile, I'm so worthless... I'm ashamed to even ask... can you ever forgive me?"

"There, there." She put her hands around his head and kissed his wine-covered forehead. "You are my husband and always will be. Despite your wayward behavior and the agony you've inflicted on me, I know that, deep inside, you still love me."

"You forgive me?"

"Yes."

"Oh, Jezebel, my Jezebel... I don't deserve you."

*You really don't.* "There, there. I'm here."

Sniffling, he blinked his tearful eyes dry and said, "How can you be such a wonderful woman? To really forgive me? I don't know how you can even stand to look at me."

*You can get used to anything if you do it long enough... even hanging.* "Hush, Ahab. You'll always have your Jezebel." *No matter how much I might wish it were otherwise.*

"Oh, Jezebel, sweet Jezebel, my Jezebel..." Struggling to rise off his knees, he managed to hoist himself up enough to wrap his arms around Jezebel's lower waist. He laid his head on her lap and wept joyous tears as she gently petted his head.

# Chapter Twenty-Eight

A̶HAB SIGHED AND SLUNK down onto the embroidered foot of his mother's bed. Staring up at the leafless pink flowers painted on the ceiling, he mumbled, "Oh, Mom, I re-eeally screwed up this time."

"You certainly screwed something, Son." His mother smiled over him and with her wrinkly, spotted hands gently stroked his clean-shaven cheeks. "Ahab, sweetie, what are you going to do?"

He shrugged his shoulders. "I don't know, Mom. That's why I wanted to talk to you. I need your advice on how I can make it up to Jezebel, to let her know how much I love her and regret what has happened."

"Have you told her this?"

"Of course! But words, no matter how contrite and beautiful, cannot atone for the atrocious deeds that resulted from my actions. I had thought Nava loved me and had my best interests at heart; I eagerly followed her siren's song, foolishly turning away from my devoted wife whom I owe for saving me from a near, self-inflicted ruin. Yet although I escaped intact, I have caused irreparable harm to my family. Were it not for me bringing in that accursed woman, our little son—too young even to have received a name!—would still be alive... It's all my fault. But that noble woman, that angel

233

on earth, can love me in spite of all that. I still struggle to believe that Jezebel so readily forgave me."

His mother furrowed her brow and looked leftwards. "She certainly seems to be taking this in stride," she said pensively.

"She's such a trooper! The past week has proven the extraordinary resilience and endurance of her constitution. By her outward behavior, you wouldn't know she is a mother grieving for a child so cruelly snatched from her. But I know, deep inside, she is suffering because of me. That's why I need to do something to let her know just how much I regret my actions."

His mother kissed his wrinkly forehead and said, "Why don't you give her a special gift? A woman likes to know her husband appreciates her."

"You mean like jewelry?" Ahab sat up and pounded one hand in the other. "I could design new regalia for her, outfit her in the finest—"

"I was thinking something more thoughtful."

Ahab cocked his head. "What do you mean?"

"Jewelry is nice and all, but don't just give her the same sort of presents that she routinely receives. (We all know Jezebel's collection of jewels is one of the largest in the world.) Rather, find something personalized, something that conveys to her that your gift is not the common sort which any royal lackey might send on his king's behalf but that it is made especially for her, coming straight from her husband's heart."

"Like what?"

"You're her husband. Surely you know something she would like?"

"Maybe she'd like... no. Oh, how about—oh, no, no, no, definitely not that. Hmmm..." Ahab, pressing his brown eyes shut, rested his naked chin on his fist and frowned.

"Maybe there's something she really wants but lacks? Has she ever revealed anything like this?"

*Wants but lacks?* "I know! Our neighbor Naboth's vineyard!"

"A vineyard?" His mother looked askance at him. "Does Jezebel want a vineyard?"

"Not any vineyard," exclaimed Ahab, jumping to his feet. His eyes were wide and he was animatedly waving his hands. "Naboth's vineyard! We used to dine at his place a lot before me and... Well, anyway, Jezebel always loved the ambiance of the vineyard itself. You should have seen the way her eyes would wander around Naboth's place, how she used to smile and lick her lips as she surveyed the property. She even told me it would make a great herb garden, a place she could really leave a mark on the land. It would make a fantastic project for her to do—something for her to improve and take her mind off her sorrows! She'll love owning it!" Ahab briskly leaned over, kissed his mother's cheek, and calling back "Thanks, Mom!" bolted out of the room.

Spurred on by this newfound conviction of how he could make amends to his wife, Ahab dashed over to his neighbor's house. Several servants tending the vines paused in their labor to observe the commotion that the king's feet were making. Naboth himself was out on his patio, seated on a couch and sipping a glass of red wine that his attendant continuously refreshed. He sat up when he spotted the king sprinting over to him.

"Naboth!" shouted Ahab, waving his hand to hail him.

"Your Majesty," answered Naboth, bowing his head. His eyes looking up to him, he asked, "To what do I owe the honor of your presence?"

Ahab placed his hand on the man's shoulder and beckoned him to be at ease. "Naboth, you're both a good neighbor and a good subject, and that is why I know I can depend on you for this favor. I need your vineyard."

"My vineyard?" said Naboth. "Are you asking for my wine? I can supply the palace with as much wine as you may wish."

"Not the wine, tasty though it is. What I want is to use the land on which your vineyard lies."

Naboth blinked confusedly and frowned. "Use it for what? Are you planning a harvest celebration?"

"No, no, I'm not making myself clear." Ahab put his arm around Naboth's shoulders. "Give me your vineyard so that I may turn it into an herb garden, because it is near my house. And in exchange I will give you a better vineyard than it. Or, if you prefer, I will give you its equivalent value in money."

Naboth shook himself out of the king's embrace and took a step backwards. With his eyebrows pressing down on his grave-looking eyes, he said, "I will not sell my vineyard in order for you to turn it into an herb garden. If you need herbs, there are many other places where they are grown."

Ahab sighed. *Naboth's always been a stubborn fellow.* He waved his hands back and forth. "It's not the herbs themselves but their cultivation that I seek. Your vineyard is not only conveniently located but it also has excellent soil for herbs. It will give great joy to the queen to have a little garden to call her own. You know how much women love nurturing plants! Because her joy is worth more than anything in the world to me, I don't want to quibble over prices with you. Sell me your land now and I'll give you double its worth."

"No."

"Triple!"

"Money has nothing to do with it!" insisted Naboth, shaking his head vigorously. "Yahweh forbid that I should give the inheritance of my father to you. My father tilled this soil, and his father before him, and his father before him. This land has been in our family's unbroken possession ever since Joshua allotted it to us in the forty-sixth year from our people's exodus out of Egypt. It was God's will that this plot of land fell to my family's lot and I will not be the first in my line to betray my forefathers' legacy and to sell out the heritage of my own sons."

"Please, Naboth. This isn't just a passing fancy of mine." He dropped to his knees and tugged on Naboth's lower garment. "I *need* your vineyard, not for me, but for the queen. For Jezebel! What will she think if I come back empty-handed?"

"I will never sell my land, not to you nor to any man. I am certain the queen will understand: she is a strong woman."

"It's supposed to be a gift. She doesn't even know I'm trying to buy it..."

"Then don't tell her and spare yourself the grief. Simple! Now, my lord, I must respectfully ask you either to drop this commercial suggestion or to return to your palace. For I am a busy man and this estate does not manage itself."

"You know," said Ahab while he idly circled one finger in the dust, "you wouldn't have to exert yourself so much if you had ten times the value of this land..."

"Please, my lord. Futile pleading does not befit a king."

With his shoulders slumping, Ahab sighed and listlessly rose to his feet. He turned his back on Naboth and uttered not another syllable to him. Then he sluggishly marched back to the palace, his legs feeling as though they were chained to two weights, twenty tons apiece, and forced to drag them up to the peak of the highest mountain.

When he returned to the palace, Ahab refused to speak to anyone who encountered him. He headed straight to his bedroom, nudged the door shut behind him, tottered over to his bed, and collapsed onto the sheets which ruffled from his giant sighs. He spent the remainder of the day alone in bed, refusing all visitors and spurning the food that his servants tried coaxing him to eat.

***

ON THE FOLLOWING DAY, as the sun was reaching the high point in the solar circuit, Ahab was still sulking in his bed. His solitary brooding was finally interrupted by the sole visitor who could penetrate the lugubrious room.

"Ahab," went the voice resonating both irritation and impatience in its cadence.

Ahab glanced up with his eyes without bothering to lift his head.

It was Jezebel. Looming over him, her eyes looking down from beside her crinkling aquiline nose, she put her arms akimbo and demanded, "Why is your mood so gloomy that you are eating no food?"

Sighing, Ahab mumbled, "It's nothing."

"*Nothing*?" echoed Jezebel, squinting at him. "Don't lie to me! Don't you ever lie to me! Do you think I'm an idiot? You've been moping in your bed since yesterday afternoon. Had you simply been loafing under the sheets, I would have thought nothing unusual about it; but I'm told that you haven't eaten since then either. If by noontime Ahab hasn't glutted his stomach with enough bread, meat, and cheese to breakfast three teenage boys toiling behind the plow, and enough wine to top off the town drunk, then he's clearly feeling ill. I want the truth from you and I want it now!"

"I'm sorry for lying, dear," answered Ahab meekly, turning his gaze away from her. "I just didn't want to worry you over something that's not really that important."

"*I'll* be the judge of its importance. Tell me what happened yesterday. Why are you in such a sorry state?"

"Well, it's because I spoke with Naboth the Jezreëlite and I said to him, 'Give me your vineyard in exchange for money; or else, if it pleases you, I will give you a different vineyard for it.' And his reply was: 'I will not give you my vineyard.'"

Jezebel's soft-angled eyebrows arched briefly before they almost instantaneously sank into a heavy squint. "A *vineyard*? Really? You got all this worked up over a piddling property dispute?"

"It wasn't 'piddling,'" protested Ahab as he rubbed his thick neck which was itching from a sudden burst of heat. "It was of the utmost importance to me that I acquire Naboth's vineyard."

"And when did it suddenly become so important for you to get this property? Was this another one of those things that pops up in your mind one moment and then the next you're off running to try to actualize your fancy before you've even thought through what might be the best way to approach it? Oh, Ahab, Ahab, whatever am I to do with you?"

Ahab made no reply to her derision except to turn his head away from her.

"When you made your offer, did you clearly preface it with the importance of remaining in the king's good graces? Did you remind Naboth of the vast distance between a king and a subject and our claims upon the realm? Please tell me you didn't just start throwing out financial offers like some common huckster in the bazaar."

After several seconds of silence, which coïncided with a feeling of clenching in Ahab's empty stomach, he finally mumbled, "Maybe."

"Ahab..." Jezebel glared and ground her teeth. Crossing her arms across her face, she leaned over the bed. "When he refused your offer of money, surely you didn't offer him even *more* money?"

Gulping, Ahab answered, "He said it wasn't because of the money he refused me: it's his ancestral land and he won't sign it over to anyone."

Her hot breath hitting his face, Jezebel said, "Did you make multiple counteroffers before you learned of this?"

"It wasn't really that many..."

"Don't tell me you made a fool of yourself by begging. You didn't debase yourself by falling to your knees or anything, did you?"

"I wouldn't exactly call it *begging*," muttered Ahab, rubbing one hand behind his neck. "It was more, like, an emphatic exhibition of interest."

"And I suppose you did all this in front of Naboth's servants, too?"

"Well, there were some servants tilling the vines and whatnot, but I doubt they heard our conversation."

"But they saw you fail pitifully. Damn it, Ahab! Are you a king or a stable boy's bastard?" She stomped her foot. "I find it hard to comprehend you at times. How many times will you behave like this? Are you *really* this inept at using kingly power to acquire what you want? Or do you just suffer from a streak of masochism and want everybody to laugh at you in your face? Why, when my father ruled Tyre—"

Slamming his fist into the bedspread, Ahab sat up and stridently screeched, "Your father, your father, your father! You're tired of my behavior? Well, I'm sick of hearing you drone on and on about how much better a king he was than me! You've been doing it since the day we were married. I don't want to hear any more about how your father was better than me."

"Infinitely better!"

"It's not possible for any man to have been as good as you make him out to be."

"He was! He didn't inherit his crown from Daddy like you; he took his crown by his own means! He took more enemy commanders prisoner than you've witnessed battles, took more towns from the enemy, took in larger tribute than even—"

"Well, for all his superiorities, there's at least one thing I took that he never got!" interjected Ahab, sitting up and pointing his finger at her. His sides heaving and pupils constricting, the spit sprayed from his mouth as he hollered, "I TOOK YOUR VIR-GINITY!"

Wiping a couple drops of his saliva off her cheek, Jezebel sneered and casually said, "Father even beat you to that, too."

"WHAT?!" Ahab's face blanched and he fell backwards onto the bed, his arms lying flaccidly beside him. Through clenched teeth, he managed to utter, "Wh-what did you just say?"

"I said my father took my virginity long before you ever had the chance."

"Don't say such a terrible thing!" pleaded Ahab through his tightened jaws. *This must be a joke...*

"But it's true! I was a girl of thirteen, just entering into the rosy bloom of maidenhood. My stature was tall, my figure curvy and slender. And I was remarkably well endowed for my age," she noted while jiggling her breasts with her fingers. "Obviously, such nubile charm could not remain unobserved. I had soon attracted the thirsty gaze of every man not yet interred in the earth. (And if what they say about male corpses is true, then probably even a few stiffs found one final pleasure in me, too.) Unfortunately, my father, being as he was the manliest of men, proved unable to rein in his manly craving for the feminine. Rushing madly across the boundaries of convention—despising them as though made by ants—he burned with great lust for me and would stop at nothing to slake the itching drive.

"And so it came to pass, one midsummer night of yore, while I lay still awake on my rosewater-scented bedclothes, observing the craters on the moon through the oval window of my room, listening to the sweet sound of the cicadae dancing outside on my balcony, dreaming of such things as young women dream of at that age, that my door suddenly flew open as though a tempest from the sea had found its way into the palace. I gasped in fright and pulled the sheets up to my quivering mouth as I suspect any other girl in my situation would do. Through widening eyes I spied a dark figure hovering menacingly in my doorway; the stench of alcohol on him reached all the way to my nostrils and was so powerful that I gagged and almost did more than retch.

"'Fear not, Daughter,' came the familiar voice. 'It is I, Ithobaal, the man who gave you life, come to claim what is my own.'

"I had no time to reflect on the meaning of my father's words or wonder for what reason he had come and in such a condition. It all happened so fast. He did not waste any time with the usual words that boys whisper into the ears of the girls whom they desire. No. Instead, he lunged across the room like a half-starved panther, grabbed me with those big sinewy hands of his, yanked me out of my bed, threw my trembling body up against the cold stone wall, and *then*, and *then*, and *then*..." At each temporal adverb Jezebel quivered and her face, tightened with closed eyelids, jolted one way and then the other.

*This is a living nightmare!* Ahab stared wordlessly at his wife's dramatic gestures.

Finally, clutching her diamond-studded necklace and working it over in one hand whilst her other hand held onto its sister's wrist, Jezebel murmured softly, "And then he had his way with me."

Ahab's pallid neck, its blue veins bulging on the sides, was stiff and could not easily move. The lids of his almost pupil-less eyes blinked in rapid succession as he gazed up at his wife. While wringing his hands, he mumbled, "D-did Ithobaal really do it?"

"He did."

"Did you not beg him to stop?"

"What good would that have done?" she asked, looking at him askance. She folded her arms across her bosom. "He was the father, I the daughter; he the king, I the subject; he the battle-hardened warrior, and I, I, I..." Jezebel's voice trailed off while her eyes stared blankly into the distance.

Ahab drew his hands beneath the sheets and wiped his soaking palms against his trembling thighs. "Your father really perpetrated such violence against you?"

"Well, just that once because he was so drunk. He was much gentler the other times."

Biting down on his fat lips hard enough to draw blood, Ahab gasped, "*Other* times?"

"Of course!" said Jezebel as her soft-angled eyebrows rose, her kohl-darkened eyelids fell, and her pupils dilated. Hugging herself with her arms, she added, "You don't think any man could have his fill of me in but a single session, do you? For the next two years, until the moment I was given in marriage to you, my father would pay twice-weekly visits to my bedchamber. He gave me kisses, caresses, embraces; he loved me as father ought not to love daughter."

*O Baal and all the gods, please tell me I'm hallucinating!* Ahab lay motionless on the bed, his face entirely white and his lips visibly desiccated. "I can't believe what I am hearing. Is it really true?" he asked with a choking voice. "Please, please tell me it isn't true! Tell me this is just one long, cruel, sick joke of yours."

Jezebel stared directly into his eyes and replied, "It is as truthful as anything ever uttered by these lips."

"Why did you never tell me about it?"

She cocked her head and pursed her lips. "When exactly do you propose I should have mentioned it? This is not the kind of thing which comes with a ready-made time for discussing it. On our wedding night, when you were straining beneath the sheets to check that everything was working properly down there, should I have allayed your distress by pulling the bedspread off you and announcing in my girlish voice, 'Fear not, my father can show you how it's done: he's an expert.' Now wouldn't that have made for an awkward honeymoon!" She tilted her head back and let out a short chuckle.

"But, but, but..." Ahab's jaw gaped open as he stared helplessly at her, the blood pounding in his ears. "All these years... You've been living with such unspeakable horrors in your memory... the knowledge thereof daily eating your mind alive... the wounds never healing but only growing deeper with the passage of time..."

"Cut out the melodramatics, Ahab." She sniffed and, turning up her nose at him, looked down on him with squinting eyes. "Although unwanted and unwished for, my father's actions did me no lasting injury. His assignations did not blind me, scar my body, nor leave me with a crippled leg that I would have to drag around for the rest of my life. (It's not as though he came at me brandishing something dangerous in his hands: that tool was made for love, not war.) So it would have been quite pointless to obsess over them: that would only have detracted from all the things I sought to do in Israel. Nor, despite your sheltered upbringing leaving you with a lack of imagination, are they as unthinkable as you suppose. These things do happen from time to time, albeit reports of them are confined mostly to tales of the ever-blissful gods and goddesses who dwell in the heavens. Then again, we royalty do bestride the earth as gods among men; perhaps it is not too unseemly for us likewise to do those things which most strike peasants' hearts with horror."

Ahab lay silently in his bed for several moments. Then, his throat constricting and jaw muscles tightening, he spat out jadedly, "Maybe it's just as well you never told me." Deep furrows appeared on his forehead as he raised his shaky fist into the air. His skin burning with the heat of rage that even his hateful tears could not extinguish, he exclaimed, "Had I known, I-I-I would have strangled your father, choked his eyeballs out, smeared his brains all over the place—murdered him!"

"No, you wouldn't. Father would have broken every bone in your body before you could have so much as laid the slightest scratch on his manicured nails. He was by far a stronger man than you. We both know that."

*She's right... God, how right she is...*

A whimpering Ahab slunk further into his bed, pressing himself deep into the sheets just as much as his chapped lips had vanished within his dry mouth. He appeared as though he were sinking in a bed made of quicksand, and there was not a vine nearby for him to grasp to safety.

*I'm a complete failure as a king, as a husband, as a man... Which god did I offend to merit so many curses in this life...?*

# CHAPTER TWENTY-NINE

H ER LEGS SPLAYED WIDELY out and her arms folded across her chest, each hand tightly clutching the opposing upper arm and digging its nails into the skin, Jezebel loomed over her husband and glared down at him.

*What a pathetic loser you are!*

"Alright," she said after a minute had passed since their last words had been exchanged, "I don't have any more time to waste with you. It's time to get Naboth's vineyard once and for all."

"Why? Just forget about it," mumbled Ahab between sighs.

"I can't 'forget about it' now. You've made that impossible. Shall people say that my husband, the king of Israel, is so useless and incompetent that he can't even purchase some dumpy vineyard? Did you never once *think* how that would make me look?"

"I guess thinking's not my strong suit..." said Ahab, covering his downcast eyes with his arm.

*You don't have a strong suit!* Her forehead furrowing with lines, she said, "We can't let the situation stand as it is or else we risk the whole monarchy falling into disrepute. Naboth's vineyard must be ours so that all Israel will know the power of the monarchy and that it ought not to be esteemed lightly. In the future, if the king makes a request, his word must be obeyed promptly and without any disputation. We can't permit all the little Naboths of the world to think that *they* get to decide when and under what conditions they will fulfill a king's wish."

"That sounds excellent, Jezebel. What would you like me to do?"

"Nothing! You've done more than enough already. I'll take it from here."

"Oh, okay," muttered Ahab, chewing on his lips. "I'm confidant you'll do a better job at this."

Jezebel turned to leave the room. But after taking a few steps, she paused and looked back at him. "Why did you even want his land in the first place? What's it to you?" *Don't we import enough wine from Tyre so as to keep you from growing your own wine? Or is even that insufficient to quench your drunken thirst?*

"It wasn't for me," said Ahab softly, looking up at her while twiddling his thumbs. "I wanted to buy it for *you*. As a gift to express my remorse for committing all those affronts against you with that Hebrew woman. To let you know how sorry—how truly, utterly, to-the-depths-of-my-rotten-soul sorry—I am for all the trouble I caused."

Sneering, she thought, *Great, I even have to go get my own apology gift. I must be the luckiest wife in the world to have* this *thing for a husband! Whatever did I do to deserve him...?*

"Why the hell would I want a vineyard? Whatever made you think it would interest me?"

"Well, I remember that time we dined at Naboth's with your brother and sister, and you commented on how great the soil would be for an herb garden. I just thought..."

She squinted incredulously at him as his faint voice trailed off. Finally, she looked around the untidy room and demanded, "Where do you keep the royal seal?"

Ahab wordlessly lifted up his limp hand and pointed at a knee-high drawer in the corner.

Her nostrils flaring, Jezebel yanked out the drawer so hard that it fell onto the floor with a loud clank. She bent down and foraged through its contents, throwing this and that here and there, until she found the royal seal under a pile of official clay tablets and papyrus scrolls. Plopping it into her sleeve, she straightened up and, her chin high, sped towards the door. But before leaving she spun her head around, fixed her eyebrow-pinched eyes on Ahab, and said in a caustic tone:

"Are you now ruling the kingdom of Israel? Get up, eat some food, and let your heart be merry! I'll give you the vineyard of Naboth the Jezreëlite."

Ahab said nothing in reply as she exited his bedchamber. After she stepped into the hallway, Elishat, who had accompanied her here and had been waiting for her while she spoke with the king, said to her:

"How is the king, Madam?"

"He's as lost as ever," replied Jezebel, shrugging both her shoulders. "Come, we have business to take care of."

The two proceeded in silence down the corridor till they reached Jezebel's room. Once inside with the doors securely locked behind them, Jezebel took out the royal seal and set it on her table.

"Is that the king's seal?" said Elishat coolly. She gazed at the crown-wearing eagle, its talons grasping ten rods, exquisitely engraved in the seal.

"Yes, and it will come in quite handy."

"I can't recall the king giving you the official seal before."

Jezebel huffed. "Well, I used to be able to count on him to sign whatever document I needed. (At least until that Hebrew woman showed up!) But now he's in no condition to do even that, so I'll have to do it all myself. That's fine. It's about time I took it from his hands. A royal seal symbolizes the supreme power and honor of the monarchy, makes even the wormiest parchment to be reverently handled by men, imbues even the most inconsequential command with as much majesty and authority as if the gods themselves were to open up the heavens and rain down fire for a sign. Ahab's proven time and again that he can't be trusted with such power. He can't even sign a real estate deed properly."

"Pardon, Madam?"

Jezebel summarized the king's interaction with Naboth for her.

"So what will you do, Madam?"

"What I always do." Her eyes went wide as she formed a vein-bulging fist. "Win!"

"Do you propose a direct attack?"

"No, not after the public spectacle Ahab made of himself." Jezebel's forehead furrowed, her long fingers tapped on her thigh, and her tongue peaked out of the corner of her mouth. "If I simply bring naked force to bear against Naboth, it will look like we're trying far too hard to compensate for Ahab's pathetic behavior."

"Then would a more subtle attack be preferable? I know a couple of gold-hungry rogues whom we could quickly get to do away with the vintner."

"No, for that would engender rumors about us. Assassinations work best when one doesn't know who's responsible (or at least can't muster a plausible conjecture). But if Naboth's killed right after he openly defied the king, everyone will know it was us. And if they'll know anyway, we shouldn't try to hide behind some drifting thugs: our duplicity would be patent while our attempts at secrecy would make us look hesitant, and if hesitant, weak, and if weak, contemptible. No, I must make it so that the vineyard—without appearing as though we were actively involved in bringing it about— will fall into our hands like an overripe apple plops down to the brown bear below."

After Jezebel sat down at her table and picked up her reed pen to write upon a fresh piece of papyrus, Elishat inquired, "How will you do it?"

A smirk spread out across her face. While chewing on the end of the pen, Jezebel stared off into the distance and said, "Easy. I'll write to a few of the important townsmen, dependable fellows who owe everything they have to me—and nothing buys men's loyalty easier than making them completely dependent on you—and command them to throw a big party to which the whole town will be invited. They will give Naboth the pride of place and extol him for his virtues, for his successes, for whatever sorts of things which gladden men's minds. Then, once he has been feted like a pig is fatted before it's led to the slaughter, they shall have a couple of lawless men—maybe even the very rogues you referenced earlier—brought in to accuse Naboth, in the sight of all the people, of having blasphemed god and king. That will do it for him! In an instant he shall have been turned into an infamous criminal; per the laws of the land, he shall have to be stoned to death for his heinous offense as well as forfeiting all his worldly possessions to the royal treasury. Thus, he'll be dead, we'll gain his vineyard, and the people will assume his execution was lawful and just." *And even if they don't, they won't dare to say that aloud. We'd only be able to plausibly deny the accusation and hang them for slander...*

With a beaming face, Elishat nodded. "It is hard to devise a more perfect plan than this."

"Yes, though it's not entirely without cost." Jezebel sighed and shook her head. "I guess this'll put an end to the occasional dalliance I have had with his son (who, damn it, is a real lusty one at that!). Not for killing his father, mind you," she added, waving her right index finger in front of Elishat. "Many a man soon forgets his father's murder just so long as the spilling of blood was the sole crime committed. Truly it's the stolen patrimony that poisons men's souls against you."

"Is that really the case, Madam?"

"Oh, it most certainly is, Elishat. As my father once told me, a ruler must simply keep his hands off his subjects' property and women and they'll put up with every other offense."

Her cheeks blushing redder than the rubies in the choker around her neck, Elishat clasped the necklace in her right hand and, her beady eyes fluttering rapidly, gasped, "It is a shame, then, that your father did not himself more assiduously obey the latter part of his wise precept!"

"Well," said Jezebel, quickly moving her hand over her mouth to stifle a chuckle, "he was only a man. None of them are perfect!"

# CHAPTER THIRTY

"**A**HAB!"

Ahab had been lolling on his couch out on the palace patio, enjoying the cool morning breeze and listening to the cooing of doves nesting nearby. A servant beside him kept him shielded from the sun by means of a large white parasol. The day had been tranquil thus far, and Ahab had done nothing to dispel his lethargy apart from eating some bacon and eggs. Yet as soon as the deafening voice of his wife pierced his ears, he pulled the lime-water soaked towel off his face and turned his neck in her direction. "Jezebel," he said, forcing a smile, "what is it?"

She had a large smirk on her face and a glint in her green eyes. "Get up and go take possession of the vineyard of Naboth the Jezreëlite, which he stubbornly refused to give you in exchange for money, because Naboth is no longer alive. He's dead."

"What?" gasped Ahab. He jumped up onto his feet almost as fast as his jaw had fallen. "He's really dead?"

"He was stoned to death last night as a public criminal."

*Criminal?* "I never suspected Naboth would become guilty of crime. What did he do?"

"Witnesses heard him speaking contemptuously about you and the gods and he was duly executed according to the law of the land."

"Hmm." Ahab bowed his head and squeezed his almond eyes shut. Puffing up his cheeks, he exhaled and ventured, "Jezebel, did you have something to do with his death?"

"I ratified the judgment of the judge trying the case."

"That's not what I meant... The other day, you said you would acquire Naboth's property... and I just thought... and now he's dead..."

Jezebel interrupted his meandering drivel with an emphatic snort. "What are you trying to say? Are you taking up my enemies' slurs and accusing me of being an evil, heartless woman? Is that what you are suggesting? And if you are, then I must ask: what did I ever do to make you hate me like this?"

"No, no, no, no!" exclaimed Ahab, grabbing her hand and planting a wet kiss on it in an attempt to soothe her. "I wasn't suggesting any such thing. You are the best of women."

"Whom will you trust, Ahab? The mother of your children, both living and dead; your loving wife, who's stuck with you through thick and thin and forgiven you for all your transgressions; your unwavering supporter on whom you have relied all these years? Her or a measly vintner—a lowborn man who obstinately snubbed your royal majesty; humiliated you in the sight of his slaves; and was himself convicted of uttering treasonous words, in open court, by the sworn testimony of witnesses lawful and true? Well?" She placed her arms akimbo and glared at him. "Whom will you trust?"

"I trust you, Jezebel, *you*! I believe in you, I have faith in you—all the faith that it is possible for a man to muster."

Jezebel smirked and, kissing his cheek, said, "Good. Now go take possession of that vineyard and we'll be able to put the whole incident behind us."

"Alright, dear," said Ahab as he reciprocated her kiss by planting his fat lips on her cheek.

After exchanging farewells, he quitted the palace and headed for his new vineyard. As his feet were bringing him there, Ahab, with his hands locked together behind his back, kept his eyes fixed on the bare ground while pondering over things in his mind.

*I must never think anything amiss of Jezebel again... it's simply a noxious habit which that wicked woman planted in my mind...*

As soon as bricks appeared beneath his feet, Ahab looked up. He had reached the patio where Naboth had entertained him and his fellow guests on so many occasions. The fire-pit, where the juiciest of meats had once been roasted, now lay cold. All around the fire-pit were ashes which the servants had not cleared away before they too were forcibly removed from the premises. There were some broken bottles and plates scattered around the patio, and in the corner next to the door of the house was a bundle of cloth. Ahab stooped to pick it up. It was a homemade doll, probably belonging to one of Naboth's younger daughters; the doll, in addition to missing an eye, had been crushed by a boot that had presumably belonged to one of the royal officers responsible for clearing out Naboth's family.

"Thus says Yahweh: 'Hast thou killed and also taken possession?'"

Ahab gasped and the doll fell from his hand.

"Because of this, thus says Yahweh: 'In the place where dogs licked the blood of Naboth shall dogs lick thy blood, even thine.'"

Ahab's squinty eyes had both dilated and their pupils contracted in less than a second after he spun around. Clenching his fists together as the blood roared through his ears, he shouted at the source of the baritone voice, as familiar to him as it was unwelcome, "Have you found me, O enemy of mine?"

Ambling slowly across the patio with a shepherd's crook, his sullied mantle flowing in the breeze along with some white strands of his scraggy beard, Elijah approached the king. "I have found you because you've sold yourself to work evil in the sight of Yahweh."

"No, I haven't! Everything I've done was what I thought was right."

"God's ways are not the ways of men, nor are His thoughts your thoughts. What you imagine to be right is greatly repulsive in the eyes of God. You have turned your back on Him, O wicked king."

"If you speak for God as you claim you do, then why hasn't He told you about the ways I've sought to worship him? I've prayed to Him!"

Elijah shook his disheveled head. "Yahweh does not listen to the prayers of sinners."

"And I've offered up the fat of rams to Him! When was the last time a king of Israel sacrificed to Him?"

"Obedience to His commandments is more pleasing in His sight than the blood of slaughtered animals. You spared the life of Ben-Hadad, a man who deserved to die; and you put to death blameless Naboth, who ought still to be among the living. You refuse to do what Yahweh commands and instead do what He forbids. That, in short, makes you an evil man."

"I never killed Naboth! If your God were all-knowing, He'd know that!"

Elijah guffawed and began pacing around Ahab in a circle. He raised one thin arm and shook it at him while saying, "No, instead you allowed your wife to do your dirty work for you, using your name and royal seal to frame the innocent. That makes you just as guilty as she."

"How dare you accuse Jezebel!" shouted Ahab, his face turning red.

"She is a murderer like Ithobaal of Tyre, and the lusts of her father she will do."

"You prophets—always rebuking, never a kind word from you... Does someone pay you to do this, or are you sufficiently requited with the joy you get from torturing me?"

"I derive no pleasure from seeing you squirm." Elijah shut his bulging eyes and exhaled deeply while still keeping his slow pace around Ahab. "I come only to report the words that my God directs me to speak."

"And what exactly does God want from me now?"

"He no longer expects anything good from you."

"What do you mean by that?"

"God is both merciful and just. Yet although He is longsuffering, he is not everlastingly-suffering. And He has reached His limit with you."

Ahab crossed his arms and pouted. "What does that babbling mean?"

"Thus says Yahweh: 'Behold, I will bring evil upon thee, and will take away thy posterity, and will cut off from Ahab him that pisseth against the wall, and him that is shut up and left in Israel, and I will make thine House like the House of Jeroboäm the son of Nebat, and like the House of Baäsha the son of Ahijah, for the provocation wherewith thou hast provoked Me to anger and made Israel to sin.'"

"You can't just blame me for causing Israel to sin!" protested Ahab, stamping his foot.

"You are right, O King. For you never would have had it in you to commit your abominations except for that wicked woman Jezebel, that heathen foreigner and witch, whom you have permitted to pollute the land with impunity."

"Again you obsess over my wife... What is so wrong with you that you endlessly speak badly about Jezebel! I forbid you from saying anything against her!"

"Your commands are overruled by God!" yelled Elijah, his eyes flashing. He raised his shepherd's crook towards the sky. "For thus says Yahweh: 'The dogs shall eat Jezebel by the wall of Jezreël. Him that dieth of Ahab in the city the dogs shall eat; and him that dieth in the field shall the fowls of the air eat. But there was none like unto Ahab, who did sell himself to work wickedness in the sight of Yahweh, whom Jezebel his wife stirred up. And he did very abominably in following idols, according to all things as did the Amorites, whom Yahweh cast out before the sons of Israel.'"

Clasping his pounding heart, Ahab sucked in a deep breath and screeched, "Get out of here, just get out! I hate you!"

Elijah ceased his circular pacing and stood still to face the king. Scrunching his bushy eyebrows, his entire forehead furrowing, he gazed intently with unblinking eyes. In a hushed tone of voice, he said, "I go now, O King, but take a good look at me. For you never again shall see me nor I you until your soul departs from this world.

As milk once squeezed cannot be put back into the cow, so are my words of prophecy against you."

"Go on then, just go," whimpered Ahab with a breaking voice. He turned his head so as not to be able to see the prophet.

Elijah turned his back on the king and, with a snort, left.

"What a wretched man, what an incorrigible rebel," complained Ahab, pacing back and forth across the courtyard for several minutes. *Prophesying our deaths... no, it can't be true. God wouldn't kill me. I am a king and have performed rites for Him, the first king of Israel to do so since the ten northern tribes seceded from Rehoboám. Regardless of what that crank says, my sacrifices must count for something... After all, every god needs sacrifices and gives to those who give. But what if He kills Jezebel? NO! Jezebel is beloved by Baal and all her ancestral gods. Surely they will watch over and can protect her from the wrath of a single Hebrew God... What is one god against so many?*

He halted. Wiping the sweat off his wrinkly forehead with his shaking hand, Ahab looked up at the sky that had steadily begun to fill with dark clouds since Elijah approached him. "O God of my fathers: You won't bring destruction upon my house, will You?"

Just as he had finished his sentence, a lone blast of thunder roared overhead.

*No, no, no!* Ahab hanged his head low and buried it in his hands. Breathing heavily, he muttered, "Baal, aren't you equally a god? Do you not have the power to protect one woman?" *On the other hand, you didn't stop Elijah from slaughtering all those priests of yours... What chance will Jezebel stand against His wrath?*

When silence was the only reply from the sky, Ahab fell to his knees and wept. "O God, God of Israel... Please, please don't destroy us." He ripped at his clothes and exposed his bare chest to the heavens. "I'm a worthless man. I know I make mistakes. (I've already seen one child suffer the consequences of my misdeeds.) Jezebel knows my flaws and, doubtless, You do too. But don't take my failings out on my family."

Sniveling, Ahab crawled over to the fire pit. He scooped up fistfuls of ash and poured it over his head. The ash mixed with his flowing tears, sticking to his face most piteously.

"I know Jezebel is hardnosed and cunning, but that's exactly what a government must have to survive. Yet she is more than that. I need her, not only for my crown's sake but also for my own sake. She's my other half, my better half, she completes me... Without her I am nothing... mere ash and dust. O God, I couldn't bear to see my Jezebel die—her body torn by dogs! Please, have mercy, have mercy on us!"

A flash of lightning lit up the sky and was quickly followed by the first drops of rain. And as the minutes passed and the intensity of the rain increased, Ahab was still kneeling in Naboth's patio. With great moaning, he finally stood up and started to stagger back to his palace. As he did so, he stared up at the sky and glared.

*If You have rejected me, then I will reject You. I will redouble my worship of Baal and all the other gods of heaven, who will save me from Your wrath. If You think You'll have time to persecute my wife, think again, God. You'll be too busy trying to save Your worshippers. For I will give Jezebel full authority and the resources to finish the task she's always desired: to wipe out Your name from among men! No god of whatever people, even my own, may trifle with me and my Jezebel with impunity....*

260

# CHAPTER THIRTY-ONE

S EATED UPON HIS GOLDEN throne, his beardless cheeks weighed down from profuse fat that had been accumulating in the many months since the incident with Naboth the vintner, Ahab was staring into the distance with weary eyes. There were others in the throne room along with him: courtiers, guards, and servants. Although they were bustling and making noise with their respective tasks—clanking javelins, gossiping about the latest news brewing in the countryside, or polishing the decorative bronze shields adorning the walls—Ahab paid no heed to them. As far as any onlooker could tell, he was alone with his thoughts. And he sat, unmoving, stewing in who-knows-what thoughts. His body suddenly jolted, however, when a familiar voice easily pierced his mental bubble.

"Ahab," said Jezebel, approaching the throne, "an important visitor has just arrived in our court."

"Who is it?"

"Your half-sister's father-in-law, King Jehoshaphat of Judah."

"Then show him in."

Jezebel, with the beginnings of a smile appearing around her mouth, shook her head. "Before you meet with your fellow king, we must discuss the reason for his visit."

"What is it?"

"He seeks an alliance against Ben-Hadad."

Ahab cocked his head to the side. "What? Is he so bold as to wish to make a go against Ben-Hadad and his Aramaic horde? And he expects me to join him?"

"He expects nothing of the sort," replied Jezebel breezily with her aquiline nose held high. "In fact, he will not even bring up the topic unless you initiate the conversation."

"I don't understand."

*Of course you don't.* "Ahab, Ahab..." said Jezebel, shaking her head. "It's simply a matter of appearances. Although Jehoshaphat is an adherent of the Hebrew superstition, his personal beliefs have never hindered him from coöperating with us in the past nor from marrying his son and heir to our darling Athaliah. Like any prudent king, statecraft is not purely a matter of religion for him. But no king is an island. His regime is backed by the priests and Levites of Jerusalem along with the Judean lords and nobles who still subscribe to their ancestral rites. These men provide Jehoshaphat with the support necessary for him to govern his kingdom; he cannot unduly antagonize them without slashing his own throat. And there's a big difference between coöperating in commercial enterprises with 'our kind' and sacrificing the lives of his subjects in a war undertaken jointly with us. While the hypocrites in Judah would find it acceptable, the true-believers among them would be *aghast* at the thought of their king coming cap in hand to beg us for military assistance. Their negative reäction would destabilize his hold on power. But if *we* should appear to make the first move, and Jehoshaphat merely takes a side in the war that is already coming regardless of what he does, then he can plausibly portray his actions to his subjects as a necessary decision amid a regional war not of his own choosing."

Biting on his fat lips, Ahab said, "So this rigmarole is just because of political appearances... Well, I guess I understand that. But tell me, why does he want to fight Ben-Hadad to begin with? After all the bloodshed and fearsome fighting it took to bring Ben-Hadad to heel, what makes Jehoshaphat think breaking the peace would be a good move?"

"Ben-Hadad has had a longstanding feud with Judah and many of his troops have pillaged the Judahites' commercial caravans on the King's Highway. It's very embarrassing for Jehoshaphat—or any king, for that matter—passively to endure such outrages without responding to them. It makes him look weak not only in the eyes of the Arameans but even in those of his own subjects, especially those less enthused with his regime."

"Alright, so he wants revenge for wrongs done. I suppose that's as reasonable a motive as any. But that leaves one thing unexplained. Why should *we* join him in his war? It's not our concern. And why are you so eager to help him? It's out of character for you to want to do so great a favor to a worshipper of the Hebrew God."

Jezebel snorted and flicked her long silky black hair back. "When have I ever helped a Hebrew?" Her bulbous eyes narrowed and a smirk spread across her face. "Despite my disdain for Jehoshaphat's religious practices, I've always managed to separate my subjective feelings from objective realities and possibilities. And I recognize in this venture the tantalizing prospect of enlarging our domain and profiting our realm. For that reason, I am inclined to expand our existing alliance with heathen Judah even to matters of war." *To take advantage of any scenario that might arise and to work with anyone who could conceivably assist me in that enterprise–that has always been the system I've followed.*

"But that would require us to defeat Ben-Hadad and his army," mused Ahab, resting his chin on his fist. "We were lucky enough to defeat him once—remember when he had his heel on Samaria's throat? Our kingdom's very existence was in jeopardy: we almost lost everything. Despite our ability now to live in security, are you seriously contemplating that we risk another war against him, and this time one of our own choosing?"

"Don't fret about the past, Ahab. The old Aram is no more and the new is not to be feared. Remember, when the Battle of Qarqar happened last year, King Shalmaneser and his Assyrians decimated Ben-Hadad's forces. His army is still in shambles and its strength much reduced from what it was when we defeated him the first time. Even by ourselves, the odds are extremely favorable for us to wipe him out; if we combine the forces of Judah with our own, then it will be impossible for us to lose!"

"Yes, we are much better off now than then, and the opposite is the case for Ben-Hadad. You do make a good point..." Ahab rested his hands on his wrinkly forehead and massaged his temples with the knuckles of his thumbs. "But even if that is the case, dear, it does not alter the fact that we are now allies of Ben-Hadad. We even sent a contingent of soldiers and chariots to assist him and the other allied kings at Qarqar. How can we renounce this alliance and treacherously make war against him?"

Jezebel swatted her hand through the air as though she were eliminating a bug. Rolling her green eyes, she said dryly, "We allied with Ben-Hadad, Irhuleni of Hamath, Gindibu of Arabia, and the other seven kings simply to halt Shalmaneser's advance. It was a purely circumstantial alliance born of geostrategic necessity. Now that that conflict is over, we owe him nothing more. Ben-Hadad is only a dangerous stranger with a long history of committing hostile acts against us. Jehoshaphat, on the other hand, has been a reliable partner for many years and, moreover, is our kinsman. His blood and yours intermingles in the veins of Athaliah's son—a testament in the flesh of the close bond between our families. Between these two alliances, Jehoshaphat alone has a claim upon our help."

"That is all true. But it is equally true that, when I defeated Ben-Hadad three years ago, we mutually swore oaths of peace and sacrificed victims to our respective gods. Am I to violate my word and offend heaven?"

Jezebel put her arms akimbo and, leaning towards him, asked, "And what of *his* word? Is Ben-Hadad alone permitted to violate his promises with impunity?"

"What do you mean?"

"You spared his life and permitted him to continue to reign in Damascus on the condition that he return *all* the territories that his father stole from your father. Isn't that correct?" When he nodded, Jezebel continued, "And has he restored it all? NO! That perjurer, to this day, yet retains the city of Ramoth-Gileäd and refuses to restore what is rightfully ours."

Ahab shrugged his shoulders. "It's just a single city; it's not that important. I'd almost forgotten about it, to be honest. So while you're right about it being a technical violation of the treaty, is it really worth it to jettison the present peace over so small a slight?"

Her nostrils flaring, Jezebel hissed, "He retains the city precisely because of lackadaisical thinking such as that! Ahab, if you allow others to take advantage of you in the small things, then they will take advantage of you in the big things. Your inability to grasp this great truth has always brought great trouble for us. Do you remember when Ben-Hadad demanded your utterly humiliating submission to his demands and (ignoring my advice in favor of the swill proffered by that whore who shall remain nameless) you submitted? And did that placate him? NO! You showed weakness to him and he instantly responded by increasing his demands."

"Well, I, I—"

"Unless you respond aggressively to this latest slight," she insisted, looming over him and taking his head between her palms, "Ben-Hadad will reason that he can push you around anytime he wishes. Once he recovers his strength, which he will do if given the time, he will steadily unwind all the hard-fought gains we made until we're left with nothing. That is why we must strike *now* while the gods favor us with good fortune!"

"Your advice does have merits—"

"When has it not? Have I not always provided you with the best counsel a king could wish? So what precludes you from accepting it?" She took a few steps away from him and turned her back on him. Slowly twirling her silky black hair with one hand, she added, "I can't think of any reason. Unless, perhaps, you wish that whore were still here to beguile you with her wheedling words…"

Hunching his head over his knees, Ahab sighed. "No, no. Not at all. To my dying day, Jezebel, you know that I will always regret the hurt I caused you because of my indiscretion. If you think that war is in our best interests, then I think so too. I will do as you say."

"Excellent," said Jezebel, licking her ruby lips. She moved in and gave him a quick kiss on his cheek immediately to the left of a bright red razor burn. Turning around to go, she called back over her shoulders, "Remember what I told you about bringing it up first."

Exiting the throne room, Jezebel passed through an antechamber lined with purple tapestries and returned to where Jehoshaphat and his entourage had been waiting. The king of Judah rose from his seat to greet her.

"Jezebel, how is the king disposed to our planned campaign?"

"He agreed to everything just as I told you he would."

"Your foresight is to be wondered at."

*That's scarcely high praise when we're talking about Ahab...* "Yes, and as I expected, his vanity also reared its ugly head. Ahab will stand shoulder-to-shoulder with you on the battlefield but his egotism positively insists that you allow him to appear as the great leader and organizer of this campaign against Aram. Just go along with his charade and let him seem in his subjects' eyes like he's the one who originally devised this plan."

"I can certainly do that. I don't need the glory. I am just happy that Ahab is willing to retract his consent to that treaty with the Aramean."

"Treaties were made to be broken," chuckled Jezebel as she speedily arched and lowered her soft-angled eyebrows several times. "They're only valid so long as their terms agree with the facts upon the ground. When realities shift, moribund treaties cease to matter."

"Especially when their provisions are detrimental to both Israel and Judah's vital interests," said Jehoshaphat, resting his hand on her shoulder. "Ben-Hadad is an ongoing danger to both our countries: he must be neutralized at once. And I am most grateful that I can always count on you as a partner in these matters and benefit from your valuable support. You and I, Jezebel, are by no means cut from the same cloth. Heaven knows that to be the case! We are divided by nationality, by the gods we worship, and by our fundamental views of statecraft. (I cannot deny that your reputation for, how to put it, ruthlessness in pursuing your objectives most efficiently do, at times, give me palpitations of moral unease.) But I appreciate your pragmatic willingness in setting aside your own antipathy towards those of my religious persuasion in order to coöperate with me whenever it is in our mutual interests to do so."

"I am nothing if not pragmatic," said Jezebel, brushing his hand away. Interlocking her fingers behind her back, she paced in front of him while keeping her eyes fixed firmly on his. "And my pragmatism is born of an understanding peculiar to rulers. For despite the ignorant masses' delusion that disputes over the gods is a driving force behind the wars of mortals—and frankly your people are especially susceptible to this on account of their stories about Joshua—we know that that is the farthest thing from the truth! Wars arise between kingdoms because of the opposing interests of power: religion is merely the patina we subsequently paint on it to rouse our peoples to action. We each have our own priests to bless our campaigns, performing their respective rites and hymns to inspire and urge their soldiers onwards." Jezebel, ceasing her pacing, slinked up beside Jehoshaphat and locked her unblinking eyes on his. "So really, there is no reason preventing us from allying in a war against the Arameans where our common interests lie. Let the peasants think what they will!"

"There is a certain truth in your words," gulped Jehoshaphat while glancing down at the floor, "albeit spoken in a harsher tone than I would put it."

"Just remember to play your part when you meet Ahab."

# CHAPTER THIRTY-TWO

*W*ELL, *I SUPPOSE IT'S time to bring it up,* thought Ahab.
Gulping, he glanced over to Jehoshaphat, who was seated opposite him at the table which had been erected in the midst of the throne room. Ahab raised his golden goblet to him. *I hope Jezebel is right about his willingness...*

He pointed to the decorative ceramic pot in the corner that Jezebel had had specially brought in. It was knee-high in the shape of a bowl, with a high foot elevating it a couple inches off the ground; its sides were adorned with concentric stripes of red slip. "That is such a lovely piece of pottery, is it not? Servants, from which of my cities is that pot?"

A servant approached the pot and, carefully so as not to break it accidentally, tipped it backwards so as to glance at the craftsman's mark on its bottom. Setting the pot back in position, the servant turned around and announced, "The pot was produced in Ramoth-Gileäd."

"Ramoth-Gileäd?" exclaimed Ahab, pronouncing the words slowly and with feigned surprise, even gently smacking his forehead for emphasis. He next turned to slowly rubbing the skin of his chin. "Wasn't that city supposed to be turned over to us according to the terms of the treaty Ben-Hadad, king of Aram, made with me? It has been three years. Has he done it?"

"No, my lord."

"He hasn't? Hmm..." Making his almond eyes go wide and opening his mouth as though genuinely astonished at what he had heard, Ahab glanced at all the men of his court in the room. "Do you all not know that Ramoth in Gileäd is ours, and yet we are motionless, and have not taken it out of the hand of the king of Aram?"

His courtiers looked at each other wearily without answering their king.

Jehoshaphat broke the silence. "Ahab, it sounds like you have been defrauded by the king of Aram. What will you do about it?"

"I will take what is rightfully mine," said Ahab, "with whatever forces I can muster." Locking his brown eyes on the king of Judah, he swallowed a little before making his request: "Jehoshaphat, Ben-Hadad is weak. Israel can defeat him. Yet victory will go so much more smoothly if Israel has allies to share both in the toils and spoils of war. Judah is our sister kingdom: it would be fabulous if our two nations could once more be on the same side. Therefore, Jehoshaphat, I ask you this: will you go with me to battle to Ramoth-Gileäd?"

Bowing his head ever so slightly, Jehoshaphat replied, "Your words are true and I concur. I am as you are, my people as your people, my horses as your horses."

"Excellent!" *Wow, I got him to say yes so easily. Jezebel will be so proud of me!* "Then we will set our heads together and plot our battle plan."

Jehoshaphat, shifting in his seat, said, "This alliance seems good in my eyes but I hope that it is equally pleasing to God. Inquire, please, at the word of Yahweh today."

A disgusted frown oozed across Ahab's face as though he had just bitten into a citron that had been baking beneath the desert sun and its sour juice was making an assault on his stomach. Coughing into his fist, he said, "I am no longer in the habit of making inquiries to that God. Do you really feel it necessary?"

"I won't feel well unless we have at least inquired."

"So be it."

***

A S THE SUN BEGAN to set, Ahab and Jehoshaphat each seated themselves upon iron thrones that had been erected in the area in front of Samaria's northern gate. In this spot, overlooking the landscape which gently receded into a lower lying plane, Ahab had gathered four hundred of his prophets. Once they were assembled, Ahab held up his golden scepter and announced:

"Shall I go against Ramoth-Gileäd to battle, or shall I refrain from doing so?"

No sooner had he asked his question but all four hundred prophets, as though they had rehearsed their answer like a well-drilled chorus line, shouted, "Go up: for Yahweh shall deliver it into the hand of the king."

With his head nodding affirmatively, Ahab said to Jehoshaphat, "See? Our success is assured."

Pursing his lips while his thick eyebrows pressed down on his eyes, Jehoshaphat said, "The prophets' response is favorable; yet I noticed that none of them is not a prophet of the gods of Sidon. Is there not here a prophet of Yahweh as well, that we might inquire by him?"

Ahab folded his arms across his chest and glared at the reddening sky. "There is one other man, Micaiah the son of Imlah, by whom we may enquire of Yahweh. But I hate him because he does not prophesy any good concerning me, but only evil."

"Let not the king say such a thing."

*If this is the only way to mollify him, I guess I have no choice...* Ahab, choking the scepter in his hand, pointed it at one of his officers, who promptly approached the throne. "Bring Micaiah the son of Imlah here quickly."

The officer bowed his head and dashed off to retrieve the prophet from the city prison.

As the minutes dragged on, the Phoenician prophets kept prophesying in unison like a well-trained choir: "Go up to Ramoth-Gileäd and prosper: for Yahweh will deliver it into the king's hand."

Despite the persistent refrain of foretold success, Ahab meanwhile brooded on his throne. *Micaiah will speak unfavorably as he always does. The god of my forefathers has utterly abandoned me... Well, He may have helped me in the last war but I don't need Him for the next one! I still have Baal, Astartë, Melqart, Dagon, Resheph, Moloch, and all my wife's other gods and goddesses on my side. And if Gad, Meni, and Ashima bless my cause, then my luck will be unstoppable! My coterie of divinities are mightier than a single holdout. I do not need Him to prevail! Yet Jehoshaphat is still a believer in Him: he might listen to Micaiah... Please, Baal, remember all the sacrifices I and my wife have offered you and hold up his spine: keep Jehoshaphat committed to our alliance.*

When the last remnant of the solar disc sunk beneath the horizon, servants lit torches around the area. They had just completed their task when Ahab's officer returned. Seated atop his horse, he kept the beast at a slow saunter as he led Micaiah along by a rope tied to the metal collar around the prisoner's neck.

Halting in front of the kings, the officer dismounted and manhandled Micaiah into a submissive posture on the ground. Needing to raise his voice to make himself heard over the laughter of the other prophets, the messenger declared, "Here he is, my lord." He dug his heel into the back of the prisoner's neck so as to make him taste the ground.

"Excellent." Ahab motioned for the officer to withdraw. He cast an uneasy glance at Jehoshaphat beside him. He looked down at Micaiah. Finally, drawing in a deep breath, he exhaled and said, "Micaiah, you've been summoned for one thing. My fellow king Jehoshaphat and I desire your prophetic services. Shall we go against Ramoth-Gileäd, or shall we desist?"

Shakily propping himself up with his bony emaciated arms, Micaiah spat sand out of his mouth. He glared up at Ahab and, sneering, declared, "Go and prosper! For Yahweh shall deliver it into the hand of the king."

*The brazen liar!* With his face blushing red, Ahab flared his nostrils, threw down his scepter with a clunk, and rose from his throne. He pointed his furiously quaking finger at the prophet and bellowed, "How many times shall I adjure you that you tell me nothing except what is true in the name of Yahweh?"

"You want the truth?" asked the prophet, looking past Ahab's finger to meet his glaring eyes. He wearily rose to his feet and snapped his fingers with both hands. "So be it. Here is the truth! I saw all Israel scattered upon the hills as sheep that have no shepherd. And Yahweh said, 'These have no master: let them return every man to his house in peace.'"

Sitting back down, Ahab glared at Jehoshaphat and acerbically remarked, "Did I not tell you that he would prophesy no good concerning me, but evil?"

"His words certainly resound ominously," murmured Jehoshaphat, dividing his eyes' attention between Micaiah and Ahab.

"He hates me and bears a great grudge against me. Pay him no attention."

Before Jehoshaphat could respond, Micaiah interrupted the royal conversation. "Hear therefore the word of Yahweh!" he declared, spreading his arms out and holding them as wide as possible. "I saw Yahweh sitting on His throne, and all the host of Heaven standing by Him on His right and on His left. And Yahweh said, 'Who shall persuade Ahab, that he may go up and fall at Ramoth-Gileäd?' And one spoke on this manner and another spoke on that manner. And there came forth a spirit who stood before Yahweh, and said, 'I will persuade him.' And Yahweh said to him, 'Wherewith?' And the spirit said, 'I will go forth and I will be a lying spirit in the mouths of all his prophets.' And God said, 'Thou shalt persuade him and prevail also. Go forth and do so!' Now therefore, behold, Yahweh has put a lying spirit in the mouths of all these prophets of yours, and Yahweh has spoken evil concerning you."

*Such insolent blasphemy!* With the veins on his sweaty forehead bulging, Ahab slammed his fist on his throne's armrest.

Without needing Ahab to command him but, as it were, accurately predicting his master's wishes, Zedekiah the son of Chenaanah, one of the prophets of Baal, went up to Micaiah and struck him on the cheek from behind. "Which way went the Spirit of Yahweh from me to speak to you?" he asked mockingly.

His action elicited a smile from Ahab's chubby face.

"Behold," answered Micaiah, spinning his head around to paralyze his assailant with his eyes that were bloodshot and revealing their scleras, "you shall see on that day when you shall go into an inner chamber to hide yourself."

When Zedekiah raised his hand to strike him again, Ahab interposed. He called for the officer who had brought the prisoner here and said, "Take Micaiah and carry him back to Amon the governor of the city and to Joäsh the king's son, and say, 'Thus says the king: "Put this man in the prison and feed him with bread of affliction and with water of affliction until I come in peace."'"

As the officer yanked on the rope to drag his prisoner away, causing him to fall to the ground, Micaiah looked up at Ahab and called out to him with a shriek. "If you return at all in peace, then Yahweh has not spoken by me!"

*Damn you and your God!*

# CHAPTER THIRTY-THREE

"AAAAHHHH! GOD SAVE ME!!! NOOOOOO!!!"

Ahab shot up in his cot as though stung by a cobra. His heart was pounding louder than a midsummer thunderstorm and his extremities were shaking. His skin was drenched from toe to head with as much cold sweat as if he had just emerged from a nighttime swim. He spun his head back and forth, as disoriented and desperately searching for some means of salvation as a flailing puppy which has been thrust beneath the surf of a lake, choking from both the water and the burly hand of its malevolent owner.

"My lord, my lord!" shouted his aide-de-camp, jumping up from his sleeping place on the dirt ground beside the royal bed. His eyes wide, casting his glance at the entrance and then throughout the tent as though attempting to make out, in the predawn light which was penetrating the flaps of the tent, whether any entity other than the sun's rays had forced an entry. After he assessed the situation, he threw his arms around Ahab and pulled him up against himself; this act of his stopped the king's thrashing but did nothing to halt the concomitant strident shrieking that continued to resonate through the tent. When his soothing words failed to calm the petrified king, he said, "Forgive me, my lord," and slapped him on his left cheek.

The smack stopped his howling. Blinking for the first time in over a minute and relaxing his arched eyebrows while the constricted pupils of his widened eyes returned to a more normal size, he gasped, "Am I alive? I'm alive? I'm alive! Oh, thank the gods, I am alive!"

Ahab freed himself from his aide's clutch and, resting his hands on his knees, sunk his head between them and sighed. "O Azmelqart, you do not know how much the sight of you relieves me: for I have just endured the most frightening dream of my life." Holding up his shaking hand, he pinched it with his other while he added, "My mind is still in doubt that the nightmare is truly over."

"My lord, what dream could cause you this distress?"

"Azmelqart, Azmelqart," murmured Ahab, reaching out for him and pulling him against his side, "I dreamt of my own death—a dream that felt as real as you and I talking!—in the coming battle. It began well. I was single-handedly slashing down one enemy after another, distinguishing myself in the eyes of my men. Then suddenly I found myself cut off from Israel's soldiers, axe-wielding Arameans by the thousands were surrounding me, Ben-Hadad himself rushing at me... I sought to raise my sword to meet him but discovered it was gone. What's more, my shield, breastplate, all my armor—even the tunic underneath—were gone. I was as naked as the day I was born. I desperately tried to turn away from Ben-Hadad's attack but my feet were frozen to the spot; every muscle in my body was trembling, chills crisscrossed my skeleton, my pounding heart drowned out every other sound, and I was so short of breath that the lack of air made it hard for my eyes to focus on anything. Then his sword went through my heart and emerged triumphantly out of my back. (I don't know how it's physically possible, but in my dream my vision returned and I could clearly see my own back and all the blood spurting from it when the blade came out.) I started falling to the ground, being only able to see Ben-Hadad's laughing face, laughing, laughing... When my body expected to hit the earth and end its fall, suddenly the ground beneath me vanished and I plunged headfirst into a black abyss. I flailed my arms in every which way but there was nothing to grasp. I just kept falling, falling, falling into the unending darkness...."

"My lord, I am sorry that you experienced so frightening a dream."

"No, no," whispered Ahab, rising from his bed and clenching his fist, "it was more than a dream. It was a vision of the future—an omen of ill-fate. I must not fight in today's battle. No, I cannot!"

Blinking in bemusement, Azmelqart cocked his head and said, "What, my lord? Shall Ben-Hadad carry the day by default?"

"My soldiers can fight him. But not me."

"But you are their sovereign commander! Will you send them off to war, thinking their king is scared of bad dreams?"

"Dreams are what the gods show us will come true."

Azmelqart bowed his head and steepled his fingers. "I know that's what the dream-interpreters say, but, pardon me for my bluntness, I've never believed that to be true. Were men's dreams portents of their future, the world would either be populated with kings richer than the gods themselves or else entirely devoid of human beings, or at least those who are not unworthy of the name of man. When I was a lad, I once dreamed a most impious dream: I had slain my father and married my mother. What foolish things dreams are!"

"I take it that your dream proved false."

"The falsest, my lord. Forty-seven years on this earth, and I'm still a bachelor as ever, although there is a little widow-woman back home who I've got my eyes on..."

"And your father?"

"Never knew him! My mother said he died before I was born. So although I have on several occasions killed men my senior in battle, I had no reason to fear any of them might have been my father."

Taking in a deep breath, Ahab said, "You speak sensibly, Azmelqart, and I don't want to yield to a preposterous fear. Yet I'm still torn about it..."

"Ignore foolish nightmares and fight like a king." Azmelqart emphasized his encouragement with a firm press on Ahab's shoulder.

"I know I ought to, but..."

"Remember also the words that Queen Jezebel said on your departure. She said the soldiers will take great inspiration under the leadership of the Hero of Aphek. And Ben-Hadad will equally fear you for having conquered him once and feel ashamed for owing his life to your gracious clemency."

Sighing, Ahab scuffed his foot on the earthen floor and said, "Yes, yes, Jezebel is right as always. I must lead my men to victory. That is my kingly duty." *Assuming I can conquer my nerves...*

With his aide having convinced him that the dream was irrational, Ahab vowed not to waste any more time on hesitancy and began his preparation for battle. He consumed a hearty, protein-packed breakfast consisting of pork chops and bacon, five hardboiled eggs, a plate of honey-drenched biscuits, and a large goblet of beer. After breakfast, Ahab rose and, bracing himself for the looming discomfort, clenched his teeth as his aide started suiting him up.

As the grieves were wrapped around his legs, Ahab did not initially cry out because of his aching shin splints; but when Azmelqart fastened the grieves' silver ankle-clasps behind his feet, tying them tight, he let out a low groan from the pain of his gout. Next Azmelqart sought to strap the breastplate round the king's rotund chest. Ahab sucked in his gut and held his breath in order to ease his aide's task. Nonetheless it was to no effect: the breastplate's leather strap snapped in Azmelqart's hands while he was struggling to tie it behind the king's back.

*Oh, how easier this went the last time I faced Ben-Hadad!* thought Ahab, regretting the extra pounds he had put on since that earlier, happier time in his life.

After a short delay a new longer strap was acquired and the breastplate was successfully tied behind Ahab's back. Then he picked up his sword, its fine iron blade freshly sharpened and its silver-studded hilt glittery, and slung it over his shoulder; he landed it in its sheath on the third attempt. His aide handed him his massive shield. Painted across the center of the perfectly round shield were nine blue roses, arranged in a square formation of three rows and surrounded by a white garland. Ahab placed his arm through the shield's strap and, gasping as its weight (which seemed to have doubled since the last time he wore it) dragged his arm downwards, barely managed to keep his balance and hoist the shield. At last Ahab received his helmet. As he lifted it upwards, the horsehair crest flopped onto the helmet's right horn but straightened up again after he had set the helmet around his head.

Ahab wiggled his arms and stepped from side to side inside the tent in order to test his armor. The armor was in top condition: the camp's smiths had removed the rust that had accumulated over the previous three years and caused it to sparkle like the day it was first cast. Although the armor was battle-ready, its warrior was less so. Puffing after moving around in his armor, Ahab grabbed an ashen spear to lean on and thought, *This is a lot more uncomfortable than I remember... How could I have gotten so out of shape?*

"You look magnificent, my lord," said Azmelqart with a giant smile.

Ahab chuckled. "Your enthusiasm is appreciated." He stepped outside his tent and looked up at the overcast sky. Grimacing, he remarked to Azmelqart as soon as he had also come outside, "Before the battle starts, I should offer up one of the sacred chickens to Baal—to remind the god of my piety." *I'll need all the help I can get.*

"Uhhh," murmured Azmelqart, wringing his hands, "I'm afraid you won't be able to do that, my lord. We're fresh out of sacred chickens."

"We can't be!" protested Ahab, stomping his spear's butt into the earth. "Jezebel sent us with a huge herd of chickens consecrated to Baal. We can't have sacrificed them all already."

"No, but a pack of wild wolves broke into their coops last night and, well..."

Ahab's dry mouth dropped inside his helmet and his sweaty palm almost let slip his spear. Wobbling back inside his tent, Ahab sat on the foot of his cot and gazed at the floor while biting his fat lips.

*First that frightful dream... now the god's sacrifices devoured by wild beasts... This has to be a sign from heaven...*

"My lord," called Azmelqart as he peeked his head inside, "King Jehoshaphat is here."

Ahab rose to greet his fellow king.

"Good morning, Ahab," said Jehoshaphat, his armor clinking as he made his way into the tent. "Are you ready for us to marshal the armies? I think the troops are anxious to depart."

"Not quite yet. I'm having a hard morning."

Removing his helmet to get a better view, Jehoshaphat said, "What could distress the great king of Israel?"

"Well," began Ahab, taking off his helmet too and holding it in both his hands as though it were a watermelon, "I had a terrible dream last night—I dreamt Ben-Hadad killed me in battle."

Jehoshaphat placed his hand on Ahab's shoulder. "I wouldn't pay any attention to it. It's just pre-battle jitters. It happens to the best of us."

"Yes, but I'm also concerned by the fact that I haven't fought in a long time; this is the first time in three years that I've been suited up in armor. I fear I may not be up for the rigors of war."

"But my lord," interjected Azmelqart as he approached his king, "you will be in a horse-drawn chariot. Unlike foot-soldiers, you'll tower over the battlefield from the safest location one could be in."

"Your servant's right, Ahab. We kings fight from where positional superiority does not require great stamina or strength and we are surrounded by our best fighters for added protection. That is why it is much rarer for us to be killed in battle than for the common man who must fight on foot."

"I know, I know," muttered Ahab. *Even so, kings do die some-times...* He slunk down on his cot, let his helmet fall with a thud, and wrung his hands in front of his navel while staring at the ground. "It's just... I was already anxious ahead of today, and that dream has only intensified my unease."

Rubbing his beard, Jehoshaphat said, "If there is anything at all that might help, you need only ask me."

Ahab did not look up at his eyes but kept his gaze down at the level of Jehoshaphat's breastplate, over which was his royal surcoat. The robe was emblazoned with the image of the royal House of Judah: a lion rampant. For some reason the leonine image captivated Ahab's eyes; and as he stared at it, the sparks of a thought soon combusted in his mind.

He shot up from the bed and exclaimed, wild-eyed, "There is something!" He tugged on the surcoat over top of Jehoshaphat's breastplate and with his other hand tugged on his own. "Switch with me!"

"What?"

"I will disguise myself when I enter into the battle and you put on my garments. That way the Arameans will think I'm the king of Judah and Ben-Hadad won't be able to track me down in the thick of battle and kill me like in my dream." He threw up his hands and threw back his neck. "The vision will be foiled!"

Raising one eyebrow and gazing at him out of the corner of his eyes, Jehoshaphat said matter-of-factly, "If the dream were a true vision of the future, I highly doubt a change of clothes could fool it into thinking I am you..."

*Though it could fool any Aramean seeking me out. My spies say Ben-Hadad has offered the richest estate in his kingdom to the man who brings him my head...* "Please, Jehoshaphat, agree to do this: it will make me feel much better."

"It is unorthodox, although I did say I'd do anything to help you, so... Alright, if it will make you feel better, I'll participate in your disguise ploy."

"Thank you, Jehoshaphat," said Ahab, taking his fellow king's hand and shaking it heartily. "This really means a lot to me." *I shall escape out of the hands of my assassins! Although I do hope the God of your fathers saves you from my killers...*

"You are welcome, Ahab. Now, if you are ready, let us go and lead our armies, God-willing, to victory against the Arameans."

Ahab followed Jehoshaphat to the entrance of the tent. As he lifted his foot to step outside, his mouth going dry and his lower intestines rumbling, he thought:

*I hope so. O gods and goddesses, do I ever hope so....*

# CHAPTER THIRTY-FOUR

A S THE AFTERNOON WAS perishing before the dark onslaught of the looming evening, Jezebel lay upon cin-
namon-scented sheets within her bedchamber at the Samaritan
palace. She had been in Samaria since Ahab set out with the army:
their capital needed royal attention during a tense time such as
this. However, with little to do but sip wine until word about the
war should come, she was languishing from inaction. She kept a
damp cloth over her bulbous eyes and forehead and blocked out
the harsh light of the sun while lying there. A cool breeze had been
blowing through the balcony into the room all afternoon, rustling
the silvery bells which were tied to the translucent canopy above
the queen's bed. But as the shadows grew longer, the breeze began
also to bring murmurings of the people from the street below that
overpowered the sound of the bells' tinkling.

When the murmurings proved not to be transitory, their sound
reaching a crescendo that was as noticeable collectively as it was
imperceptible individually, Jezebel suddenly snatched the cloth off
her green eyes and bolted up from the bed. "What on earth is going
on?" she exclaimed, strutting out to the balcony.

Looking down at the undulating crowd as it was swarming the street, she spotted a palace guard stationed below and called out to him: "What hornet has stung the people?"

"Oh, my queen," exclaimed the guard, crossing his heart while struggling to lift his heavy eyes to meet hers, "we've just received news from the front that has spread through the people like fire through a summer forest: King Ahab's army has been routed by the enemy."

"NOOOO!" gasped Jezebel as her lips curled into a snarl and her pupils shrunk tight. She spun around and hurried through the halls of the palace, clenching her fists and thinking, *That damned bastard screwed everything up! I should have known he would... just like he's screwed everything up!*

Amid the chaos of distant defeat but present fear, a half dozen guards had instinctively rushed to Jezebel's defense and now surrounded her as she emerged from the palace. Not allowing her guardians to block her view, she nudged past them and proceeded the short distance across the courtyard to the gate leading out to the street. She put her hand above her eyes while leaning her neck forwards to peer through the gate's iron bars. The crowd of onlookers which filled the street was slowly being dispersed by other guards and royal officials; as it dissolved, a chariot was slowly making its way through the crowd and coming closer to the gate. Jezebel squinted at what was unmistakably Ahab's chariot.

"Is that your lord the king?" said Jezebel dryly when the charioteer had driven within hearing distance. She crossed her arms and scowled as the gate was opened.

The charioteer drove his team about twenty feet into the courtyard. Then he tugged on the panting, sweat-covered horses to halt.

He descended from the chariot and went over to Jezebel. Lowering his head, he said, "My queen, I do not know how to tell you…"

Ignoring the charioteer's faltering, Jezebel brushed past him and peered at the chariot's vacant back. "Where's Ahab? Why'd he send his chariot ahead?"

"My queen," said the charioteer, his voice breaking. He knelt down before her and rested his forehead on the ground. "I have the sad duty to inform you that our king, your beloved husband, was seriously wounded in the battle. During the course of our retreat, the king… died of his wounds."

Jezebel's face blanched and she momentarily choked. "Ahab… dead…" she spluttered at last. She glanced at the sky, then the charioteer, next the palace, and finally the ground.

Recovering from the shock, she staggered over to the chariot, clenched its cold metal side, and peered inside. At the bottom of the chariot, rising out of the shallow pool of his own blood like a noxious egg floating in a bowl of water, lay Ahab. His almond eyes were shut but a long frown spread across his face that was now scarred more from battle than from his razor's edge.

*You bastard!* she silently cursed as her red nails scraped the chariot's metal. *How* dare *you die on me like this!*

Scowling heavily, Jezebel, upon taking a closer look at Ahab's corpse and how it was dressed in foreign apparel, turned to the charioteer and demanded, "What is this?! Why's the king of Israel dressed in Judahite garb?"

"My queen, the gods sent the king a dream of ill omen before the battle, presaging his coming death in battle. As the omen had not yet come to pass and its interpretation obscure, our king sought to forestall its fulfillment by switching garments with the king of Judah, in the hopes that he might escape the will of fate. Unfortunately, the fickle fates cannot be deceived by the ruses of men."

*As though he could pull off deceiving a teething toddler, let alone the gods!*

She flashed a futile glare at her dead husband. "Come, we mustn't leave the king in this state." She snapped her fingers at some guards and said, "Get the king out of this defiled chariot and bring him into the courtyard. We will have to ready the body for a burial befitting a king." *No matter how unworthy of that sacred name he was, the monarchy must not be dishonored...*

Ahab's body was conveyed from the chariot into the center of the palace courtyard where a military tent was hastily erected to protect the unfeeling flesh from the rays of the setting sun. With the servants and other denizens of the palace dismissed by their curt queen, Jezebel secluded herself within the make-shift sepulcher. She stood over the body, which lay sprawled across upturned mangers from the royal stables in lieu of a proper bier. Fingering his Judahite garments as though touching an obsidian arrowhead whose sharpness would bloody her entire hand, she gritted her teeth and glared at him with unmistakable hatred.

"You sniveling, gutless worm! Even in death, you couldn't maintain your dignity in your own kingly robes! Did you really hope that, by exchanging your bepissed garments with Jehoshaphat's, they would make you invulnerable to enemies' blows? No more than they'd clothe you with his muscles, courage, prudence." She spat on the corpse's pale face. "I thank the gods my father did not live to see how his worthless son-in-law turned out. He would be ashamed to share the name of 'king' with the likes of you."

Having turned her back on him, Jezebel swayed her vein-bulging fists beside her and sprayed the tent's side with her saliva as she hissed:

"You worthless excuse for a man! Too scared to face the enemy without feebly trying to play a coward's trick?! Did another one of those 'very bad dreams'"—she imitated Ahab's shrill tone of voice as she repeated a phrase that he had uttered many times to her—"upset the oh-so-delicate king of Israel? (A choleric baby disturbs its parents' sleep less than you did mine on those nights I deigned to share your bed.) Well, if you were so overcome by your fears, why did you ever lead our men into battle? You should have stayed behind in camp like other cowardly kings do, allowed the real generals to wage war without having you as a millstone hung around their necks. Why did you do it, Ahab? Did you think you'd win glory for yourself, have all the maidens singing your praises, become a warlike hero in our men's eyes? Idiot! The palpable stench of your fear probably infected our soldiers and caused them to lose heart in battle and thus cost us the war. You may have played pretend when that Hebrew whore was around, acted the part of the brave man for her (and the gods know what other sordid rôles as well!), but you could never fool me... You've been exactly the same since the day your ghastly mother relieved her tortured womb by thrusting you out upon us all! What supreme folly it was for *you*, of all men, to dare go into battle! You selfish, self-centered, egotistical bastard! THIS IS SO TYPICAL OF YOU!"

Spinning around to face the accused, her eyes wide and nostrils flaring, Jezebel suddenly fell to her knees from her unmitigated anger. She crawled over to the body and, her limbs shaking with rage, repeatedly slammed her fists on Ahab's chest as she screamed:

"Why, why, why?! Do your subjects mean so little to you, do the sons whom I bore you mean so little to you, do *I*, your one and only wife for these long years, who has patiently endured your each and every flaw, defect, shortcoming... mean so little to you that you chose to abandon us—throwing away your life, never pausing for a moment to consider what might befall those, whom you were obligated to look after, without you? You bloody turd! You damned, bloody turd!"

Her limbs and her anger going limp from exhaustion, Jezebel collapsed over Ahab's body and laid her tearful head upon the cold unfeeling corpse. Staunching the flow of tears with some of his blood-blackened garment, she moaned, "Just look at what you've reduced me to...! Now that you have selfishly chosen death for yourself, O my husband, what shall become of me? I am beset by enemies on all sides... Aramaic soldiers must surely be heading this way, hoping to capitalize on their victory and put our capital to the torch. At home I am still a stranger in a strange land, whose inhabitants are as stubbornly treacherous as they are heathenish. Home? Bah! What kind of home is Israel to me? Even if I should escape Ben-Hadad's clutches, I will still find myself drowning in a sea of infidels, led by that godless man thirsting for my blood, his appetite unquenchable despite spilling the precious blood of my priests, my Pygmalion, oh, sweet Pygmalion..." Her voice dropping to a whisper, she looked at Ahab's dead face and asked, "Is this the end of Jezebel?"

As the seconds dragged on without a response, she shut her eyes, pursed her lips, and clenched her fists.

"No, I am the daughter of a king!" she cried, her arms thrusting herself upwards onto her feet. "And not just any king but Ithobaal, the kingliest of kings, begot me. It was at his knees that I learned true kinghood. Surrender is not in the blood that flows through my kingly veins!"

Looking down at Ahab, Jezebel smirked. "I don't need you, Ahab. Not anymore! Even if you were alive, I know you'd be as useless to me as you are dead. So just lie there and rot!"

She turned her back on him, shoved the tent's flaps open, and stormed outside.

*We have sons. (At least there was one department he excelled at!) Ahaziah shall take his father's place on the throne. As he is still of tender years, I will have to guide him in the way of kingcraft and make him the king his father never was. Thankfully, he's always been very obedient to me, like a good son should. With the assistance of my counsel, Israel will finally have a strong, competent ruler, one who knows both what must be done and also how it can be done. And this time I won't have an Ahab around to screw things up...*

A medley of panting soldiers and courtiers, their wild eyes exuding terror, dashed past Jezebel as she ambled across the courtyard. Their yells and feet thudding loudly upon the pavement made no impression upon her; despite paying no attention to the oncoming hordes, she suffered not a single collision because even amidst the specter of invasion—of city walls breached, buildings burning, their wives taken captive, and themselves slain alongside their sons—no man had been driven to such a state of fear that he would be so foolhardy as to run into his queen. Instead Jezebel, while rubbing her hands and, with a lick of the lips, thinking of the future, stared into the distance without focusing her eyes on anything in particular.

*Ben-Hadad may wish to advance on Samaria, but after suffering those losses to the Assyrians his forces are far, far weaker today than they were three years ago. Even if he wants to, he cannot take this city, let alone conquer the whole kingdom. Once the remnant of our army reconvenes, I'll renew its ranks with a fresh round of conscripts from the countryside: farmers and shepherds are always willing to fight when it's their farmlands and flocks at risk of plunder and flames. We'll check the Aramaic advance and force them to negotiate. Holding my brother's refreshed strength over him, Ben-Hadad will realize the prudence of making peace. With the foreign front temporized for now, I'll be able to return my focus to consolidating my strength at home and* wipe out *the last maggots infecting this land with that contemptible superstition. Then there'll be none left to question me! And this time no whore can save them from my wrath! I shall finally have a kingdom amenable to me, whose resources and manpower will, in due time, recover and allow me to blot out the memory of the victory of the Arameans... of even the Arameans themselves. Yes, yes, tomorrow is already dawning brighter.*

As the last reddish slice of sun sank beneath the horizon, ushering in the twilight hour, Jezebel reached the wall enclosing the courtyard. Without a word, javelin-wielding guards streamed over and protectively flanked her sides as she had approached the gate leading out to the city's streets. She sniffed with disgust as the scent of mudded swine and mangy alley dogs wafted her way. She glared at the filthy creatures, which were eagerly licking the ground outside the gate where Ahab's blood had sloshed from his chariot not long ago.

"Soldier," said Jezebel brusquely, looking at no guard in particular as she spoke, "where did they take the royal chariot?"

"To the Great Fountain, Your Majesty. It was brimming with so much blood that the servants thought it best to immerse it in water rather than try to wipe it down only with cloths."

*Did they?*

An idle curiosity caused her lips to form a smirk. She ordered the gate to be opened and pointed at the beasts that were still licking at the dried blood. With a few whacks from their javelins' butts, the guards dispersed them so that the queen could proceed out into the street. Jezebel had to walk only a short distance down the street before she reached the public square where the Great Fountain lay. This colossal fountain, whose granite-edged pool spanned fifty feet in diameter, dominated the square. Arising in its center were six stone columns that circled the spring from which gushed clear water down the granite side's two-foot drop into the waterline of the pool below. These columns stretched twenty-six feet into the air and supported a white marble dome; the pinnacle of the dome was graced by a gilded statue of the goddess Astartë who was depicted standing naked upon a horse.

Jezebel laughed.

The king's chariot was submerged in the fountain's knee-high water, resting just against the granite side underneath one of the columns. It had already been cleansed of the blood that had earlier pooled inside it and one palace slave was still atop it, rubbing it down with rags. But the sight that had made Jezebel let out an unexpected chuckle was what else the spacious fountain held within its waters. Several young women, clearly marked out as prostitutes by their gaudy apparel and shameless eyes, had climbed into the fountain to bathe themselves and their clothing.

*You were always a selfish son of a whore, Ahab, prizing your own whores over me, your lawful wife. After a sordid life of lechery, it is somehow only fitting that in death common harlots should bathe in your blood. Perhaps the gods do have a sense of humor after all.*

Having had her fill of the sight, Jezebel retraced her steps and withdrew into her palace.

## A REQUEST FROM THE AUTHOR

I greatly appreciate the time you took to give my book a read.

If you have 60 seconds, it would mean the world to me to hear your honest feedback on Amazon. It does wonders for the book and I love hearing your thoughts on it!

To leave your feedback on the Amazon website specific to your country or region, please visit this universal review link:

https://authorhelp.uk?azr=B0CW9XMPTD

Or

1. Open your camera app

2. Point your mobile device at the QR code below

3. The review page will appear in your web browser.

Thank you!

## About the author

Joseph Bringman was born and raised in Seattle, Washington. He loves studying the history and cultures of the ancient Mediterranean, reading works of classical literature, and learning ancient languages. Joseph received his PhD in Classics from the University of Washington.

*Ahab and Jezebel: A Match Made in Hell* is his début novel.

More about Joseph, including his social media presence and newsletter, can be found on his website:

www.BringmanPublishing.com

## ACKNOWLEDGMENTS

To all who had a hand in helping me bring my book to market, especially my mother Laurie for her superb proofreading, thank you.

**Keep on the lookout for...**

## Periander the Avenger: The Fall of Atlantis

KING PERIANDER TENDED THE flames of his fire. The stars of the heavens shone upon the makeshift campsite, illuminating Periander's platinum hair while starry Leo up above observed the earthbound band. All of his companions, after another day's trek across the Libyan plains, had reached the nocturnal pastures of dreamland. Periander, however, remained awake, the sweet embraces of sleep far-off from his whirling mind.

His eyes—an emerald-green hue on the left and a right shining as sapphire—watched the gently heaving body of his teenage son beside him. With fatherly affection he pulled back up over the boy his tattered blanket, which had been shaken loose. Hot were the desert days yet the nights were so cold! And as Periander kept watching him, it almost seemed as if an outline of his wife appeared at their child's side, holding him close so that nothing could dislodge her. He lifted his hand and grasped at the air.

She was gone.

Periander clenched his fist, and cursed it for its failure—not for this time, for he knew that it had been only an apparition, a faint glow of his memory deceiving his eyes. No, rather he cursed the hand that had let Cornelia slip through its grasp, his beloved spouse, who ought still to be with him.

Dreadful was that night, that horrible night when he was forced to flee for his life—he, his family, and his closest companions too.

The abandonment of hearth and home. Speeding in the hovercar. Flashes of lasers. Explosions. Running up the stairs. Panting. Just a few more steps! You can make it. Help! Cornelia hit. Falling. Grab my hand! NOOOOOOO!

While these dark memories stewed in his mind's vengeful juices, Periander snatched up a purple flower from the desert earth. His fingers strangled it, pulverizing it into pulp; the liquefied plant bled out all over his hand, the sticky juice rolling down his wrist. He ground it so hard that his knuckles scraped against the palm. Finally he stopped. With the slime sticking to his hand, he wiped the plant guts on the earth.

*I will avenge you, Cornelia,* thought Periander, his blazing eyes trained on his hand. *By the Deity Who created the world, I do swear that Critias and Eudoxia shall answer for your death. When I return to the land of my fathers, I will liberate it from their ravenous gullets. Every offense and insult they have committed against our family and our country shall be repaid double, treble, quadruple. By our son's head, Cornelia, which I will safeguard better than I did yours, your murderers shall pay life for life....*